Death of John Tait

A Chief Inspector Pointer Mystery

By A. E. Fielding

Originally published in 1932

Death of John Tait

© 2014 Resurrected Press
www.ResurrectedPress.com

Published by Intrepid Ink, LLC

Intrepid Ink, LLC provides full publishing services to authors of fiction and non-fiction books, eBooks and websites. From editing to formatting, to publishing, to marketing, Intrepid Ink gets your creative works into the hands of the people who want to read them.
Find out more at www.IntrepidInk.com.

ISBN 13: 978-1-937022-79-2

Printed in the United States of America

Other Resurrected Press Books in *The Chief Inspector Pointer Mystery* Series

RESURRECTED PRESS CLASSIC MYSTERY CATALOGUE

Journeys into Mystery
Travel and Mystery in a More Elegant Time

The Edwardian Detectives
Literary Sleuths of the Edwardian Era

Gems of Mystery
Lost Jewels from a More Elegant Age

Anne Austin
One Drop of Blood
The Black Pigeon
Murder at Bridge

E. C. Bentley
Trent's Last Case: The Woman in Black

Ernest Bramah
Max Carrados Resurrected:
The Detective Stories of Max Carrados

Agatha Christie
The Secret Adversary
The Mysterious Affair at Styles

Octavus Roy Cohen
Midnight

Freeman Wills Croft
The Ponson Case
The Pit Prop Syndicate

The Uttermost Farthing: A Savant's Vendetta

Arthur Griffiths
The Passenger From Calais
The Rome Express

Fergus Hume
The Mystery of a Hansom Cab
The Green Mummy
The Silent House
The Secret Passage

Edgar Jepson
The Loudwater Mystery

A. E. W. Mason
At the Villa Rose

A. A. Milne
The Red House Mystery

Baroness Emma Orczy
The Old Man in the Corner

Edgar Allan Poe
The Detective Stories of Edgar Allan Poe

Arthur J. Rees
The Hampstead Mystery
The Shrieking Pit
The Hand In The Dark
The Moon Rock
The Mystery of the Downs

Mary Roberts Rinehart
Sight Unseen and The Confession

Dorothy L. Sayers

Anybody but Anne
The Bride of a Moment
Faulkner's Folly
The Diamond Pin
The Gold Bag
The Mystery of the Sycamore
The Come Back

Raoul Whitfield
Death in a Bowl

And much more!
Visit ResurrectedPress.com
for our complete catalogue

FOREWORD

The period between the First and Second World Wars has rightly been called the "Golden Age of British Mysteries." It was during this period that Agatha Christie, Dorothy L. Sayers, and Margery Allingham first turned their pens to crime. On the male side, the era saw such writers as Anthony Berkeley, John Dickson Carr, and Freeman Wills Crofts join the ranks of writers of detective fiction. The genre was immensely popular at the time on both sides of the Atlantic, and by the end of the 1930's one out of every four novels published in Britain was a mystery.

While Agatha Christie and a few of her peers have remained popular and in print to this day, the same cannot be said of all the authors of this period. With so many mysteries published in the period, it is inevitable that many of them would become obscure or worse, forgotten, often with no justification than changing public tastes. The case of Archibald Fielding is one such, an author, who though popular enough to have a career spanning two decades and more than two dozen mysteries has become such a cipher that his, or as seems more likely, her real identity has become as much a mystery as the books themselves.

While the identity of the author may forever remain an unsolved puzzle, there are some facts that may be inferred from the texts. It is likely that the author had an upbringing and education typical of the British upper middle class in the period before the Great War with all that implies; a familiarity with the classics, the arts, and music, a working knowledge of French and Italian, an appreciation of the finer things in life. The author has also traveled abroad, primarily in the south of France, but probably to Belgium, Spain, and Italy as well, as portions of several of the books are set in those locales.

The books attributed to Archibald Fielding, A. E. Fielding, or Archibald E. Fielding, are quintessential Golden Age British mysteries. They include all the attributes, the country houses, the tangled webs of relationships, the somewhat feckless cast of characters who seem to have nothing better to do with themselves than to murder or be murdered. Their focus is on a middle class and upper class struggling to find themselves in the new realities of the post war era while still trying to live the lifestyle of the Edwardian era. Things are never as they seem, red herrings are distributed liberally throughout the pages as are the clues that will ultimately lead to the solution of "the puzzle," for the British mysteries of this period are centered on the puzzle element which both the reader and the detective must solve before the last page.

A majority of the Fielding mysteries involve the character of Chief Inspector Pointer. Unlike the eccentric Belgian Hercule Poirot, the flamboyant Lord Peter Wimsey, or the somewhat mysterious Albert Campion, Pointer is merely a competent, sometimes clever, occasionally intuitive policeman. And unlike, as with Inspector French in the stories of Freeman Wills Croft, the emphasis is on the mystery itself, not the process of detection.

Pointer is nearly as much of a mystery as the author. Very little of his personal life is revealed in the books. He is described as being vaguely of Scottish ancestry. In *Death of John Tait* it is revealed that his father was a coastguardsman. He is well read and educated, though his duties at Scotland Yard prevent him from enjoying those pursuits. His success as a detective depends on his willingness to "suspect everyone" and to not being tied to any one theory. He is fluent in French and familiar with that country. He is, at least in the first two books, unmarried, and sharing lodgings with a bookbinder named O'Connor, in much the manner of Holmes and Watson though this character disappears in later books. One intriguing feature of the Pointer mysteries is that they all involve an unexpected twist at the end, wherein the mystery finally solved is not the mystery invoked at the beginning of the book. I leave it to the reader to judge whether Fielding is "playing by the rules" in this, but it does keep the books interesting up to the last chapter. *Death of John Tait* comes in the middle of Fielding's career, the twelfth book in the series of 23 that feature Chief Inspector Pointer. The author had perfected her style. The book remains part police procedural, with the following up of clues and shadowing of suspects, but much more attention is given to the characters surrounding the crime and their interactions with each other. There is still a certain amount of dressing up in disguises and impersonating tradesmen on the part of the detectives, but it seems less forced than in the earlier books, and it was, after all, part of the typical style of the period.

In *Death of John Tait* Pointer is confronted with the death of a man in front of the house of his step-mother. John Tait was about to be married, and at first brush, the changes his marital status will bring about seem the prime motive for murder; his three cousins will find themselves pushed out of a comfortable home and left to live on fairly meager resources. But other possible suspects quickly appear, and Pointer must decide which are real and which are red-herrings. In typical Fielding fashion, another crime appears to be behind the first, leading to a quite surprising turn of events at the conclusion. Of course, in the end, the inspector comes to the right solution.

Despite their obscurity, the mysteries of Archibald Fielding, whoever he or she may have been, are well written, well crafted examples of the form, worthy of the interest of the fans of the genre. It is with pleasure, then, that Resurrected Press presents this new edition of *Death of John Tait* and others in the series to its readers.

About the Author

The identity of the author is as much a mystery as the plots of the novels. Two dozen novels were published from 1924 to 1944 as by Archibald Fielding, A. E. Fielding, or Archibald E. Fielding, yet the only clue as to the real author is a comment by the American publishers, H.C. Kinsey Co. that A. E. Fielding was in reality a "middle-aged English woman by the name of Dorothy Feilding whose peacetime address is Sheffield Terrace, Kensington, London, and who enjoys gardening." Research on the part of John Herrington has uncovered a person by that name living at 2 Sheffield Terrace from 1932-1936. She appears to have moved to Islington in 1937 after which she disappears. To complicate things, some have attributed the authorship to Lady Dorothy Mary Evelyn Moore nee Feilding (1889-1935), however, a grandson of Lady Dorothy denied any family knowledge of such authorship. The archivist at Collins, the British publisher, reports that any records of A. Fielding were presumably lost during WWII. Birthdates have been given variously as 1884, 1889, and 1900. Unless new information comes to light, it would appear that the real authorship must remain a mystery.

Greg Fowlkes
Editor-In-Chief
Resurrected Press
www.ResurrectedPress.com

CHAPTER ONE

"JOHN is going to be married." Alysia Naylor said the words sharply, almost between clenched teeth, as she stared at her sister across the pleasant breakfast table in Chelsea Gardens.

"So Lady Ida has got him at last," her sister observed calmly.

"Lady Ida! He's going to marry some widow woman or other of whom no one has ever heard" They were talking of their cousin, in whose house they were living.

"Indeed" Her sister put more sugar on her grapefruit with an air of absorption. Only after it was well powdered did she look up "How do you know?"

"I've a letter from Aunt Norah She simply gloats over the whole affair. A Mrs. Burnham, designing thing, has used the time while aunt was recovering from her accident to rope John in."

"But surely you are pleased for dear John's sake?" Etta Naylor looked pained surprise at her sister. Both women were past thirty. Henrietta was the younger, a handsome woman, tall and fair-headed and as plump as her dressmaker and tailor permitted. Alysia, the elder, was thin and dark, with an ugly, passionate, vivid face. Her hair, dark too, seemed always to float around her temples. giving her an air tragic and muse-like. An appearance which some said was carefully cultivated.

For goodness' sake, Etta, don't always be so smug!" Alysia broke off a piece of ryebread, and snapped it down on the table as though it were the highest trump. "It's perfectly damnable. And you think so, too! Of course we looked on John as a confirmed bachelor. Since he evidently wasn't going to marry Ida Westmacott after all. Besides, he always spoke as though he would never marry."

"But haven't you found"—Etta spoke with an air of imparting an interesting and quite original discovery of her own—"haven't you found that people don't always do as they say, or think they will? I have." And she tackled her grapefruit again.

Alysia pushed her chair away from the table.

"It means the end of everything between Reggie and me." she said under her breath.

Oh, surely not!" murmured her sister in a shocked voice.

"Surely not indeed!" scoffed the other. "you and I, Etta, have three hundred a year between us. Between us!"

"Claud has exactly the same," Etta threw in brightly. Claud was their brother.

"And don't you suppose he's feeling just, as we are about this blow? Though he's got his profession. A clever barrister can earn thousands."

"Personally, I'm glad for dear John's sake that he's going to have a real home of his own. I never did think that Lady Ida would suit him. And since Aunt Norah is pleased, you did say that she's pleased, didn't you?—why, I'm prepared to like this Mrs. Burnham very much indeed."

Her sister flashed a look of scorn at her and smacked the table again, this time with her aunt's letter, which Etta took and carefully read, murmuring, "May I?" while her sister raved on.

"Three hundred between us with this house of John's to live in, with his car to use, with him always willing to entertain one's friends, was one thing, but three hundred, or, rather the half of it, with no house, no servants, no car—why, it's starvation—beggary—of course, Reggie and I can't marry on this!"

"My girls' clubs will have to be given up," Etta murmured sadly. "But don't you think, dear, it's rather selfish of us to look at this piece of news just from our own standpoint?" She gave a bright, brave smile. Her sister made a sound in her throat, suggestive of being strangled.

"Reggie!" she called suddenly, as a step sounded outside the door.

"Any one call me?" asked a rich baritone voice, and Reginald Claridge came into the room. "I told Tompkins that it was a waste of breath to announce. Morning, Etta. Morning, dearest thing" He waved a finger at Etta, and kissed Alysia's dark, thin check. Alysia held on to his hand and sat looking up at him with something yearning in her face, something real and genuine. There was nothing real or genuine in the handsome debonair one looking into hers

Seldom does a face show one purpose in life as clearly as did this young man's, and that purpose was to do the very best for Reginald Claridge that circumstances permitted. So far, no very good chance had come his way. A penniless chemist working in a beauty parlor's laboratory, he had been immensely flattered at being taken up by Alysia Naylor, who was hostess at the big old house where money evidently was plentiful, and where he had an entrance into circles which otherwise he could never have reached. That Alysia had had the good taste to fall in love with him was very pleasant too. True, she was older than he, but she was in "the swim" as he called it, and that counted for everything with him. It had been a cold douche to learn that her father had halved six hundred a year, and given one pittance—so Claridge called it to himself, and as the son of a struggling Durham chemist, he knew what that word meant—to be divided between the two sisters. But Alysia had explained with thoughtful promptness her cousin John Tait's position, for whom she and her sister kept house, and where her brother had a couple of rooms.

Tait had a wealthy step-mother, the Naylors' aunt, who intended leaving him the whole of her late husband's wealth. He was certain to do something really handsome for Alysia, who had acted as his hostess for nearly five years now, even if he did marry Lady Ida Westmacott. A very pleasant connection she would prove, while supposing he did not marry her then Alysia assured him that John would never part with his freedom, in which case, eventually, something still more handsome might come their way.

"You're looking a bit on edge," he remarked, stroking her hand and eyeing the sideboard attentively. He disliked kidneys, but the grilled ham looked uncommonly good. Standing on a hot-plate wasn't going to improve it, however. He tried to free his hand with a lover-like little pat, but Alysia only held it tighter.

"John is going to be married," she said briefly, and her eyes still clung to his face. Not to his eyes, for he had dropped them immediately.

"So Lady Ida has pulled it off. Well, he might do worse," he murmured.

"He has done worse! He's going to marry an odious, designing creature, a widow my Aunt Norah has picked up in Vichy It's not exactly like winning the Dublin sweepstake, is it?" She poured out another cup of black coffee for herself. Alysia's breakfast consisted of cigarettes and black coffee.

"Perhaps it won't make so much difference, after all," Etta put in, as Claridge resolutely moved away from Alysia and towards the sideboard.

"John has sent a line, too," Alysia said on that. "He says"—she pulled a folded sheet from a bag dangling on her wrist—"he says that he hopes we won't find it short notice, the wedding won't be for another couple of months and the honeymoon will last quite that, but that as the builders will have rather a job to put in central heating, and so on, Etta and I might like to move down to Tor

Cottage. Tor Cottage!" she repeated, raising her eyes to the ceiling.

"And where is Tor Cottage?" Reginald asked in rather an absent-minded voice. He wanted time to digest the news of this marriage.

"It's a pretty place" Etta rang for fresh toast for Reginald "Quite charming And John is making a hard court down there. It was just for our sake really. I do hope he won't stop it. But very likely Mrs. Barnham—"

"Burnham," snapped her sister

"—is keen on tennis. Aunt Norah writes that she's about John's age, though one wouldn't guess it. You may be sure one wouldn't!" came from Alysia, whose age was clear to see in spite of the most liberal make-up. "Tor Cottage is at the end of the world," she said contemptuously.

"No, dear, only near Canterbury," amended Etta placidly.

"And even Tor Cottage is only thrown in as a temporary perch," Alysia went on, "for he writes that it won't be wanted till the autumn... there you are, we're turned out like servants who've been given notice!"

"I'm sure he said some kind things, words of regret," put in Etta, but her. face had flushed, and her eyes glittered for a moment before she resolutely fastened them on her plate.

"Of course! Plenty!"

After Alysia's bitter reply, a silence fell, broken only by the steady crunch of fresh toast. Suddenly Etta said gently:

"But perhaps his marriage won't take place after all. You never, know."

"Only death ever stops what Aunt Norah approves of," retorted Alysia.

"Death does stop many things," murmured Etta in her tone of having just discovered a new planet and being anxious to impart the news to a listening universe.

"Will you murder John for us, Reggie darling, since after all he is a cousin, while I cross over to Vichy and attend to the widow? Let me see, what did I say her name was?" Alysia made a pretense of scanning the letter again. "Lucy Burnham."

"A pretty name," Etta murmured.

"And a very pretty woman, your aunt says" Without troubling to ask permission, Reginald had taken the letter from his fiancée's hand and was reading it very carefully indeed.

"Lust John!" Alysia said with a short laugh

"In one way I'm glad," Etta now announced "I've always felt that the attraction to Lady Ida was only a passing one, and John needs some anchor—"

"You think marriage will act as one?" Reggie spoke with careless laugh His teeth were too white and too even. Just as his hair was a shade too wavy, and too thick, and grew in too much of a peak on his low forehead. "But I don't feel like murdering your cousin to stop it. Murders need such a lot of preparation nowadays, or they turn out wrong. Like that Welsh rabbit you made for us last night, Etta."

He was very polite to Etta as a rule. She had some really influential friends. More than Alysia had. He admired her more, too, but Etta had turned down Reggie Claridge with a firm hand in the beginning of their acquaintanceship. She now said reprovingly:

"You're like Claud. You read too many detective stories."

"Granted. Still, if you're thinking of bumping off any one, Etta, either your cousin, or this interloping widow, I should advise a course of them just the same."

"Certainly Claud could lend a hundred volumes with ease," Alysia said. "His shelves are littered with corpses. *The Corpse in the Attic, The Corpse in the Cellar, The Corpse in the Arm-chair, The Corpse in the Bed, The Corpse—*"

"I'm hardly likely to kill any one," Etta interrupted her sister's list of dead bodies, "but if I did, I shouldn't need to read up silly ways of doing it. I should think out something fresh for myself" And picking up the cat, Etta left the two together She was a remarkably, handsome woman, Reggie thought, he had rather expected that she and this same John Tait would make a match of it, once the affair with Lady Ida seemed to hang fire and then slowly die out, but apparently the two cousins had only rather a tepid feeling of family affection to share between them

"By Jove, Etta could!" he now said, rising, and going towards the silent Alysia "She preaches like a parson, but I always feel that she's pulling my leg really."

"It's some ridiculous affectation of hers, talking like that," Alysia said shortly, "she never used to do it. I can't think why she's taken to it lately. But about this coming marriage, Reggie, I wish you'd go to Vichy and save the situation—for us all—" She hesitated for a second, her burning eyes on his, "Aunt Norah writes that this widow woman has lived an entirely secluded life, and is frightfully impressed by the certainty of John's getting a really big diplomatic post some day. You're ridiculously good-looking," she went on. "Oh, don't pretend you don't know it..." She stopped, then she went on again. "It's just a possibility, you're going for a holiday anyway tomorrow, why not try Vichy? Go to the Imperial Hotel and see what you can do. It sounds horrid, but, as Etta would say nowadays, if dear Mrs. Burnham really loves dear John, why you won't be able to do anything, but if she doesn't, you might—might flirt with her sufficiently to come between them... No one knows we're engaged. I'll wager Aunt Norah has never heard of you. And to John and Claud you're only one of a crowd."

He stood thinking.

"Let me read your aunt's letter again," he said finally, and read it over with great care a second time.

It began with an account of the motor smash about a month ago which had left Lady Tait and the hotel chauffeur senseless on the road. Fortunately a visitor to the hotel, a Mrs. Burnham, had seen the accident and taken them both back in her own car. Lady Tait knew. that Alysia had heard all about the smash. Claud Naylor and John Tait had been wired for at her wish, and had stayed on with their aunt until her complete recovery. But Norah Tait did things thoroughly, and she wanted "the girls," as she still called her nieces, to have a clear idea of how Mrs. Burnham came into John's life. There was a great deal about the little lady in the letter, how pretty she was, how delighted the writer felt that John had fallen in love with her. Mrs. Burnham was further mentioned as wealthy, the widow of a well-known solicitor.

Reading it all through once more, Reginald stroked his neat little mustache, then, his neat little head, handed it back, and smiled.

"Your idea is that I come between these lovers? Just long enough to separate them? Not a bad notion. I see they're all staying on for another week..." Before his mind ran the phrases about the widow being very pretty and wealthy. That latter word used by Lady Tait should mean at least some thousands a year, one would think.

"But there's one drawback," he went on, as though it was one that would prevent his pursuing the matter further.

Alysia turned swiftly, a glow in her cheeks. He was going to say that the drawback was that he loved her, and could not even pretend successfully to love another, but Reggie went on.

"Funds, beloved, or the lack of them. The Imperial sounds a trifle dearish. And I'm absolutely cleaned out, Last night's poker! Evidently unlucky at cards for the good old reason," he finished with a pat on her cheek.

"I thought of that. I can manage to let you have fifteen pounds, Reggie. It ought to see you through the journey and let you stay a week at the hotel. It's the best I can do."

He studied her averted   head stealthily and shrewdly, then he said with an air of casual good-nature:

"Well it's only a try-on, isn't it? And as I am going purely on your account, darling, so as not to let any one prevent our getting married, I'll take the fifteen, and try to use it to the best advantage. After all, a wealthy widow can always find consolation, and one must do the best for oneself —and one's friends—one can."

"Spoken like Etta!" Alysia said contemptuously, with a travesty of a smile. as she went to her bureau and drew out her checkbook.

Reggie took the check, talked a little about the route, said that he would start this very day at noon, and took his leave, professing to think it all an amusing little joke.

"And when John has lost his widow, we'll have our wedding," he called back softly before he open the door and left her.

Etta, entering a second later, found her sister with her head down on the Bradshaw, her hands twisting the leaves into dog's ears.

"I heard what he said as he left," Etta murmured. "I take it that you're sending him to try and get Mrs. Burnham to fall in love with him instead of with John. It seems to me a very unkind idea, and not very wise."

Alysia jumped up and shut her bureau with a thud.

"I've sold Reggie for good food, the use of a town house, a car, and my accounts settled for me every now and then. For ease and comfort, in other words, and I shall never have a happy day again."

Etta said nothing.

"Of course he'll marry the woman. It's the only way. I shall always hate myself—and him. Oh, curse money! Curse it!"

"Why, I thought you wanted more of it," Etta said with a smile that was frankly satirical. "But as to Reggie trying to separate Mrs. Burnham and John, if she loves

him she won't look at Reggie. And if she does let Reggie
wheedle her away from John, well, wouldn't it be just as
well for him to find out, before marrying her that her love
wasn't worth having?"

"You always can find some smug reason for doing
anything." Alysia squirmed in her chair. Suddenly she
jumped up.

"I'm going too! I won't let him go alone. After all, this
widow woman is very, pretty, Aunt Norah says; that
means nothing, but—"

"Now, don't be silly," Etta spoke firmly. "Don't go to
Vichy, too. You'll only spoil things. You've decided that
it's worth while giving up Reggie for the sake of staying
on here, living in John's house. Having decided it, stick to
it. You'll spoil everything if you go."

"It's all very well for you," her sister fairly tore the
Bradshaw between her groping fingers, "it's I who suffer.
I who give up the man I love, not you, and yet you'll
benefit too."

"The widow may not take him In which case, you
won't give up anything that is yours," Etta reminded her.

"I'd like to see the woman who can resist Reggie when
he tries to be charming."

"He'll make no headway with Aunt Norah," Etta
observed dispassionately. Even Alysia laughed. "I didn't
count her in. No, I don't think Aunt Norah will become
one of his admirers. But this other little simpleton, oh,
she'll never have seen anything so handsome and so
marvelous! He sweeps you off your feet, Etta, with that
voice of his."

"He may sweep the widow off hers," Etta conceded,
"and after all, there's no harm in Reggie. He would make
a rich woman quite a good husband. The pity is, that like
Becky Sharp, he needs five thousand a year to be good
on."

"If only there were some other way!" Alysia said.

"Short of waiting till Aunt Norah has given John the
thirty thousand she writes of as her wedding gift to him,

and then killing him off at once, I can see no way," Etta said pleasantly, "and somehow one doesn't feel like committing murder even for the sake of keeping Reggie in the family. But to be serious, there may be no marriage. There's Lady Ida to reckon with, too, you know. She's seemed quite determined on getting John back. And what she's determined on getting John back. And what she's determined on getting —" Etta's unfriendly smile finished the sentence. "Personally I should have waited, before sending Reggie off, to see what she would do."

"Oh, Ida!" Alysia fairly snorted. "She's no earthly chance of getting John back. She had him at her feet once and he got up again and walked away. When a man does that—"

"I've often wondered why he did do it." Etta murmured with retrospective curiosity. "If he did. I'm not so sure that there wasn't something else between them— not love, but business—"

"Same thing with her!" snapped Alysia. Etta gave a reproving shake of the head as she hurried off in answer to a telephone inquiry.

It was two days after she had sent off her letter to the Naylor sisters, and Lady Tait was installed in the hotel lounge for the first time since her accident. She looked about her with the vivid interest of one who had not expected ever to see a lounge again. After all, she was over seventy. But the present day seventy has plenty of fight and pluck. Silver haired, black browed, slender, handsome, energetic, she had come through with flying colors, and now, barring a limp, and a liking for chairs, was very much her old despotic self again.

To any one else, or to her at any other time, Vichy at this hour is insupportable. The papers had just arrived from Paris, and each vendor was shouting the name of his sheet in the peculiarly penetrating French twang.

"V'la La France!"

"V'la L'Intransigeant!" reached her most clearly in the national daily Eisteddfodd held outside and around the so-called Parc of Vichy. A moment later and the most penetrating howl of all cut through the others. It was *Le Matin*. Its vendor even managed to make himself heard through the hooting of the motors, which consider it a point of honor to sound their horns at their loudest and longest when rushing through Vichy.

Lady Tait picked out a macaroon from the plate and frowned. It was a most excellent macaroon. Such as only seem to grow in France. Grudgingly she admitted that much. But she regretted having come. Vichy water is all very well when drunk away from the springs with which she believed it to have no connection other than name, but she detested the place itself. She was not inclined to be pro-German, but when she compared French and German spas, her heart warmed to the Teuton.

Her English doctor hadn't wanted her to come. She had thought this insularity. Now she called it wisdom.

The French doctor to whom a friend had given her an introduction as one of the leading men there had just been in. Lady Tait's aquiline nose quivered with indignation. To stand behind her, put both his arms around her suddenly, and press his two outcurving thumbs hard into the center of her waistline, and then look grave because she gave a small howl of pain, was really not cricket.

Lady Tait was positive that Doctor Precheur would have shouted a great deal louder than that, if she had suddenly tried it with him. And then to talk about her solar plexus needing toning up, and to write out fussy ordinances for hot spinal shower baths and rubbings.

Fiddlesticks, thought Lady Tait, ruefully aware that her accident had at least saved her from the necessity of having three weeks of that sort of thing. As it was she had agreed to try them for a week, coming back next year for the regular cure should she find herself benefited. Her maid Rainer, came for her now. It was time for the first of the week's baths. Rainer wanted to go with her mistress, but Lady Tait did not want her. She liked exploring by herself. Lucy Burnham, too, would be at the *Etablissement des Bains*, and they would come home together.

A minute later and the hotel car put her down at what looked like a Moorish palace of white stucco, a big building just behind the Pare. Lady Tait stepped into a vast, vaulted hall, made her way to a businesslike looking desk, showed the doctor's *ordonnance*, and was given a ticket. She was directed down a passage which started with Eastern magnificence, but increased in simplicity with every step, until finally she was asked to wait in a ladies' waiting-room, which was a very creditable copy of the same room in an English country station. Here she was kept only a second, for two cheerful, smiling women pounced on her, declared themselves as Doctor Precheur's *baigneuses*, and took her into a tiny hall opposite. Here three wooden cubicles met her eye with a sort of sun blind across each doorway.

Lady Tait, as she undressed, wondered how stout women fared. Even for her the box was a tight fit. The next compartment was empty, the third apparently occupied.

"A lady, who comes frequently, had this, but we asked her to let Madame have it, as Madame is still a little lame from her accident," the woman had said on showing Lady Tait in. A very dashing garter on the floor suggested that the late occupant was young.

Lady Tait was undressing in her rather slow, methodical way, when she heard the door of the waiting-room open, and a swift step on the tiles. To her surprise, a second later, a hand, fat, pudgy, thrust something through the side of the sun blind into her cubicle without a word. It dropped on the floor on one of her shoes, a plain, closed envelope. Lady Tait supposed it to be some toilet advertisement, or fortune teller's address, but she slit it with an incurious finger preparatory to tearing it in half.

Inside, on a half sheet of paper, was written *Reginald Claridge*. Then came the following: *"Lives by his wits. Penniless. Small salary with Decor, Ltd. No money. No family. But knows some good people."*

That was all. Lady Tait turned the paper over. Nothing was written on the other side. The message, whatever its meaning, was all that the envelope contained. It struck her as extraordinary, this singularly brief and unflattering resumé of Mr. Claridge, written in English, and dropped into her cubicle here on the first visit that she had ever made to the baths. She read it again. Surely it was not some new form of advertising, too subtle for her to grasp?

She heard a voice speaking close beside her in French, a very trim shadow crossed her door blind. As she stepped out in her loofah shoes, and thick toweling wrap, the *beigneuse*, pocketing a departing tip, murmured to her *"La jeune anglaise"* who let Madame have her cabin.

"Could this have been meant for you?" Lady Tait called, as she held out the envelope with its odd enclosures. She had quite forgotten that there was another occupant of the little boxes. "It was dropped into this cubicle just now. It's certainly not for me;, as I saw when I opened it."

She found herself looking into a very striking young face, but, to her, a very repellent one. Lowbrowed, loose-lipped, hair rakishly parted on the side, gray-yellow eyes that were hard, and bold, and calculating.

"And it certainly isn't meant for me!" the stranger said, with almost rude negligence, as she skimmed over the words. "More likely for a detective, I fancy. I'll give it in at the Lost Property Office as I pass, since you say it isn't for you." The eyes rested impudently on the elder woman before she went on. Lady Taft felt that every white hair, every wrinkle, was noticed and scorned. That impression soon passed, but the incident itself stuck in her mind while one attendant played a hot water spray from across the large room up and down her spine, and the second rubbed her with Eau de Cologne.

She went on into the waiting-room and related the little happening to Mrs. Burnham who, her own carbonic acid bath over, looked fresh and charming as usual in her shady hat and frock of colored embroidery.

Lucy Burnham was a very pretty, sweet-faced woman with a gentle, timid glance and manner that suggested that life had not allowed her much independence as yet. Her unpowdered skin had no need to fear the light. Her curly hair still kept the gleams of a child in it. Figure, hands and feet were exquisite, and she was the kind who looks her best of a morning.

She burst out laughing at the account of the note, and refused at first to take it as true. But she was all eagerness to talk about a letter that John had handed to her from, his cousin, Alysia Naylor.

"Ah, yes, Alysia." Lady Tait's tone did not suggest great affection. "A note of congratulation, of course."

"Such a charming letter." Lady Burnham handed the sheet to her companion, who glanced it over.

"She's very popular, so is Etta," their aunt said, handing back the letter. "Etta was my favorite until just lately. She's adopted a most trying pose of saintliness which is too much for unregenerate me."

"But I should have thought!" Lucy Burnham opened her eyes very wide.

"Oh, real saintliness, is one thing. Every one admires that. But I can't stand goody-goodiness, which is quite another matter. I couldn't have Alysia here without her sister, and Etta would have paced my bedroom floor murmuring texts or sweet resigned words of consolation to me. I should have gone mad."

Lucy laughed again.. "It's a charming letter," she repeated, putting it away in her bag. "The two have kept house for John for years, haven't they?"

"Around five, I think. But as to keeping house—I left my own old housekeeper when my husband died, and John took over the house. I don't care for Chelsea. Never did. But the two girls have played hostess for John. Claud has a couple of rooms there too. He's moving into the Temple. As for the girls, they'll be a bit at a loose end for a while, I fancy."

"That's why I think it's such a sweet letter. I was very much afraid they would be a little bitter about his marriage."

Lady Tait did not reply that, however bitter Alysia Naylor might he feeling, she would nevertheless write just that sort of letter under the circumstances.

"She says her sister is quite looking forward to making my acquaintance. John tells me that Etta is a regular Juno. I rather wondered—" It was Lady Tait who laughed this time.

"No need to wonder, puss. John and the Naylor girls have never been particularly fond of one another. Besides, in confidence, my dear, it once looked as though Etta was about to make a very good match indeed." Lucy looked interested, but as Lady Tait's face suggested that she intended to say no more at the moment about any unfortunate love affair that her niece might have had, she too fell silent, only to reflect that, because Etta Naylor had been unable to marry where heart and interest led, it by no means followed that she would not have been quite willing to take second best—to wit, John Tait, and that that might be why only one sister had written.

CHAPTER TWO

BACK at the hotel, Lady Tait settled herself in the lounge to wait for her step-son, who was to pick up Lucy Burnham and take her for a drive to the heights around the hot, close, little town.

Suddenly she saw the young Englishwoman to whom she had spoken in the bathing establishment come into the hall. She moved to the manager's desk, and stood a moment waiting. Now that she could study it through her powerful lorgnette, Lady Tait, unenvious of the youth that she would not have again, if she could, liked the face even less than she had before. Give and take is the law of life. This girl belonged to the takers. Lady Tait doubted if she could ever give—unless it were something which she herself no longer wanted. The girl spoke to the reception clerk. Her words reached the elder woman "Madame de Souza likes the rooms. I will register now."

At that instant John Tait came into the lounge. He was a tall, well-set-up man, looking a good deal less than his age, which was between forty and fifty. It was a determined looking face, and yet with something about it that suggested the possibility of some hidden weakness. Lady Tait made an instinctive gesture at sight of him John Tait, her dead husband's only son, and since her own son had died, the only son of the house, was as fond of her as she was of him. He did not see her now, but stood a moment, buying some cigarettes. Then turning, he caught sight of the face still bent over the register.

Tait stood as though rooted to the spot. His step mother smiled a trifle grimly. John had once spoken of himself to her as a case-hardened bachelor, but that was just after he began to avoid Lady Ida, and Lady Tait had never taken him at that valuation. Quite the contrary, her private conviction was that Ida Westmacott must have made some very stupid blunder, otherwise any woman who was not positively ugly could lead John on a string.

Fortunately, he had rather a severe look and manner that quite misled strangers. But he had generally irreproachable manners. This absolutely gaping stare and pause in the middle of the hall was only to be excused by the girl's extreme, good looks, but even so, Lady Taft wondered at it—just now, with Lucy Burnham under the same roof. Then she wondered a great deal more. He came a step towards the girl, a step which brought him to her. Without looking up, still fingering a pen, her lips moved. Lady Tait watched the scene intently. The moving lips said something—gave some message. Tait nodded, his eyes swept around the lounge. When they caught sight of his step-mother she was apparently reading a novel. A moment later he stood beside her, smiling and cheery as ever, but he was quite pale, as she noted with sudden, swift suspicion.

"The sun was hot on the links," he said, as though conscious of his pallor. "I think for once I'll share your pernicious cup of before-lunch tea."

"What a lovely girl!" Lady Tait said, as she beckoned a waiter and gave the order. She looked deliberately across to the receptionist's desk. "English, I fancy. Who is she? Do you know?"

"Not the faintest idea," Tait said, rather shortly, and, with his back to the vision, he began to talk politics, a subject which Lady Tait as a rule loved. She answered a trifle at random now, but if her step-son felt a chill in the air, he gave no sign, unless he exerted himself more than usual to be agreeable, and he had great charm when he chose.

Lady Tait was not over-fond of unnecessary frankness. She considered it a very tiresome virtue, but a deliberate lie, such as he had just told her... However, perhaps it was just as well. But it was a most extraordinary incident. She knew well that there were two strains in the man, as there had always been in the boy. He was fond of work, ambitious, and endowed with the sense of worldly values which, as much as principles, helps to keep a man straight. This was the larger strain. But in all the Carfilds, and his mother was one of that ill-fated family, runs another streak, hidden most of the time, but now and then cropping out, a wild, reckless strain that had led to some black pages in the family annals. Of course there was very little of this strain in John, his step-mother hastily told herself. Still there was, yes, she must acknowledge it, there was a certain incalculable twist to him, a wild kicking up of his heels after a long and seemly trot along the beaten track, which had twice before, to her knowledge and therefore doubtless more than twice in fact—nearly ruined his career. But he had also a very keen sense of honor. Perhaps it was a narrow streak, but it was very rigid. And that, she told herself with the wisdom of seventy, was what counted in the long run. Not how wide, nor how high, but how inflexible, were the standards.

A minute later Lucy Burnham appeared. There was a look in John's eyes as he jumped to place a chair for her that quieted Lady Tait's dim alarm.

"I met such a lovely girl just now," Mrs. Burnham began—she looked like a girl herself under her big hat—"coming out of the lounge. I wonder if she is staying here?"

Neither of the two others made any reply. Lady Tait turned the talk to the drive up towards Royat.

John rose, and with a laughing word of excuse about the American bar, left them. He did not go towards the bar, but to the ballroom, deserted at this hour except for "the lovely girl" whom Lady Tait and Mrs. Burnham had both noticed. She was at the further end, where the orchestra usually played, ostensibly looking at the new ceiling.

"Mr. Tait," she began earnestly, as John joined her, "first of all, I'm here by the merest chance—with Mrs. de Souza, you know. But I was just going to write to you. You must help me out again. I've got to send in another fifty or he'll tell Mrs. de Souza, and I daren't risk that!".

John Tait said nothing. He stood looking gravely, searchingly at her with tight lips and brooding eyes. "And it's not only my own future that's at stake," the girl went on, as though desperate, her eyes big and pleading, "it's my father and mother too. I told you, when I had to ask you to pay the first time he threatened me, that my salary just lets, them live." Her lip trembled, but Lady Tait would have noticed that her eyes did not soften. They were as calculating as a croupier's. She must have known it herself, for she dropped her glance swiftly, to her beautifully-manicured hands, whose shape was not worthy of the rest of her, for there was something cruel about the deep valley that outlined each polished, orange nail.

"Poor Dad!" she repeated, her face working, "he's a cripple and mother can't leave him, nor is she strong enough to go out to work. Everything depends on my sending them in my salary regularly. I wish, oh a hundred times a day, that I'd never gone with you to that horrid night club. I lost all the money I had saved for them, and then—then—" she gulped.

"What made you come here?" Tait asked sternly.

She opened her eyes at him "I didn't come here Mrs. de Souza came here We were staying at the Cosmopolite first, but she didn't care for the food. I hadn't the faintest idea you'd be here. If I had, do you suppose I would have come? You flatter yourself, Mr. Tait, and suspect me quite unnecessarily of running after you. I don't need to run after men" She spoke with spirit. "If I hadn't met you in the lounge out there I should have sent his horrible letter to your club I can't pay him!" Her voice had changed to a note of despair. Tait said nothing for a long minute.

"Let me see the letter," he said finally.

She opened a dainty handbag, which had, however, an unusually good clasp, and held it out It was addressed to Miss Gillian Dundas, Hotel Bristol, Cannes. Inside was a note that ran:

"DEAR MISS DUNDAS,:

It was very good of you to buy the little sketch I offered you some six months ago. I had hoped to use the proceeds to go to America, as I wrote you at the time, but alas, a distressing illness has taken every penny of it. And once again I wonder if you would care to buy the accompanying sketch from me at the same figure—£50. This time I shall not delay with the precious money, but shall leave Marseilles at once with it. Or perhaps Madame de Souza might care for the picture? The snapshot, on which it is based is in New York, but I can easily have it posted to me at once. should you prefer this."

There was no signature. Tait stood for a while looking down at the familiar paper and writing. He had had one identical in practically, every sentence except that in his case the price had been five hundred, and that it had been his step-mother's name which the foul creature had used. He had paid. The first time a photograph had accompanied each letter. A copy of a snapshot taken by artificial light, and it showed John Tait walking across a floor in an apparently half-tipsy condition, one arm around the neck of Miss Dundas. In reality the floor had been as glass, and the arm had been thrown out but for a second, to help him keep his balance, as, turning, he had all but fallen on the slippery soles of his dancing pumps. It was this twist that had given his body its look of sagging knees and instability. But Tait also knew that on the night in question he had drunk a good deal, that he could not deny this. Besides, the snapshot really was absolutely damning, with his arms flung out, one clasping the girl's neck.

A line had been enclosed with the snapshot, giving a *poste restante* address in Nice. Tait remembered how Miss Dundas had rung him up. She had telephoned in tones of anguish her utter inability to find fifty shillings, let alone fifty pounds. He had sent the two sums of money, on his own and her account. He saw the abyss in front of him, but his step-mother frequently spoke of making him a gift of a sum large enough to let him live on, apart from his small salary and private means. Once let him have that firm ground under his feet, and he would snap his fingers at the blackmailer, and as for Miss Dundas, he would help her to find another situation if need be, but, in her case too, the payment would not be repeated. It was at her suggestion that they had originally gone on to the *Eye of Lucifer*, a mysterious, beautiful night club opened at Nice, where Gillian had pleaded that she wanted a flutter with an unexpected pound note her employer had given her on her birthday. John Tait that incalculable streak in him uppermost, knowing that no one he cared about was at Nice just then, had offered to take her there He was immensely struck with the girl's beauty, a captivity that did not last long, as he found her as stupid as she was good looking. Next day Mrs. de Souza left Cannes, taking her companion with her. Then, a week later, had come the telephone conversation and imploring letters, followed by a grateful note. That was six months ago and now this unexpected meeting in Vichy. Just day or two after he had received a second letter, a second hidden menace and demand for money.

Unfortunately his father's will had been made when he married a second time, when John was but a child, and well provided for by his mother's fortune. This fortune consisted of shares in a great shipping company, considered as almost a gilt-edged security, which suddenly and unexpectedly came to grief. The elder Tait meant to alter his will on that, but his own unexpected death prevented this, with the result that all his money went to his second wife, on whom John was dependent for the comforts of life, if not its necessities. A fact evidently known to the blackmailer.

This last was not surprising, for our extraordinary system of leaving wills open to any curious possessor of half a crown is of the greatest help to the underworld.

"I'll settle again this time," he said now, "but it is a final settlement."

"And he means it," she said about an hour later when relating the whole interview to a young man who sprawled facing her, in an armchair. The two were in the young man's private sitting-room at the *Hotel Splendide et Superbe*, a horrible new erection much, frequented by South Americans.

"But the point is, he's going to pay, and fifty pounds will be very convenient to me just now," she finished, "so you might as well hand it over now."

"You shall have it as soon as he pays," he assured her. "Just at the moment—" He waved a cigarette in the air to describe a naught. She laughed.

"Run of bad luck at the Casino, I suppose? I'm rather lucky. At least, I have been." She touched the wooden back of her chair hastily. He had passed a box of very expensive cigarettes over to her. Getting up for some matches, one saw how tall he was. But he carried himself so badly that he had a misleading look of suffering from slight spinal curvature. Moving a chair out of the way, one saw how strong he was with his abnormally long arms, how flexible his muscles. He was apparently on the young side of thirty, and had a very peculiar face. One sees lined faces, but this man's was not so much lined as folded. The forehead, the cheeks, the neck, all showed in numerable creases. It was rather a dismal face usually, but when he laughed, he did so so immoderately that one got the idea of an idiot. But the eyes were far from being an idiot's eyes. Something in their glance, though the balls were far from clear, certainly suggested a very swift and sly intelligence.

"So he doesn't like the style of my letters," he said, lighting her cigarette with a lover's lingering, a lingering she put an instant end to by throwing her head back with an impatient flip.

"They do the trick," she observed, and, picking up a weekly, turned to the fashion page and was at once absorbed in it.

"You don't think he suspects the truth?" he asked, after lying back, with his unhappy, creased face turned to the ceiling above him.

"Why should he? Innocent little lamb straying into strangely wicked places... bleating to be let out again... that was me that night."

"I wonder what would happen if he did suspect me though?" She asked the question idly, the underlying stupidity in her face showing for a second.

"Prison," he said shortly. "Penal servitude. Long spell." She flung the magazine from her, jumped to her feet, and whirled around on him in terror. Then her mood changed, she threw back her head and laughed incredulously.

"Quite right," he said approvingly, "something unpleasant would be much more likely to happen to him than to you...Much more!"

"I'm off," she said to that, drawing a lovely coat towards her with her foot. She had tossed it down on the floor beside her chair. "I hate talking, about being found out, and silly things that will never happen."

"You're an extravagant little spendthrift," he said reproachfully, picking it up for her and holding it. "I don't treat my clothes that way."

"Half the time you don't have any, probably." She laughed again and flung out of the room before he could reply.

Meanwhile Tait had taken Lucy Burnham for their drive. His step-mother sat on awhile, then she went to the desk.

"Who was that young lady who was talking to you just now? Very fair. Very pretty. I heard her mention the name of a Mrs. de Souza."

"Her name is Miss Dundas. Is she not beautiful? They are but just arrived. From the *Splendide*. A noisy place quite unfitted for visitors of distinction. She is traveling with the elder lady. A relative evidently."

"Dundas..." Now Lady Tait knew some Cheltenham Dundases, and some Dublin Dundases, a some Northumberland Dundases... "Do you happen to know her first name?"

The reception clerk opened the visitors' book and pointed to where, in a sprawling, slovenly hand, was written *Gillian Dundas*. The place from which she came was given as London. Just before hers was the name of Caroline de Souza. Also from London. Lady Tait was handing the book back when a name leapt out at her. Reginald Claridge—from London.

"And when did this gentleman arrive?" she ask, laying a finger on the name.

"Early this morning. Milady knows him?"

"I've seen the name before." Lady Tait turned away.

Obviously Mrs. de Souza and the young girl were traveling about to capture a wealthy husband for Miss Dundas. Lady Tait thought it must he the maid who had been instructed to find out particulars of all young men arriving at the hotel, so as not to let the lovely Gillian waste her time But that exchanging with John of a quick furtive sentence was not so easy to understand. Not by any means. As a picture painted by a master becomes more and more intricate, shows more and more lights and shades the longer it is studied, so this little scene grew more and more complex to the woman who had inadvertently watched it

After a rest in her own rooms, she decided to have tea in the lounge. John and Lucy might go on to Montdore. Lady Tait was stirring her cup meditatively when a young man dropped into the chair near her. He was very good looking indeed, she thought, quite unusually so. She caught his eye on her, and he bent forward with an effect of youthful impetuosity.

"They tell me you're Lady Tait. I happen to know two nieces of yours quite well. Alysia and Henrietta Naylor."

"Oh, so you know the Naylor girls, do you?" Lady Tait by a look invited him to take the chair beside her.

"I saw them only a couple of days ago, and when I told them I had booked a room here, they told that Naylor and Tait were both staying here with you. I hope your accident has left no ill effects? By the way, I should have introduced myself at once. My name is Claridge. Reginald Claridge," he murmured as he took the seat. "I say this is jolly! Making your acquaintance, I mean. I've so often heard the girls speak of you," and Reginald Claridge began his best entertainment form. He amused Lady Tait with his easy chat and talk of mutual acquaintances, which they seemed to have several.

"Knows some good people" returned to her mind more than once. As for Claridge, he was desperately bored. Lady Tait was not at all the kind of spiteful raffish old thing he liked to talk to. But there was still the young widow. So when, a little later, Mrs. Burnham came in, smiling from her drive, he looked at her with interest. But his heart, or, rather, his astute little brain, sank. She was quite, pretty, little woman with the charming complexion and the shining gold in her hair, but she was not his kind either. Simple. Foolish. Good. He summed her up to himself. The first two were all right, but they were quite wiped out by the last. You might as well make love to the curate's wife, he told himself disconsolately, as he smiled and bowed, and did his best to be interesting when Lady Tait introduced him.

John was detained, Mrs. Burnham said, but would come in shortly. Claridge noticed the way in which Lady Tait's eyes at once roamed the lounge as she heard this. He wondered why. But at that moment a young man and a girl came into view, at sight of whom Claridge nearly swallowed a gulp of tea. Here was something worth coming to Vichy for. What looks! What style! Nothing goody-goody about this damsel. His glance flicked contemptuously over "bread-and-butter Mrs. Burnham," as he called her to himself, and Lady Tait. The young man talking to the girl was Naylor. His clever, rather hatchet face was alight, and yet his eyes as they rested on the girl beside him were critical. There was something a little off-hand in his manner too as he walked over with her to the group around the tea table.. Claridge felt that he was stressing the off-handedness, as a man might struggle against his bonds, or pretend that they were not there.

Lady Tait was gracious but a trifle persistent in her inquiries as to which of the Dundases Gillian belonged. The girl modestly claimed a distant kinship with the Northumberland family. She spoke easily, she said the most correct things, yet Claridge felt even surer than ever, from something in her eye and smile, that this lovely young creature was no prude.

But prude or no, he found that Miss Dundas would have none of him, when he tried later on to improve the acquaintance. Not being Lady Tait, he had no clue as to why she barely tolerated him, refused to laugh at his most risque jokes, and generally stiffened whenever he joined her.

As to Mrs. Burnham, further acquaintance only deepened his conviction that he would never be able to cut John out from the little widow's affections, nor would want to achieve that feat. She bored him stiff and apparently he had the same effect on her. So the journey to Vichy was a washout as far as the plan was concerned, but it had shown him Gillian Dundas, and to her he devoted himself. That he was playing false with the woman who had sent him to Vichy, did not trouble Claridge in the least. He was always playing women false. He determined that he would make an impression on the cool, disdainful beauty whose yellow gray eyes fell away from his own passionate ones so indifferently. Something hot and ugly stirred in him at her ignoring of him. An ignoring that told him, quite rightly, that for some reason or of she did not take him at his own face value. It stung Claridge. He had hitherto found his good looks that was needed to capture a young woman of Gill Dundas' type, and he could not understand why the assets of his did not avail now. As to having misread the girl's type, he knew better! That Mrs. Burnham should be quite patently indifferent to him he could understand. She was about to make a much better match, and, moreover, Claridge could not get up steam where she was concerned. But that this girl, with that in her—black spots—which he felt and knew were kin to his own stripes, that she should pass him over so negligently was intolerable. It could only mean, he felt sure, there was another man. Jealousy flamed and smoked in Claridge. It was not Naylor. The girl exerted herself to please the young barrister, it was true, but Naylor refused to become a victim. However desperately he flirted, his manner always underscored the fact that it was but a flirtation, and Claridge was sure that Gillian herself was not in the least moved by Naylor. That meant that it was some illicit, or at least clandestine, love affair. He had twice come on her and Tait in an out of the way place at the Casino or in the hotel. Each time they had had some easy careless explanation, but each time Tait had looked stirred—moved. Dimly Claridge saw a possibility of pleasing Alysia, justifying his own mission as an irresistible Adonis, without the bother of making love to Lucy Burnham.

Claridge watched Gillian Dundas as a cat watches a mousehole. Unknown to her, he even moved into the room next to hers, the better to spy and listen. There was no result. He decided to leave Vichy as soon as his week was up.

Going down to the lounge to post the letter to Alysia, which would tell her of his return with his mission unaccomplished, he nearly ran into Lady Tait's group which, for once, Mrs. de Souza and Miss Dundas had joined. Mrs. Burnham was chatting pleasantly to the

young girl, who met her rather shy advances with an air
of bored hauteur. Lady Tait made no advances. She spoke
to Miss Dundas as little as possible, and, answered her as
briefly.

The manager bustled up. Would the ladies and
gentlemen be interested to see a real Moroccan sorcerer?
There was one in the hotel for this evening who had been
chief soothsayer to Abd-el-Krim himself. He was said to
be marvelous. Paris was wild over him. Later on, he
would give a sort of midnight show for all the guests, but
if the ladies would like the chance to see and hear him
first, perhaps to try him, eh? These things, one did not
believe them, of course, oh no! But they were rather
amusing, were they not?

Now Lady Tait, oddly, enough, was rather interested.
She had once met a man in Egypt, a snake charmer, who
had told her two events, both of capital importance in her,
life, which had come true within the, year. Mrs. Burnham
demurred. She was not quite sure that she approved of
such things. Either the man was an out and out fraud,
and one should not encourage frauds, or there might be
something in it, in which case it rather frightened her...

Mrs. de Souza was all aglow at the idea. She was a
rather plethoric silent woman who eyed any one talking
to her with a somnolent good humor that was occasionally
belied by a glance of quite unusual sharpness. Gillian
Dundas, too, begged to see the marvel.

"Come this way," the manager murmured, leading
them around into his private sitting-room. He left them
there, and a minute later a tall, thin figure in an Arab's
flowing robes bowed gravely to the group.

"You wish to know the future?" he began briskly, in
perfect French. Without waiting for the affirmation he
unrolled, a strip of oil cloth that he carried under his arm,
and laid it on the table after glancing at a wrist-compass.
"I face Mecca," he murmured, as he stood behind it rather
like a salesman. From his bosom he drew out a little red

bag, an opening it, placed it by his side on the cloth. It contained—he said—sand from the desert.

"Now will you all stand around the table?" he asked. "I will then read the sand as it falls, as to the future, and in general terms. After that, I will go into that inner room, and whoever of you likes can have a private reading, when I will tell the whole truth, for I am one who sees the whole truth. But for the moment I speak in general terms, and each of you can judge how much I could tell—in private?'

There was no mistaking the fact that Mrs. de Souza now looked distinctly uneasy. It was only when she saw Lady Tait eyeing her with rather malicious enjoyment, and caught the surprised look in Lucy Burnham's eyes, that she assumed an air of indifference.

The Arab dipped his right hand into the red bag and dribbled some sand in front of each. "I will start with you, sir." Tait was the one nearest to him on his left. The Arab bent forward, letting more sand begin to dribble through his fingers. Then he gave a sort of convulsive start, and did the same in front of the next, then rapidly round the circle. In an instant he had stepped back from the table, swept the sand on it back into his red bag, caught up the oil cloth and vanished.

The group around the table waited. This was part of the show. Lady Tait began to laugh, it was so absurd.. "How long do we wait here, until cock-crow, or, something of that sort? I hope he hasn't gone to sacrifice the cock, by the way." Lucy Burnham did not laugh. She had an idea—absurd, of course, that the man had fled.

The door opened, but it was the manager only. And a most apologetic manager.

"Miladi, mesdames, messieurs, I am desolated! Figure to yourselves that idiot has left some important charm behind him in Paris and cannot tell fortunes without it. He has gone to wire for it to be sent him —the toe of some holy man probably—but until it comes he is just an ordinary Arab, he says, and can no more tell the past or the future than you or I."

Lady Taft found the idea of an Arab Moslem necromancer using a telegram with which to summon his magic working charms distinctly funny.

The manager escorted them to the lounge and finally left them with many apologies. Then, he returned to his office. The Arab rose from a chair, at a table. In his hand was an envelope.

"I have written and sealed this. If you open it this time next year you will know why. I refused to tell the fortunes of those ladies and gentlemen." Ibrahim ben Mahrnoud ben Jussuf, Head Sorcerer of Abd-el-Krim, would have glided softly from the room, but the manager stopped him.

"You can't give any show tonight. It would be an insult to those other ladies and gentlemen. As it is, I had to invent some absurd story to excuse you..."

"They are leaving shortly," the Arab said in his thick guttural French.

"Tomorrow."

"Then I will give my show tomorrow night. I do not care to be in the presence of those about to die."

The manager was impressed and uneasy against his will.

"*Voyons,* if a calamity is coming, say a railway accident or another motor smash, the elder lady has already been in one—a word of caution, perhaps—"

"No word can stop what is coming," the Arab said indifferently. "It is not evil of the kind avoided. *Mektub—* it is written," and this time did not pause again, but passed on out, like some figure of fate.

Lady Tait went early to bed that night, her last night. She had an idea when she woke next morning that she had been dreaming badly. Something about John Tait and that Dundas girl... She shared Claridge's certainty about her character it, and, like him, could find nothing

on which to hang her conviction. Not that it would seem
to matter.

She watched her maid collect a few last trifles of
books and cushions from the sitting-room.

"There's a very lovely young girl staying at the hotel,
Rainer, Miss Dundas by name. I suppose my nephew has
been quite aware of the fact?"

Rainer looked at her mistress over her spectacles.
She coughed a little coyly.

"Well, my lady, I didn't like to worry and, after all,
why shouldn't the young gentleman see a good deal of
her? Lovely she is, and they seem to have plenty of
money. Not that I think he lost his head if you take my
meaning."

"Mr. Claud wouldn't do that easily." Lady Tait spoke
dryly. In common with most women, caution in a man
was not a trait she prized.

"And that's a blessing, my lady," Rainer said
fervently. "As for Mr. John, he hasn't eyes for any one
except for Mrs. Burnham."

"Who is Miss Dundas, do you know?"

Rainer did not. "The ladies seem quite all right,
respectable I mean, and that. But not in the swim. Not at
all in the swim. Mrs. de Souza's English herself, her
husband was the foreigner, but I got it out of the maid
that she had applied for tickets for the Royal Enclosure
but didn't get them. Which shows—"

"Very little," was Lady Tait's private comment. Aloud
she said: "You'll be late for your dinner, Rainer." She was
not interested in Mrs. de Souza nor in anything, beyond
hearing that John had not been seen about with Miss
Dundas.

Rainer tossed her head.

"And a funny time to have it," she plumped up a
cushion afresh, "and the meals themselves! I didn't want
to worry you, my lady, but they really are the limit!"

"The management wrote that they were very careful
of the food served at the housekeeper's table. It's a bit

late in the day for complaints, in any case." Lady Tait disliked grumbles.

"It's not the food, it's the way it's served. Oh, they're quite mad. They serve the meat by itself and the vegetables separately. Would you believe it, my lady!" And with this specimen of foreign insanity Rainer vanished.

Lady Tait should have felt entirely at ease. But a memory would not be dismissed. A memory of words without any sound. As for Claud, her nephew, she was profoundly indifferent as to whether he was interested in Gillian Dundas or not. He would never do anything foolish. Catch Naylor marrying a nobody! But those soundless, moving lips... Lady Tait could not shake that burr out of her mind, try as she would.

CHAPTER THREE

CLARIDGE left Vichy on the same day, and by the same train that carried Mrs. de Souza and Gillian Dundas to Paris They stopped there for a while. So did Claridge, but he dropped a line to Alysia. She read his note twice, the first time with a pleased smile, the second with a hard frown

"He couldn't do it." She announced briefly. "So I'm fifteen pounds out. But it seemed worth trying And had he really put his heart into it, he ought to've turned the trick."

"Put *what* into it?" Etta asked in a tone of stupor.

Alysia flushed. "Tried harder!" she snapped. "Well," she drummed her fingers on the table. "I'm not beaten yet. Not till the marriage actually takes place. But I see you have a letter from John. What does he say? More gush about the Silly Widow?" This was Alysia's latest name for Mrs. Burnham.

"What an unkind way to talk of her. He writes me just what he wrote you."

"A second notice to quit, eh?" Alysia bit her thin, flexible lips.

"He repeats what he wrote you, that we might like to stay at Tor Cottage until we have time to make our plans."

"What plans? The only plans I want to make would be how to separate him from that designing woman."

"You haven't been gambling on the Stock Exchange, have you?" Etta asked suddenly.

"I have, and with the very damnedest kind of damned bad, luck."

"I do wish you wouldn't swear," Etta said plaintively.

"Nothing to the language you used to use," her sister, retorted, around a cigarette holder. "I've done awfully well, you know—as a bear, of course. And that made me reckless. It seemed so safe. I ought to've gotten from under a fortnight ago... But I had a direct inside tip. It was Mayer, Card and Tully, and instead of the negotiations falling through, they've been ratified and on splendid terms. The shares have soared. Soared!" She steadied her voice with an effort to level calm. "Of course I told them to buy at the lowest possible and they did so And—well, it's the end for me. But perhaps by selling everything I have in the world I can just about clear myself."

"When is settlement day?"

"It's a three weeks' account. In a fortnight's time. Why?"

"What about John helping you out? As a loan, of course."

"John won't help now. Nor have I anything on which to borrow. The bank is selling the shares it holds of mine, and of course they're down. They would be. I knew from old experience that it's no use coming to you."

"I haven't a farthing," Etta said promptly. "I never can make ends meet. I could spend double my income and still leave any amount of deserving cases unhelped."

"You and your charities that no one knows anything about!" Alysia bit her, lip. This was becoming a vulgar squabble, and Alysia was not vulgar as a rule. "At any rate," she went on more quietly, "you're interested too in stopping this wretched marriage of John's. Something must be done."

"If it is to be stopped it will be, and if not, it's no use trying to do anything," Etta said to that.

"You used to be good at thinking out ways and means in the old days and little you cared as to the means you used!"

"Just so. In the old days," Etta repeated with a sigh that sounded regretful.

"I notice, you always get what you want," her sister said tartly.

For a second Etta's eyes seemed to double in size and glow with fire. Then they fell. "That must be because nowadays I only want what's right," she said sweetly, "and as I only want what's best for John here, it's rather difficult. Let's hope it's best for him not to marry." She rose with an air of closing the conversation. "Where's Claud?"

"Not up yet, I fancy."

Their brother had arrived back from Vichy the previous night. John was not with him. He had stopped on the way up from Dover to meet some of Mrs. Burnham's relatives.

But Claud was not in bed. He was walking briskly towards a one-man picture show in Bond street. Claud was not particularly fond of painting, but, as a rising young barrister, he considered that it behooved him to know something about everything that was on in town, and he was lunching with one of the show's patrons. He was thinking, as he walked, of the flat which he would take in the Temple, if he could get one that suited him and his purse. If only his aunt would make him an allowance one-tenth as generous as she made her stepson. True, the bulk of her money had belonged to her late husband. Naylor wondered how John liked being under her thumb to such an extent, having to take an allowance, for instance, when usually the money would have been his, and the allowance would have been Lady Tait's. His step-mother had been generous. But for that John could not have taken the post of unpaid private secretary to Lord Parkington, and that selflessness was now about to be rewarded by the Consular Generalship of Rangura. One of those Consular appointment which are diplomatic, and are only given the lesser title to avoid offending the vanity of some neighboring state. And events were shaping Rangura into a mile stone on the road to the Embassy of Paris. Yes, it had paid John well to keep in with his stepmother, Claud reflected. A most promising future was vaguely outlining itself, and as a wedding present a sum of thirty thousand pounds was to be paid into his banking account. The necessary papers were to be signed at the wedding breakfast. Thirty thousand pounds a very pleasant outlook for John Yet John had had to pay for the gift. He used to like a good time on the quiet as much as any man, and Aunt Norah, well, Aunt Norah's idea of a good time would have seemed dull even on board the Ark. Five years ago there had been a dreadful rumpus between the two. She had threatened to cut down John's allowance. And she was the kind to have done it too. Claud had thrown himself into the breach. He and John had always been pals, and things had been glossed over, and soothed out, and tucked neatly away, and John had had the lesson of his life, at any rate as to handing over the wrong letter to be read. And doubtless as to the folly of folly. Lady Tait had told Claud only last week that John had never given her a second's worry since. Which was just as well, seeing that she had assured John that if ever anything of that kind happened again, his allowance would be halved. A most unfair threat, Claud considered, seeing that his cousin had never had a chance to be self-supporting, and seeing that it was his father's money.

Aunt Norah—John—it was but a step to Gillian Dundas, or had she been in his mind all along? Claud told himself that it was not fair. He had definitely parted from Miss Dundas "over there" and here she was, walking down Bond Street with him, thrusting herself into his mind again.

At this point, Claud pushed open the door of the show with such violence that he almost flattened out the commissionaire, who looked surprised. As a rule, smartly turned out young men did not burst in to see the paintings with such an air of determination.

Claud soothed his feelings, took a catalog, and walked on. He spent an informative half hour memorizing pictures which would probably have the most success, then he turned to go. But he saw Lady Ida Westmacott also looking at some of the paintings. Poor Lady Ida, she must be feeling her nose most awfully out of joint. And it was such an imperious high-bridged nose, too. It would have been a splendid match for her. Obviously. Poor as a church mouse. Married to a man who had died after losing all his money. Nothing but a brother-in-law's generosity to depend on until her son should some day inherit from him. And she must be... Claud did some ungallant arithmetic. Close on forty. Well, Mrs. Burnham was as old as that. But the difference! Where Lady Ida was coldly handsome, Mrs. Burnham looked both kind and gentle. Gentle.... Claud lingered on the word.

He, too, meant to marry that kind. Good family, of course, plenty of money of course, but gentle too. Gentleness, he reflected, with one of those streaks of acumen which made him a rising young man, was the one thing in a woman that never let you down.

Lady Ida was not gentle. The blue of her eyes told you that. The cut of her cheek-bones. She was clever, very, intellectual and witty, but a first-class fighter had been lost when Lady Ida was born a girl. And she was reputed to have the determination of a mule. Certainly if that quality could do it, her son would be prime minister in time.

Yet, with all her determination, she had lost her hold on John. Claud had been puzzled by his cousin's relinquishing of the lady who so plainly cared for him and for whom he had appeared to have a genuine attachment. Three years ago or a little less, their engagement was as good as announced, then John had cooled off steadily—unmistakably...

Turning suddenly, Lady Ida caught sight of Claud and came forward. As always, she was beautifully turned out. Her fine eyes were bright as polished agates.

"Back already? I thought Lady Tait was keeping you to draft her last will and testament in Vichy?"

He replied on the same bantering note, and they discussed the accident.

"And so you've had the chance of getting to know John's fiancée," she said finally. "I hear she is quite charming."

Claud murmured an assent. "And he's certainly devoted to her, judging from the letter he wrote me," she went on. "I'm so glad. For really poor John is one of those men that some woman or other would marry out of pity and that is a pity, isn't it?" She flashed a brilliant smile at him. "By the way, how do your sisters feel about this marriage of John's?"

"Charmed, I suppose," he said indifferently, stopping before another picture. "That's rather good!"

"Not bad," she agreed without, a glance. "But do tell me what Etta says about this engagement."

"Etta?" Naylor looked at her coldly. "Of all the infernal cheek," was his unspoken thought. But then, Lady Ida had the cheek of the devil; "She's delighted," he said. "That's a nice bit of color," and apparently lost in artistic appreciation he drifted away, turned a corner and passed into another room. Ida Westmacott had a sharp tongue, and a sharp tongue in this world invariably cuts its owner's throat, besides gashing other people.

Claud did the gallery methodically, marking a few of the pictures that interested him most. There was one in particular... it reminded him of... its price turned out to be a little beyond the sum at which he had assessed it in his mind, and it was characteristic of the young man that he wasted no time in tergiversations or dallying with the thought of buying it in spite of that. With a civil word of regret that his finances would not permit him to follow his fancy, he walked away. Many another man in his place would have considered that he could well afford to buy the thing, but Claud was caution itself. Back at the house in Chelsea, John and his step-mother found the two Naylor "girls" busily superintending the packing of their own effects.

Lady Tait insisted on her nieces taking up their quarters with her at Great Cumberland Place until the wedding, when they could both go down to the cottage, and there make further arrangements. She included Claud, too, in this invitation, or rather summons. In his case he was to stay until his chambers should be ready for him.

That done, she left the younger generation to talk about hidden lighting, and geometrical furniture, and busied herself with the morning papers and her letters which she had brought with her. She wanted a final word with the decorators as to putting all this down to her account. Until then, she shut herself into the library, thankful that there is no modern substitute for books and bindings.

John came in presently. He was charmed with everything Delighted, as he said, that his cousins were so pleasant about leaving this house—his father's house— which had been a home to them for some years now.

Lady Tait was not in a good humor, he found. She was annoyed at finding that some of the more gossipy papers had published her intention to settle thirty thousand of his father's money on John when he married, and still more annoyed at a letter which had arrived for her this morning as a result of that announcement. It was one of those that she had brought with her.

"I didn't intend to show it to you," she said as she produced it, "but I have every confidence in your good sense." Still she fingered it. Something startled showed for an instant in John's clever but rather reckless looking dark eyes, but the look passed as he saw the writing on the envelope.

"Is it from the Ricci's?"

She nodded almost fiercely.

"From Hudson's wife?"

"She never was a wife." Lady Tait spoke in a low tone, a tone of positive loathing. "She was a horrible vampire.

She took everything from my boy and left nothing but the drunken shell of him. Yes, the letter is from her."

Stretching out his hand for it, John read:

"YOUR LADYSHIP,—

"I have read in the paper just now that you are giving your step-son thirty thousand pounds when he marries next month, and that all the rest of your husband's money is coming to him when you die. This is a wicked thing to do. That you would like me to die of hunger I can understand. You have always hated me. You were jealous that it was me and only me your son loved. I knew that the one time I saw you. But why should you hate the child of your only child? Why should your son's son have nothing, and this stranger to you have all? Give him the thirty thousand if you like, but give your own grandchild something too. If you do not you will be sorry, and this John Tait will be sorry too. I give you a warning. You had better take it.

"Maria Ricci."

Tait laid the letter down slowly, thoughtfully.

"You mustn't mind my saying that one can understand why she feels a little bitter," he said quietly, looking at her with something placating in his smile; "thirty thousand pounds is a splendid wedding present to Lucy and me, but after all, wouldn't it be possible to make some sort of an allowance to her boy, Hudson's son? The fact that she married her cousin so soon after Hudson's death—"

"Makes no difference at all." Lady Tait flashed hotly. "I'm not an unjust woman. But neither am I a simpleton. That child wasn't Hudson's child! Don't let yourself get sentimental, John. I was afraid of this when I hesitated about showing you that letter.   Maria Ricci and her cousin and all her family lived on my son, sponged on him, battened on him. They taught him to drink. You know what we went through during the four years before he died. Four years during which he was never sober."

She turned her anguished face away, tears in her keen eyes.

"It was that hurt to his head when he was hit by the falling chimney," John said, laying a gentle hand on her twitching fingers. "And one can't but allow that they were very good to him at the time."

"Of course they were!" she had conquered her softer emotion again. "They guessed how profitable a young man struck senseless just outside their wine-shop might be. And, of course, he fell in love with this Maria. And, of course, they got him to stay with them so that they could all live on him. Oh, don't talk of it!" She shuddered. "It was horrible! Horrible! You, too, tried to get him to come home and give her up, and you, too, failed."

"Just so. He loved her. He married her," John reminded his step-mother.

"It wasn't love at the end." Lady Tait spoke in a stifled voice. "She frightened him. In some way she dominated him until he had no will of his own. Horrible! And all the time there was this cousin, Guido Ricci... and that dreadful child, his image! Even Hudson never ventured to talk of him to me after the once. Even he guessed the truth. The child is the image of the Italian."

John stuck to his point. It was one he had often broached before and always in vain.

"That would be a good argument if Ricci weren't her cousin. As it is, the boy might merely take after his mother's people —a grandparent, say."

"A cousin, I say!" There was the flush of anger in her cheek "Not another word, John. Don't you suppose I know what I'm talking about?" John did not. He very much doubted if any one except Maria and her cousin knew the truth. But something in his talks with the Italian woman had made him think that she had really adored the young Englishman whom a tragic fate had literally flung into her arms one warm summer evening when he turned a, corner, was caught by a falling chimney, and was never the same again. Some injury to the brain or nerve cells too deep for medical knowledge to find, had turned a pleasant, level-headed young man, who had taken a good degree the month before, and intended doing something with his talents, into an ineffectual drunkard, whom nothing could rouse, who drank himself steadily to death after four years of life in the gutter.

John privately believed that the boy, born six months after the marriage in a registry office, really was Hudson's child, and as such the only descendant. of the woman facing him.

"In law the child was his," he said stubbornly.

"Law!". Lady Tait's tone was scorn itself. "Let her go to law, then. She had the thousand that his grandmother had left Hudson, unhappily. Or the Ricci's would soon have let him go. He and she and they together spent every penny of it—"

"Still," he urged, as she fell silent, "couldn't you do something for them as a matter of prudence? These Sicilians, the Riccis are Sicilians aren't they, can be very vengeful."

He himself had long ago offered to provide a good school for the boy, but the ex-Mrs. Hudson Tait had refused his offer with scorn. John thought that she had an idea that any taking of money from him might invalidate her claims to the fortune of her dead husband's parents...

"Nothing this woman can say—or do—nothing any of her family can say or do, would make me alter my determination not to let them have one penny. One farthing! On the contrary." And this time there were glints of fire in her quick brown eyes. "On the contrary! It would be only by the grace of heaven that I could give one of them a crust of bread if they were starving. They ruined Hudson. Would you ask me to help her, if, she had held my son down underwater till he was drowned? Well, that is what she did. Held him down in the mud till he died of mud. Strangled by her, and mud. Oh, don't talk of it! Give me that letter!" Her fingers quivered as she took it back "Let her threaten! Let them do what they like! Let them and mind you, John, no yielding on your part. You've a soft streak in you that you must fight. That something in you I can't quite count on. You must stand firm in this." Her eyes, inexorable, held his. He only sighed and shook his head stubbornly.

"If you feel any scruples about accepting my wedding present and ultimately the rest of your father's money—" Her forbidding tone finished the sentence. What could John do? He was dependent on his stepmother for his luxuries at any rate, and the very fact that Lucy was so well off made him the more grateful for the promised gift which, added to his other means, would enable him to be independent of his wife.

He hastily expressed these feelings. She looked, at him shrewdly, and yet kindly. She was very fond of John.

"Something's bothering you. You haven't been yourself at all lately, except by an effort."

"I haven't felt quite up to the mark," he replied hastily. She looked at him a second longer, her head on one side, playing with her beautiful rings. Privately she was certain that it was connected with money troubles. Whether rightly or wrongly, however, truthfully or not, John always suggested a certain indifference to money. He gambled in a mild way, she knew, and suspected deeper plunges.

He did not come to lunch, excusing himself over the telephone to Lucy in a voice and manner that suggested that something was worrying him. But he gave no explanation of his absence, not even when he arrived at three to drive her to a furniture sale in Hanover Square that she had wanted to see. He was late, and apologized, with a rather forced humor for it. He was all on edge, she thought, so was his driving. Finally, when he tried to turn into a "no entry" street, he turned to his companion.

"Do you mind if we do the rest on foot, darling? My road sense seems to've deserted me for the time being."

Lucy was thankful to get out. It had not been John's fault just now that there had not been a rather nasty squeeze between two buses. She hinted as much, half laughing up at him. Suddenly her smile left her. She made a half clutch at his arm with a little gasp.

Tait followed the direction of her eyes and stood still too. Facing them on the pavement was a news-vendor's stand. And directly in front of them was the announcement on one of the boards: "Lord Mills found shot. Arrest of valet."

In a second Tait had bought two copies of the paper, motioned to a taxi, and helped Mrs. Burnham in, jumping in after her.

"Where to? Oh—the park. Just keep on driving round and round till I say when." After which he handed his companion one paper and unfolded the other. Each read how Lord Mills had been found shot through the head in his study, a revolver beside him And that the police had arrested his valet on suspicion of having had a hand in the death.

"How terrible!" Lucy was the first to speak. Her eyes had been as much on her companion as on the paper. "He was a fellow chairman or director or something with you on some of your tea companies, wasn't he?" He nodded. His face was gray. She slid one of her soft little hands into his. He had a delightful hand, had Tait. The sort of hand that belongs to a good friend. Firm and warm.

"I didn't know he was such a friend of yours," she said sympathetically.

"He wasn't. But that valet of his saved my life at Paschendaele. I got him the place because he can't take a situation where there are stairs. To've arrested good old Brown for Mills' murder! Darling, I must leave you." He stopped the taxi. "Sorry, but I have some things to see to at once, that can't be put off."

"I'll go back to Great Cumberland Place. But you'll come to dinner without fail," she insisted.

He shook his head. "I'm afraid I can't. I've several very important things to do. Besides—I should be no fit company for you today."

"But your cousins will be there!" Her voice was aghast.

"Well?" He contrived to smile. "They like you immensely. They must."

She smiled back a little wistfully.

"I'd like to think so. But I am stealing you from them. Taking their home from them they might say."

"They'd die before they thought, let alone said, such a thing!" he retorted with affectionate exaggeration.

She touched his hand again.

"I've met them at lunch, you know. Alysia dislikes me officially as it were. Oh, yes, she does. But Etta dislikes me personally."

"Nonsense, darling!" he said firmly, but for once rather as though his mind were elsewhere, and when she had driven off, his face might have been set on a swivel, so swiftly did it alter, so dark and brooding did it become in an instant.

Claud Naylor, too, was reading the same piece of news in the same edition of an evening paper. He, too, was much shocked. Mills was a typical *bon viveur* when he had last seen him. Somehow murder—and it was obviously a question of that since the valet was detained—seemed very far, from that good-natured, easygoing man of the world.

Mills had apparently been quite alone in the flat except for his valet. Lady Mills and his daughters were in Yorkshire. She belonged to the county, a member of a very rich and powerful old family. Mills was but a self-made man's son, and was credited with having long ago run through the fortune that gave his father his peerage. The paper was very guarded as to exactly what had happened in that lonely study in that empty fiat.

John would be shocked too, Claud reflected. Mills was on some of his companies, besides being an acquaintance.

The news would startle Miss Dundas as well, if, or rather when, she should learn of it. For some one had told him only yesterday of having seen Mills about a year ago, driving about a good deal around Trouville with a remarkably lovely girl in his car. A few adroit questions, and the girl had certainly sounded unmistakably Gillian Dundas, added to the fact that she had been to Trouville. Claud hoped grimly, that the news of Mills' death would shock Miss Dundas very much indeed. The idea of her allowing a man old enough to be her father to drive her about alone in his car. Claud nearly stepped off the curb into a passing bus at the thought—general thought, of course; Applicable to any girl and any elderly man. His indignation, he assured himself, carefully, was strictly impersonal.

But at the moment Miss Dundas was far too busy to look at newspapers.

She had just arrived at Victoria with Mrs. de Souza, and they had found that two trunks which had been despatched beforehand could only be cleared through the Customs when the luggage on the boat train had been examined. Mrs. de Souza and her maid left Gillian to see to this and drove off. Now Reginald Claridge had stayed on in Paris at the same hotel, and had crossed with them to Folkstone. He had tried to talk to Gillian on the boat, but the snub he had received was so unmistakable that after it, even he effaced himself for the time being.

He was sulkily watching the trio, saw Mrs. de Souza and her maid drive off, heard, for he was just having his own things put into a taxi, her employer tell her to bring the trunks on with her, and then, to his surprise saw her motion to a taxi, once they were well away.

"Follow that taxi over there," he said to his own driver. After one look at the girl in it, the cabman gave a most understanding nod.

Claridge was driven round the corner of the station into one of those streets that call themselves Belgravia but are spoken of as Victoria. Here Gillian pulled up, and said something to her. driver, who gave four toots on his horn. Instantly the door of a tall house, that. had once been a good one, was opened, and a young man ran down the steps and bounded into the taxi. All with a speed that might have been due to a lover's ardor or to a criminal's reluctance to be seen by a passing policeman.

For a quarter of an hour the taxi with Gillian and the stranger in it drove round,. followed by Claridge. Then it returned to the house, and the young man let himself in with a key. Gillian, Claridge found, now went back to the station, and proceeded to carry out instructions.

He himself was deeply disappointed. This was no good. He had not the brains to wonder what conversation could be so important as to need such secrecy. He had had a good look at the young man as he jumped into and then when he left the taxi. A very loose-limbed big young man with enormous breadth of shoulder and long arms who slouched as he walked till he looked half deformed. He certainly had a good tailor, an English one. Yet the astute Claridge did not think that he was his tailor's favorite. Something suggested very superior cutting negligently put together, as though for a man of no social importance. He, Claridge, would not have accepted the fit of the collar, for instance. Yes, he thought ruefully as he turned away from the station, his outing had only been another wash-out. Yet he still felt certain that if he could only get behind the painted curtains of Gillian Dundas' life, he would come on something discreditable. He was as sure of this as he was of the innocent and dull background of Lady Tait and Mrs. Burnham's past lives. And if he could find out just what it was, he would have the haughty beauty at his mercy.

He drove back to the house from which he had seen the stranger come out. There he rang the bell. The door was opened by a man in a jacket, a servant of some kind. He looked Italian. Claridge was feeling in his pocket for a non-existent card. He withdrew it empty with a gesture of annoyance. He had met a gentleman in the boat-train today; they had talked business and the other had given him his card and asked him to call on him here. Unfortunately, he had lost the card, though he had remembered the address. As to the gentleman in question—Claridge here described the man whom he had seen a few minutes before. That would be Mr. Strange, the servant said at once. "Ground floor flat. He's in." Apparently the man considered that his duties were done with that announcement, for he went downstairs again pointing over his shoulder at the door beside Claridge.

Claridge opened it and stepped into a typical sitting-room of this kind of house. He had expected to find the man inside and intended then to back out after a good look at him with some sort of an apology. But as it chanced, the opening of the door and his entry had both been noiseless. He looked about him surprised to find himself alone. Then he saw a door was ajar leading into what was presumably the bedroom. Claridge had no fixed plan of action. He always gave way to the impulse of the moment, if he dared, and he thought that he did dare here. One swift step and he was looking through the half open door. He looked into the sort of room that he expected, but the occupant kept him rooted to the spot, while the hair on the back of his neck began to rise.

Something hardly human sat huddled up on the further side of a table staring at itself in a mirror on the wall. Something that mouthed and showed the whites of dreadful eyes rolled up until only the whites were visible. From the puffy, loose lips saliva drooled. Just for a second the face grimaced, then the head was turned a fraction and the rolled-up eyes evidently caught sight of the open door and the white, appalled face of the intruder. The eyes rolled down. The two men stared at one another before, with a bellow of fury, the man, for it was a man, leapt up and forward in one spring as a baboon leaps. Claridge was never brave. And now he had excuse for his terror. A look had come into those eyes, a silent determination in his rush which leant wings to Claridge's nimble feet.

He was out of the house before the other could have leapt into the corridor. Panting, mopping his face two corners away, Claridge finally ventured to pause for the first time. That was a madman whom he had watched just now. Most people would have wondered whether some tragedy, not necessarily ignoble, might not lie here. But Claridge had never felt pity in his life—except for himself. All he knew, all that interested him was the knowledge that Gillian Dundas had an insane, or partially insane, brother, or lover or husband. He decided promptly that any idea that this was an actor whom he had surprised while rehearsing an effect was negatived, first by something terribly accustomed in the very way the features seemed to fall into that dreadful, bestial look of themselves, as it were, and then by the desperation which he had rightly divined in the rush made at him by the man on whom he had intruded. There had been what shone like murder in the glare of the eyes that had looked into his own popping blue ones, and a ferocity in the spring right over the table into the center of the room, which made him feel that he would have been torn limb from limb had he been caught. He dropped on the instant, and quite definitely, any idea of ever trying to make headway with Miss Dundas. Claridge loved his own skin and his comfort more than anything else in the world. Since the girl had a madman in tow, his interest in her was gone for ever. He decided to see Alysia at once and make love to her. She would be cross at the waste, as she would call it, of the wretched fifteen pounds handed to him as a gamble on Mrs. Burnham's affection for John Tait.

CHAPTER FOUR

'THE first place to which Tait was driven after parting from Mrs. Burnham was Hay Hill, where were the chambers in which Lord Mills had been found shot a couple of hours before. He found the flat on the first floor in the hands of the police, but on sending in his card as a friend of the dead man's, was at once admitted. A rather thickset man of middle height, with a pair of very keen blue eyes, was apparently in charge of affairs, though Tait only knew it from the fact that his card was handed to him, for the stoutish man's voice and manner were singularly gentle.

He looked pleased to see the newcomer, but not half so much so as did a man standing in a corner, though there was a chair beside him on which he had twice been asked to sit down. This was Brown, the valet, who had been kept at the flat in order to explain a few oddments which bothered the police.

"Oh, Mr. Tait, sir!" Brown fairly sprang at him. "I'm in a terrible position, sir. Lord Mills has been found dead and the police think I done it. I'm under arrest. Oh, sir, can you do anything for me?"

"You're not under arrest, Mr. Brown," Superintendent Dartmoor said quietly, for it was one of the big five who had slipped Tait's card into his pocket. "I explained that to you. You're being detained while we look into your story."

"But it's the same thing!" wailed Brown, a slim, worried-looking man with, just now, a complexion the color of underdone potatoes. "It's the same thing exactly!"

The policeman beside him suppressed a grin with difficulty.

"If looking into your story means that—," he muttered under his breath.

"A friend of Lord Mills, sir?" Dartmoor asked Tait in his quiet voice.

"I'm afraid I only put it that way in order to be shown up at once," Tait murmured. "Apart from business interests—he was on several tea and Eastern produce companies with me—I didn't know Lord Mills well. It's Brown who's brought me here. I do know him well. I got him this post. He was with me first as a batman and then in my service as a houseman for over a year. I should never have parted with him but for the doctor saying that he must give up stairs."

"Oh, thank you, sir!" came in almost a sob from Brown. "I'm in a tight place, sir, but I swear to you that I never—"

"You don't need to waste time in oaths of that sort," Tait said, fearing that a more sympathetic tone would break the man down. "Now, suppose I have a word with the superintendent." Tait gave him a half impatient, half affectionate pat on the shoulder. The superintendent nodded to Brown's companion, and the two disappeared into an adjoining room.

"Now, Superintendent," Tait said as the door closed, "I can tell you one thing. Brown never murdered any one He's a trustworthy reliable fellow. Honest as the day, and a lot kinder. If you found him bending over a heaving corpse—if a corpse can heave —I should still say you'd be wasting your time thinking him the criminal"

"Very possible, sir," Dartmoor said equably, "but I should also be right in detaining him under those circumstances, just as I am under these. I can't do otherwise—given the facts."

"And the facts are?" Tait asked anxiously. This man did not look the sort of man to have blundered. Superintendent Dartmoor was broad with the breadth of a sedentary middle age. He had a plain, rather careworn face, chiefly noticeable for its look of unusual quiet. The eyes, the voice, the gait, the lack of gestures all were stamped with the same tranquility. No-one had ever heard Dartmoor raise his voice one tone in anger or excitement.

"Well, first, there is the fact that Brown had been given notice this morning after a loud scolding on the part of his master. A most unusual occurrence."

"He's growing rather hard of hearing," Tait put in.

"Quite so," agreed Dartmoor. "So that he would have found it impossible to get a job again unless Lord Mills recommended him. Then there's the fact that about thirty-seven pounds was found on Brown, among which are four five-pound notes, which passed, into Lord Mills' possession only this morning. Brown says Lord Mills rang for him at ten-thirty, handed him the money, and told him to consider it a parting present He said his master pressed it on him, told him that he was sorry to part with him, but that he was starting at once on a long journey where he would need no servant, and handed him a most glowing testimonial, which, in a moment of emotion, he flung into the fire, and asked his master to take him with him or at least let him come back into his service on his return On which he says that Lord Mills seemed to consider a moment but only told him to go to his club— the Devonshire—for his letters and to wait until the twelve o'clock post should be in in order to take charge of a registered package he was expecting. Should it not come by that post he was to return here. Brown, according to his own story, thought he was being kept on, went to the club, waited there for the post, nothing arrived, and he hurried back into the house very keen indeed on having another word with his master, so he says. Meanwhile Lord Mills had been found shot through the head from a little in front of the right ear. According to our police surgeon, death probably took place around the time when Brown supposedly left the house, judging by the time he arrived at the club. For that part of his story we have of course verified. He got there when he said he did, and acted there according to his statement."

"Brown always would," Tait said instantly.

"This room," the superintendent went on placidly, "is so situated that, in all likelihood, a revolver shot would be considered as some tire backfiring in the street outside. It was but little used by his late lordship, I understand. Of course Brown, who acted as single manservant, could easily inveigle him in here on the plea of something wrong with something—window, fireplace, ceiling—a dozen things."

"Superintendent, Brown is not a criminal," Tait said again, very earnestly. "Surely you with your large, experience of criminals must see that he's not the criminal type?"

"There isn't such a thing, sir.'

"So I've heard say, but I don't agree with you. But, leaving that on one side, we all of us know that there is a distinctly non-criminal type. The kind who under no circumstances—not for any consideration—would steal from or murder their employer. That's Brown's type."

Dartmoor looked at him with those keen, blue eyes of his, but all he said was:

"The porter's well known to us. Respectable man with a respectable wife. They run these flats as service flats with a handful of dailies. He gives Brown rather a bad-tempered character. Says he's moody and drinks a bit at times."

"Liar!" snapped Tait.

"He says that's why Brown was being dismissed. As he was cleaning the stained glass of the door, a job which he is supposed to do himself, he heard loud voices from inside the flat."

"Loud because Brown is slightly deaf."

"That's what Brown says too." Dartmoor permitted himself a fleeting smile at the indignant protector before him. "But the porter says loud because of anger.

According to him Lord Mills' voice was unmistakably indignant."

"No fingerprints on the revolver?" Tait asked after a pause. Many a detective officer would have refused to answer. But Superintendent Dartmoor never hedged. He wanted the guilty, not merely the unlucky.

"No. And it's not been wiped. Whoever used it left no prints, and that, Mr. Tait, speaks—slightly only—for, Brown. For, in my experience, many a suicide has cold hands when he fires the fatal shot, but the murderer's hands are generally clammy."

"Yet, even so, you think Brown, with £30 and over in his pockets, would come back here to be arrested?" Tait asked.

"He would not expect the body to be found. But for the chance of its being the day the windows are cleaned, the corpse would probably have lain undetected for the rest of the day. Or at any rate for some hours."

Tait took that in silence, and after a warm word to Brown about seeing him through, left, looking very grave.

"I rather think we shall hear from him again," Dartmoor said, when, back at the Yard, he mentioned the affair to Chief Inspector Pointer, who had come in to hand over a report on a case which he had just finished. "He looked to me like a man who has a piece of information which is burning a hole in his pocket. Certainly, he either really believes that Mills shot himself, or intends to take that line. And as he's a co-director of his, that's rather odd. Rather odd. But then Mr. Tait himself was odd. Very."

Pointer was putting his papers away in a filing cabinet. Evidently the superintendent was waiting for something, and wanted to fill in the time with talk.

"In what way, sir?" the detective. inspector asked.

"That's just what I can't make up my mind about," Dartmoor replied. "He gave me the impression— impression only, of course, not opinion—that the death affected him tremendously, so much so that he wanted time to think over things. Afraid lest he might say something. I don't think he would have come near us but for Brown. Because of that impression of mine, I talked Brown all the time. And I'm sure of one thing, whatever thought is disturbing him isn't connected with the valet. In fact—" Dartmoor's own ideas were beginning to clarify in talking them over, as he had hoped would be the case. "In fact, I rather think Mills' death had staggered Mr. Tait, and that he wants time to think out, or find out, whether something he knows, not merely suspects, should be told us or not."

"You say they're co-directors. Could that be the reason for the caution?" Pointer suggested.

Dartmoor shook his head. "I shall be very much surprised if it's not something that affects Mr. Tait much more than business would ever do. Unless I've read him wrong. If it's suicide, or rather since he thinks it's suicide, I should rather expect it to be some woman who is, or who he thinks is, mixed up in the tragedy."

"You don't think it was the valet, sir?"

Dartmoor was not prepared to reply to that yet. "But there are two facts that look as though some one else might have seen Mills, and therefore been able to shoot him, while Brown was away. On a chair by a table near the window we found a glove. Not one of Mills'. Too small for him. Made, so the expert tells us, from Peccary-hog hide. Only one firm makes these in England, and they're not in much request. It may be possible to trace the owner. The glove was a right hand one, too small for Brown. Nor can we find its mate in the flat. Brown knows nothing of the glove, and assured us, when he looked around the room after we had taken it, that nothing had been altered, and he looked very carefully."

"What kind of gloves was Mr. Tait wearing or carrying?" Pointer asked with a smile.

"None. But this one that we found should fit him, I fancy, as it would fit me. I don't mind telling you that I dropped one of my own gloves on the place where the other had lain, just to see if he seemed interested in it. But he never glanced at it, let alone made any effort to pick it up. No, as far as one could tell by merely watching him, Mr. Tait came really, as he said, to help Brown out by giving him the best of characters. And also, as I said just now, with something—some knowledge or suspicion in the back of his mind which—to him at least means suicide."

There was a short silence.

"When I asked him when he had last seen Lord Mills, he gave me an evasive reply. I didn't press the question, for I feel pretty sure he's only turning things over in his mind, before himself making an important statement to us. Nevertheless, I'd give a good deal to know where the mate to that glove is at this moment. It may have nothing to do with the case, of course, but apparently we can feel fairly sure it wasn't in the flat when Brown left it... "

"And what was the other thing that bears out Brown's story?" Pointer asked. He was a tall, brown, youngish-looking man, with a grave face and fine dark gray eyes, of that shade that has no admixture of blue in it. They were the eyes of a man who would be guided by reason rather than feeling. He was a coastguard's son, and something about Pointer always suggested open spaces and wide horizons.

"The other thing," Dartmoor answered slowly, were some smudges on the marble flooring just outside Mills' own front door. The halls had been washed just after Brown hurried out. The charwoman responsible is certain that she left it spotless, and, judging by the rest of the landing, she is probably to be trusted in saying so. The marks look as though some one had hurried in with dusty shoes while the marble was just not dry. They aren't prints, but they are smudges, and suggest that they were made by some one entering rather than by some one leaving Mills' flat. Now at this hour in the morning, the house is practically thrown open to people. Nor are they at any time fussy, I take it, as almost all the people have

their own valet, or maid, who answers the doors. There
are only two known keys to Mills' flat. One was on his key
ring. One in his valet's pocket. The porter, of course, has
a pass key. So that if any one stepped on the marble flags
while they were still damp, it must have been Mills
himself who let the visitor, or visitors, in. There were no
signs of cocktails. And, by the way, Brown says that no
visitor has come to the flat for a week, as Mills was away
for that time. He, Mills, I mean, only dropped in two days
ago, and was to be off early next week to join his family in
Yorkshire."

Pointer now looked inquiringly at his superior.

"You're wondering why we detained Brown?"
Dartmoor guessed rightly. "Personally, I always detain
servants if there's anything suspicious. They're so easily
hidden, and so difficult to find. But in this case—well,
Lady Mills says that of course her husband didn't shoot
himself—of course he was murdered and of course the
valet did it. She very much dislikes the man apparently—
judging by the talk I had with her over the telephone. She
was so insistent that the A.C. was glad to hear we had
our hands on the man. But between ourselves, Pointer, I
shouldn't be surprised if we lift those hands very shortly.
Certainly it'll need more than we've found. out so far to
make us really arrest him. Ah, here comes Dobbins—"
and the superintendent plunged into work again.

Lady Tait looked at Mrs. Burnham in a silence that
conveyed volumes. The latter had just returned from her
outing with Tait, the outing cut short by the
announcement in the papers that Lord Mills had been
found shot dead in his flat

Lucy Burnham returned the look with a half-
entreating, half quizzical glance "Don't say you think me
mad! You'd have done the same in my place."

"Never" Lady Tait spoke with emphasis "Take a
young woman in just because I found her crying on the
doorstep! My dear Lucy, who is she? Companion to Mrs.

de Souza? That's nothing to go on. What is she? How can you possibly tell?"

"I'm not clever like you," her guest replied promptly, "but I can read faces, and a nicer one than this pretty girl has, I've never seen. I thought so at Vichy when I first saw her there, you remember."

"Nice!" Lady Tait's very voice seemed to throw up hands of horror. "Beautiful, yes, very remarkably so And I should say a nearly perfect figure. But Oh, Lor'!" She would have added had she been given to such language "If ever I saw a weak, sly, pleasure-loving face, that girl has one. And what are you going to do with her?" She went on "People are easier picked up than dropped, as well you know. Even the best of them. Especially when one's got your kind heart. Really, I'm afraid you'll find yourself saddled with an incubus, and perhaps worse. What reason did she give for being on my doorstep, pray?"

"She hoped I would be in. She came to me for help as some poor little wild animal might, have done." Mrs. Burnham's voice was moved. "She has left Mrs. de Souza. A nephew, has turned up who is quite impossible She didn't know where to go she thought I would be kind. Few women are kind to her, she says—"

"Very few, I fancy," Lady Tait agreed grimly. "Forgive me being impertinent, dear, but oughtn't you to consult John now?"

"I hadn't time" Lucy looked as if tears were not far off. "I had to do something. She won't go back to Mrs. de Souza's flat. That dreadful young man is there, she says, and Mrs. de Souza has gone off to stay with some friends in the country. She seems to think poor Miss Dundas can remain on with him. I always did think her a frightfully selfish thing Of course I don't want to land the girl on you Lady Tait. She has some little studio of her own in Fulham, it seems, where she works at china mending and so on, only she can't afford to pay the rent if she's out of a place. It's all a rush, of course, and I know it's dreadful of me to bring her in here, but—until I can turn round I really don't quite know what to do with her."

"Take her to a G.F.S Lodge, pay a week's board for her, and let her find another place," Lady Tait said briskly.

"They're always full," Lucy reminded her reproachfully, "and generally frightfully uncomfortable. You know the kind of beds they give the girls. Lady Tait, believe me, she really is in great distress. You'd have done just as I have, had you seen her standing there like some pathetic, stray cat in the rain."

It was not a poetical simile, but Lady Tait looked uncomfortable. "As for John, I know he will feel exactly as I do," Lucy went on. "Would have done just as I did."

There was a little pause.

"Where is she at the present moment?" Lady Tait asked.

"I told her to lie down. She, looked worn out with worry and fright. Evidently the nephew was an absolute cad. Don't think that I intend to inflict her on you indefinitely. It's just for the moment." Lady Tait rang the bell and ordered tea to be taken up to Miss Dundas.

"Though I fancy she would prefer a cocktail," she said to Lucy. "Now, my dear, I'm no Gorgon. Besides, the girl is here as your friend. Of course she's welcome under that heading."

"I couldn't quite make out about her studio as she calls it, but if nothing else turns up at once, I'll find someway of making her useful to me."

"Such as?" Lady Tait asked dryly.

"Well—eh—companionship, and so on. With her good looks only a respectable girl would have been so utterly helpless."

Lady Tait acknowledged that argument with a rather grudging nod.

"Still, to take a girl as your companion, even though but for a couple of weeks, a girl you know nothing about..." she protested afresh.

"But what else can I do!" Lucy's tone was a trifle impatient. "I'm not prepared to adopt a daughter yet awhile. But seriously I felt as though some lovely bird had flown onto my window sill for protection from the storm, and God knows what, outside."

"Ump!" was Lady Tait's only comment, but she kissed Lucy. She liked a soft heart in another, though she pretended that her own was Bessemer steel.

"And you're accepting her story as gospel truth?" she said finally. There seemed no way out of the difficulty. But quite apart from disliking Gillian Dundas, she would have much preferred not to have had her cross John's path again until his wedding.

"Oh, no!" Lucy, was shocked. "Dear me, no! I shall go, out this afternoon and see Mrs. de Souza, or at least find out where she is, and so on. Oh, no, I intend, of course, to check up her story."

And when the two met at dinner, Mrs. Burnham told her hostess that, so far as she could find out, Gillian had told her nothing but the truth.

"As to the young man, Mrs. de Souza's nephew, he has tried to make love to Gillian often before, and each time Mrs. de Souza pretends that it's her fault, and refuses to do anything about it. I spoke to her on the telephone She seemed to think Gillian was making mountains out of molehills. And she's most indignant over her leaving her. But Miss Dundas very naturally feels that nothing would induce her to go near the place again."

"And this studio of hers?"

Mrs. Burnham went on to explain. It seemed that Gillian's mother had bought the lease of it some years before, and let it intermittently to artists or craft-workers. "Gillian has done pottery work and intends to go. in for mending old china. I think, with a little help, it ought to do very well. She's clever with her fingers, you know."

"I don't" But Lady Tint was smiling affectionately. "She seems, however, to be clever with her tongue. There,

there, my dear, if you like, I'll let her try her hand with my cracked Sèvres dish. Is she going to stay there entirely?" Lady Tait spoke with open, hopefulness.

"Not to sleep there," Lucy said promptly. "It's all very well by day. The studio, I mean. I've just left her there. But the weirdest sort of people seem to live there —I don't think it would he at all the sort of place to leave her in, without any one to look after her."

And Lady Tait, against her will, let it go at that. After all, she might be quite wrong in attaching so much importance to that odd little scene in the hotel lounge...But John was acting very oddly just now again. He had excused himself from luncheon for which he had meant to be back. He had not turned up at a friend's dinner which he had accepted. And, later on, he had telephoned to Lucy that he would not be able to go with her to a supper somewhere or other. The Ham Bone, Lady Tait believed, was the name of the club, where a party of the Naylors' friends were taking Mrs. Burnham.

Next morning, Lady Tait's maid began fussing about the bedroom after she had set down the cup of tea. She quite needlessly burnished up the back of one of Lady Tait's tortoiseshell brushes with her hand. When she adjusted a stand of dangling manicure instruments, her mistress knew that she had something on her mind, which she wanted to get rid of.

But Lady Tait was too interested in reading in the paper about Lord Mills' death to speak for a moment. She had heard of it last evening, but there Were one or two fresh items.

"Lord Mills' death must have been a shock to Mr. John," she said, finally laying the paper down. "Both are interested in the same tea companies." Then a thought struck her. "I didn't see him last evening. When did he get in?" The thought that had struck her was of Gillian Dundas under the same roof.

To her surprise there came a little pause. "My lady," Rainer said under her breath, "Ewart thinks he got in around half-past twelve." Ewart was the footman who acted as John Tait's valet. "But Mr. John had been in the house nearly half an hour by then," the maid went on.

"Oh?" Lady Tait knew what was expected of her, and besides, a premonition of something unpleasant, something probably connected with Gillian Dundas, had come to her.

"In the library—" the maid went on, "talking to Miss Dundas." She said the last two words importantly, as one who puts the final stone to the pyramid they have been building.

The effect on Lady Tait was all that could have been hoped for. Turning, she stared silently at her maid with eyes that demanded an explanation.

"Well, my lady, this is what happened. Miss Dundas came in around nine. She said she had had dinner, and went straight to bed. Mrs. Hopkins has given her the room looking onto—"

"I know! I know!" Lady Tait for once showed her impatience.

"Well, just before twelve I heard the front door open. I thought it was Mallard again. He's always slipping out the front door when he gets the chance and Mr. Hopkins isn't looking. I peeped out, but it was Mr. John. He stepped into the library, and he couldn't have been two minutes in there when Miss Dundas come slipping downstairs. In she goes into the library too. Well, I don't mind owning, my lady, that I—well—I just happened to pass the door and there wasn't any Fancy meeting you here! Or—oh! Are you staying here? Or anything of that kind as you might expect. No, it was a meeting. And then, hardly a minute or two passed, before the front door opened again. This time it was Mr. Claud."

"Oh?" Lady Tait's tone showed her lack of interest in Claud Naylor. As it had once before in Vichy.

"I think he just happened to come in, my lady. For he sort of started when he heard voices in the library. He must have recognized Miss Dundas, my lady, for he turned the handle. My lady"—Rainer was not even pretending to adjust anything now—"it was locked! And he says quite quietly, 'Open the door, John.' Excuse me, my lady, for speaking so familiar."

"Go on! What else did he say?" Her mistress really was startled.

"Nothing. Well, after a second, the door opened. Mr. John flung it wide—and there was no one in it but himself to be seen! I had come a step out into the hall. Well, Mr. Claud, he says nothing but he I gives the other one look, and then steps right across to the heavy curtains over the bay window, and as he does so, Miss Dundas nips out from behind the door, without a sound, and is out of the room and across the hall and up the stairs like some one moving in a film, my lady. Not a sound from her. Why, even her dress didn't swish. Give me the creeps it did, my lady. Can't say why, but it did. She moved like nothing human. And that quick! And that light!"

"What about the gentlemen?" Lady Tait interrupted.

"Well, Mr. Claud turns round from the window and he says, 'Where is she?' Just like that, and Mr. John he says, 'Who?' And Mr. Claud he says, 'You know who.' And Mr. John, without a word, goes striding out of the room, and leaves Mr. Claud standing there, staring after him, as though he didn't rightly know what to think. Or no," Rainer corrected herself. "It wasn't like that. He knew what to think, all right. He thought Miss Dundas had been there, as she had been. But he couldn't see how she got out. I could have told him. But he never saw me. None of them saw me." Rainer gave a faint, twisted smile, "Pity, ain't it, my lady, if the two, as has always been such friends, is to fall out because of a young lady."

"Jenny," her mistress moved her hands abruptly among her letters, "I can't understand things at all. You know"—she looked at her maid almost helplessly—"you know, I'm partly responsible for the engagement between Mr. John and Mrs. Burnham, and if anything happens...

There were lots of men she could marry, and lots of women he could marry. But it was through me—through my accident—they met." There was a short silence; The use of her maid's first name marked the stress of the moment. It carried both women back some thirty years to when Jenny had been an under-housemaid.

"I'm going to ask you a very odd question," Lady Tait said again, after that momentary pause. "But I know I can trust you. I hinted at it in France—Are you quite sure that Mr. John and Miss Dundas at Vichy didn't see much more of each other than the rest of us knew about? When the thought they weren't noticed?"

Jenny Rainer stroked the bristles of a hair brush reflectively, as though it were a cat.

"The other way, my lady. I thought he disliked her. He certainly tried to avoid her. And she the same. I thought... I wondered at it a bit, in our Mr. John. I mean, he likes the ladies, doesn't he, until of course he met Mrs. Burnham. That's what I finally put it down to my lady. The effect of true love."

"Rainer, don't fuss with my hair. I want it done quickly. What on earth does it matter if the wave is over, my right or my left temple!" Lady Tait was under no illusions as to the youthfulness of her looks.

"I refuse to be done out of the comfort of being seventy," she had once explained to the shocked Rainer. "Where's Mr. John?"

"Out, my lady. He left after his breakfast. On foot."

Lady Tait finished her dressing in silence. That interview with Gillian Dundas last night. What could it mean? And Claud evidently aware of it and indignant about it. It would be no use asking Claud for an explanation. He and his cousin had always been good friends. But John... could she learn anything from him? He was, softer clay. Meetings at night in her house with his fiancée's protégée called for some explanation. Yet she shrank from asking for that explanation. What she would do instead, she told herself, was to get Gillian Dundas out

of the house—out of John's way, out, dared she really
think it, of unsuspicious Mrs. Burnham's way. But how to
do this?

CHAPTER FIVE

IT was twelve when the door of her morning room opened and John himself, came in. He looked very grave.

"I found Miss Dundas staying here in the house when I came in last night," he began, after the swiftest of good-mornings. "She tells me that Lucy got you to let her stay here, as she has left Mrs. de Souza, and doesn't know where to go. That she's a sort of temporary companion to Lucy?" His tone and eyes questioned Lady Tait almost anxiously.

"Yes. Lucy found her on my doorstep and brought her in. She could hardly do otherwise. As Miss Dundas very well knew."

"She can't stay here," John said decisively, with something almost fierce in his tone, and eye.

"I quite agree." His step-mother spoke coldly, but in reality she was glad of at least that much agreement with her own ideas.

"Lucy should have consulted you, or me," John went on.

"She did consult me. But only after the girl was in the house But why is Miss Dundas not to stay here, John?"

"Because we none of us know anything about her," he replied shortly.

Lady Tait said no more. She thought it was only too plain how things were, in which case, the less said about them the better. After all, John was doing his best to keep anything that had happened in the past away from the present—the future.

"Lucy's out at the moment," she went on, more happily. "I wish you could get this young person out of the house at once, John, for I'm rather afraid Lucy will take her side. I detest the girl, and her barefaced effort to get in here I consider a form of housebreaking."

"No wonder she's terrified," he said on that, a grim note in his voice.

"What of, pray?" Lady Tait did indeed stare at him.

Of being without a situation." He replied at once, but she wondered if, that had been what he meant to say. Some day she would have all this cleared up, but not now.

"Well, I must be off." He had not sat down throughout the talk. "This death of Mills—" He seemed to pull himself up.

"Don't be late for lunch," she reminded him, turning to her letters. "Remember it's a Family Function. You and Lucy are the guests of honor."

A horrified look crossed his face. He knew his stepmother's love of that sort of thing.

"I'm afraid I shall be a trifle late. An engagement that I can't possibly put off...I made it without remembering the lunch," he explained.

"Put the engagement off," she said promptly.

"I'm awfully sorry—" and he looked it. "If it were any ordinary engagement I should. But it happens to be something I can't alter. However, I shall be back before you've quite finished."

Lady Tait was too vexed to say anything.

"I take it for granted Miss Dundas won't be there?" he went on.

"At the family lunch? Oh, no. You and she will both be away." It was a nasty speech, and meant to be so. But John did not seem to notice, and he was generally quick to catch undertones.

He looked at her with a sudden charming smile. "I've got to do a couple of things between now and then, and you may be sure I shall rush them if possible." With that he was off.

Lady Tait was extremely annoyed, but she had a feeling that things were too serious for careless speech. It was at the lunch that she intended making a sort of stately, presentation to John of the Deed of Gift to be formally signed after his wedding, when he would make his own new will.

She had loved John Taft the elder, and for that reason in her secret heart nothing that his son could do would have prevented her dealing anything but generously with him. Fortunately, she reflected, John did not know that, nor the others of the family, except perhaps the Naylor girls. They, might guess that nothing but death would ever prevent her carrying out any promise she had made John. Evidently there was some unsavory entanglement with Gillian Dundas. Past, of course. And she had tried to revive it again at Vichy, and failed. She looked that kind of young woman. But her effrontery in coming to the house where John was living till his marriage of getting in under the wing of the woman he was going to marry. Poor, generous-hearted, blind Lucy Burnham. But after all, a woman of her age should know better than to throw such a disturbing type of good looks into the way of any man. A sudden fear of the future came to Lady Tait. A middle-aged little silly, however sweet, and kind, and good, was hardly likely to make John Tait a good wife, and John needed careful handling, at times. This lunch, for instance, it was most trying of him to absent himself. What engagement could it be that kept him? Made with whom? Suddenly she remembered another occasion when he had refused to keep an engagement made in his name by Etta, which was very important indeed, but which he had said would be impossible for him. There too he had spoken of another appointment that he could not break, but which he. did not specify more clearly. Etta had told her about it. Funny... Lady Tait turned resolutely to a letter to her solicitors about some property. Claud came in as she was finishing it. She read it to him. But for John, all that she had would have gone to Claud and his sisters. Lady Tait believed in keeping money together in one family if possible. He did not seem to pay much attention and, as ,a- rule, in money matters he was most helpful.

"You're looking poorly, Claud," she said before she thought—thought of her talk with her maid this morning.

"Really? It's a special gift from Heaven, then, for I'm feeling uncommonly fit," he answered her rather rudely.

"Something's upset you," she said to that, hoping he would drop some word which might untangle things a little, for she suddenly felt as though, under the surface of life around her, were coils, and knots, and twisted ends.

"Where's John?" he asked, instead of replying.

"Out."

"Back to lunch?" he asked in a casual tone.

"Only for coffee probably."

She could have put off the lunch till two, but, as it happened, the Naylor girls had several times asked her to move her lunch hour, and she had refused. Half-past one was the latest at which she herself cared to lunch, and to that she adhered.

"Mrs. Burnham will be there, of course?"

"Of course."

"And—eh—Miss Dundas? I understand that she is staying here with Mrs. Burnham for a while."

So that was it. That explained his interest in the coming meal.

"How did you know she was here?"

"I found her in one of the rooms yesterday afternoon. She told me that she is staying on as a sort of temporary companion to Lucy till the wedding."

"Very temporary, I hope. However, she's out for the day, at a sort of studio she claims to possess somewhere in town. What are you fidgeting so for, Claud?"

"Sorry. I've just thought of something I've forgotten. Be back for lunch." He made for the door.

"You'd better be!" she said firmly, "or I shall begin to think you only looked in to see Miss Dundas."

He looked extremely indignant at that as he stalked out. Lucy met him.

"He looks quite cross," she said with a half smile. "Have you been scolding him?"

"I'm afraid he'll get entangled with your Miss Dundas," Lady Tait replied disingenuously. She was not in the least afraid of such an unlikely eventuality. But she told herself that here was a most excellent "hide." "As was only to he expected," she went on, "when you brought such a pretty girl into the house where a young man also lives. Of course, he's bound to get entangled."

"Entangled," Lucy Burnham repeated reproachfully. "What a horrid word."

"It's a horrid state of things, puss. And not at all fair on Claud. He can't marry—yet awhile."

"But how could I stop to think of possibilities when the poor child was in such a dreadful predicament?"

"So she says!" Lady Tait said meaningly.

"You skeptic! You destroyer of all confidence!" remonstrated the other. "I think it tremendously to Gillian's credit that she felt so desperate. A girl as pretty as she is could easily have stayed on and tried to inveigle young de Souza into an engagement. He's very wealthy, apparently."

This was true. Ordinarily Lady Tait would have allowed as much. But she did not soften now.

"And is it tremendously to her credit to wear the kind of clothes she does? Do you think they're the usual garments of a companion?" Her voice had become tart.

"She explained that very sweetly once at Vichy. When I chaffed her about her golfing turn-out. She's found a place where ladies' maids, and shops, sell soiled models."

"And you think that frock she wore the last night at Vichy was a soiled model?" Lady Tait spoke with warmth. She very much objected to being thought stupid.

"Didn't she look a duck in it!" Lucy said rapturously. "She told me that that frock was practically given away for a few francs."

There was no more to be said on that subject evidently. It was all very well for gullible Mrs. Burnham to be taken in, but if ever a frock was designed for its wearer by an artist, that dress had been for Gillian Dundas.

"Well, my dear, if you chose to believe her, I won't argue that matter. But, frankly, I don't want her in the house."

"Lady—Tait!" came in an aghast tone from Mrs. Burnham, who looked as though she had not heard right. "You mean—not even for a short time—until we can find some nice quiet spot for her to live?"

"Not even for a short time," Lady Tait went on determinedly. "It's not fair on Claud." She finished maternally. "I thought so last night but I know so this morning. No, don't ask me for chapter and verse. Just take it from me that I do know what I'm talking about."

"It's a curse to a girl to be as pretty as she is," Lucy said sadly, "without any family or means. But do you mind explaining just a little more? Is it because you dislike her, or because you think Claud may fall in love with her, that you want Gillian to go at once?"

"Neither." Lady Tait decided on greater frankness. "It's because I don't like the way she came here. Don't believe her story."

"But why should she come to me if her story is not true?" Lucy's voice was a tone study in bewilderment.

"Just so! Why should she? That's what I don't like. There's something about Miss Dundas I actively mistrust, my dear. I have from the first moment our eyes met."

"You do surprise me!" came rather helplessly from her guest. "I think she has such a nice, frank glance."

"Arrogantly indifferent," corrected Lady Tait. "I'm sorry, Puss. But we must see about getting her rooms elsewhere. I know of quite a respectable boarding-house, kept by a cousin of Rainer's, in fact, where she would be quite comfortable. Not expensive. And not far from this so-called studio of hers."

"Oh, but it is a real studio!" wailed Lucy. "I saw it, you know. It's much too uncomfortable for anything but a studio. There are only three chairs, all wood, in it. She's working there at this moment. Working her hardest on that Sèvres plate of yours. But of course asking her to stay in a boardinghouse—" Lucy looked rather dismal.

"Why not? For one thing, she's not a lady, my dear."

"Her father's a regular officer, her mother's a Welsh landowner's daughter—" Mrs. Burnham's tone was growing more and more bewildered. "She... knows the rules and usages of ordinary good society—"

"Oh, yes, she knows them. No, what I mean is that she's artificial through and through. I don't think she ever makes a movement that isn't thought out beforehand."

"But lots of girls nowadays are like that. They pose frightfully."

"Yes, but... well, there's a difference."

"Poor child," murmured the younger woman, "that's because she's been a paid companion ever since her school days. Of course she has to think over everything she says, before she says it. And of—"

"Puss, she's not like any. companion I've ever met. No, believe me, there's something wrong about her.. And I think you very unwise not to let her go. At once. We can arrange. it so that she doesn't lose by it. Except, of course, the very pleasant life she would have with you. No duties. No!"

"Oh, she was to keep my things mended."

"You little fraud," laughed her hostess. "Much your things are mended." And Mrs. Burnham had to laugh herself. "You'll tell me next that she's going to darn your stockings."

"But I can't turn her adrift." Mrs. Burnham spoke with unexpected firmness. "I have no fault to find with her. I like her. I think she's a thoroughly nice girl. But, of course, since you feel like that about her, I'll let her stay with some one else until I'm back from our wedding trip. Though it will be awkward." She was thinking hard.

"I have a strong feeling that she's unreliable—all through," Lady Tait persisted. "Or I wouldn't have ventured to speak as I've done. But to me she spells mischief—trouble—worry."

"But I can't do it at once!" protested the other. "She only came to me for help yesterday. And she's frightfully upset over this affair of Lord Mills."

"When had she met Lord Mills?" Lady Tait demanded.

"After we left Vichy. Or no, before she came on to Vichy she and Mrs. de Souza had been at Trouville."

"Much more in her line than Vichy!" threw in Lady Tait, and again Mrs. Burnham laughed, half agreeing, half in protest.

"Apparently Miss Dundas had met him once or twice on the links. In a nice, fatherly way, you know, he quite took to her," Lucy went on.

For a moment Lady Tait looked at Mrs. Burnham in open exasperation. Then her brow smoothed, and, leaning forward, she kissed her future daughter-in-law, for so she called her. "You're rather a darling, Puss. Nice, fatherly way! Hanson Rydings—Handsome Rydings, as we used to call him—well, Lady Mills could tell you that she's close to the end of her tether as far as he's concerned. But have it your own way. Let her stay on here until the wedding, then dump her on some other confiding lamb. But for heaven's sake do tell her not to throw back her head when she laughs so as to show the line of her throat, nor to fold her cloak round her and then mince towards the car. It got on my nerves in Vichy."

"I think it's the films," Mrs. Burnham explained. "I think these young things see some one they admire tremendously, and then come home and practice. But you know, Etta wouldn't have taken to her, as she tells me she has, if there was anything really wrong with Gillian. Etta's awfully clever, I think."

"Etta!" Lady Tait's under lip shot out dubiously. "My dear, it's not always easy nowadays to be sure of what Etta likes or doesn't like. It used to be simple enough!"

"Let's hope that all these worries are quite needless, and that she'll marry soon. With her youth and beauty, she ought to." Lucy Burnham was speaking of Gillian Dundas.

"Well, she mustn't marry Claud," Lady Tait said, trying to laugh.

"I don't think she cares for him," Mrs. Burnham said placatingly. "But, of course, I do see... I really forgot about him being here. I only thought of John and me in the house...

Lady Tait could stand no more. "Lucy," she said suddenly, against her better judgment, "don't you think there's something odd about the way Miss Dundas has followed you around? She came to the hotel where you were in Vichy. She comes to the house where you are in town?"

She stopped, rather appalled at what she had done. "Cursed be he that moveth his neighbor's landmarks." Had she moved Lucy's too far? Moved it so as to show to the gentle little thing a glimpse of that rather grim landscape—reality?

But Lucy only looked worried, perplexed.

"I can't quite make you out. I met her in Vichy, and because we had met there and she felt that I liked her and really wanted to be her friend, she came to the as to a refuge. Liking is usually mutual."

Lady Taft decided to do the thing to which she had set her hand as thoroughly as possible.

"But are you sure she does like you?" she asked now. "I happened to see her face yesterday afternoon when you brought her down and were telling me about helping her to start work in this studio of hers—" She hesitated. She intended to be quite truthful but she did not want to exaggerate.

"Well?" Lucy asked with very natural curiosity.

"You were turned to me, and Miss Dundas's eyes, which were on you, were as unfriendly as can be

imagined. There really was positive ill-will in them,
Puss."

"Oh, no, Lady Tait!" Lucy shook her head with a little,
confident laugh. "One always feels ill-will, you know.
Frankly, I feel it in Etta. I don't say that Gillian Dundas
is an easy character. I don't say she doesn't grudge me, a
little, the pleasant time I have, in contrast to her own lot.
But that's only natural, and will pass as she finds I really
want to help her."

Lady Tait hurriedly rang the bell for the butler. Her
excuse was that she wanted to see him about some wine
that was to be ordered for the big supper and dance next
Thursday. But, though she turned the pages of his cellar-
book, her thoughts were not on what she was doing.

The lunch was not a success. Something almost
tangible seemed to weigh on the little group of five at the
table. All Lady Tait's and Mrs. Burnham's efforts—and
both women made them—to lighten things, seemed to
flicker out like matches in the rain.

Alysia and Etta were galvanically sprightly, but with
the same result. Only Claud refused to play up.
Saturnine of face, monosyllabic, he remained until John
hurried in. As it happened at that moment the talk,
struggling up the wall of ice, had fastened for a moment
on Lord Mills' death. Claud was emphatic in his belief in
the valet's guilt.

"The man's innocent," Tait said harshly. He looked
very strange, his step-mother thought. Deeply angry, or
was it merely deeply disturbed? At any rate, she decided
to say nothing for the moment about the handing over to
him of a slice of his dead father's money. There was
something in the air today...

"It was suicide," Tait went on, "and I shall see to it
that there's no mistake made about it. I happen to *know*
it was suicide."

"You'll have hard work to make Lady Mills accept
that idea," Naylor said. "She'll spare no expense to have it

anything else—Brown for choice. With two girls not yet off her hands..."

"Personally, it seems much more likely to have been murder than that a man in Lord Mills' position should have killed himself," Mrs. Burnham said a little timidly. "I don't wonder his wife finds that impossible to credit."

"No, Lucy," John looked at her with great affection and sadness in his eyes and a greater envy, "*you* would find suicide incomprehensible, but—" He seemed half-inclined to. finish his sentence, half unwilling to.

"What a tragic subject!" Alysia said reproachfully, and tufted the talk to a card scandal that was running through the clubs. Neither of the men took it up. Coffee was to be served in the library, where all were to hear broadcast a very important speech from Downing Street before going on to a special charity matinée for which Lady Tait had taken a box.

"One moment, Claud, can I have a word with you?" Tait laid a detaining hand on the other's arm as the meal was over. Just as the door closed behind Etta, they heard him say as he shut it, in a deeply moved, and therefore carrying, voice, "Do you believe in a devil?"

Claud replied that he did not. His voice was half - puzzled, half-scoffing.

The women paid due attention to the address from the Prime Minister—or appeared to do so. Neither of the men showed themselves. When it was over, as they would not leave the house for another half hour, Lady Tait wisely suggested dispersing until that time.

The butler entered. Could Mr. Tait have a word with Mrs. Burnham?

"What can it be?" Lucy asked of her companion. The two were now, alone, on their way upstairs. "I had an idea in the dining-room just now that he was frightfully worried."

Lady Tait thought that she could guess what about.

"My dear," her voice was very kind and, for her, coaxing, "I want you to listen carefully to John.

Remember, apart from being the man you're going to marry, he's a very clever, astute man of the world. Don't forget that side of him." And she gave her a little motion towards the door.

Lady Taft herself lay down, but her usual would not come. Not though she had recourse to her ordinary unfailing device of counting counters on her lap. She heard the library door below open, and John say tenderly, "I won't be long. Just a minute, darling." Then the door downstairs closed, and a second later, after a tap which was at once responded to, Mrs. Burnham came into Lady Tait's room, a troubled look on her face.

"John is frightfully upset," she said, "and most mysterious." She eyed Lady Tait as though the other's insight might help her. "He didn't tell me what was the matter—he only walked the floor and looked as though he were going to have all his teeth out. He wants me to wait for him. I don't suppose, from the way he spoke, he'll be more than a couple of minutes—but I confess—I can't think what's coming. Have you any idea what it can be about? Oh, how you startled me!" Lucy's tone was sharp for once.

"I've just got back from the studio. I knocked twice," Gillian said composedly. "I couldn't find Lady Tait in the other rooms and I heard her voice. Here's the plate. I don't think you can see where it's mended."

"No, no. I'm sure I can't." Lady Taft took it hurriedly. "By the way, would you be kind enough to do me a great favor? I want a book changed at the *Times* Library, and there's no one to send. Might I ask you to take a taxi there for me and choose me a nice chatty book of Memoirs?" For once Lady Tait smiled as she held out a volume, but Gillian did not take it.

"I'm so sorry," she said in her usual uninterested way, "but I've a most frightful headache. That's why I came back here. I must lie down or I shall be blind to the world tomorrow." And without waiting for another word Miss Dundas left the room.

Lady Tait was indignant at the way in which her effort to get the girl out of the house for at least an hour or so had failed. "I hardly think Miss Dundas has the making of a satisfactory companion in her," she said with some acerbity to Lucy, who was staring after Gillian with a look of surprise on her face.

"Not if she often answers like that," Lucy agreed, "but of course, if she's really feeling ill—she looked very white—" Gillian had. White and ill.

"But about John and what he has to say " Lucy spoke as though that were miles away from Gillian Dundas. But Lady Tait had no intention of being betrayed into some indiscreet words. Better that John should break his own trail, however bad it might be.

"It's time we all had something before starting." She looked at the clock. "Tea for you and me, Puss, and cocktails for the wicked rest."

Lady Tait told herself that this was supposed to be a pleasant family party, though John had seemed quite unable to remember this.

Claud was standing in the drawing-room as the two came in. Both stared at him. Something about him suggested high tension, though his face was quite devoid of expression.

Etta first, then Alysia came on in The cocktail tray was standing ready for them. Tea came in now, and Lucy poured out some for Lady Tait and herself at the latter's request. A service that her nieces had always done hitherto for their aunt.

They heard the front door open.

"That'll be John" Lucy ejaculated, turning from the tea table with a smile that suddenly made Naylor feel lonely.

"I thought I heard a knock first," Etta said

"I must go down now," Lucy spoke to Lady Tait "I won't be long behind you others—" She stopped the door of the room opened. It was the butler, and his face was very pale.

"Can I speak to you a moment, sir?" This to Naylor.

"Certainly" Claud was at his side in a moment, but Lady Tait intervened.

"What is it, Hankins? What has happened?" She, too, had risen to her feet.

"It's about Mr. John, my lady" The man spoke in a choked voice. "There's been an accident. The constable below wants to see some relative. Some gentleman relative—"

In a second all four women had swept the men aside, and were down the stairs. But Lucy was first in the hall. First on her knees beside a figure which had been carried in from a taxi.

"John! John!" she half shrieked, half whispered. "Oh, John, speak to me! It's Lucy! It's me!" There was a passion of tenderness in voice and face that made the constable turn his back on her. But Lucy would not let him move away.

"What's the matter with him? Oh, what is it?" She was fondling a hand that lay inert, heavy, clay-like, though still warm, in hers. "Bring some water! Do something! Don't just stand around." For once she was as imperious as Lady Tait. That lady turned to the policeman. She had been stooping over her stepson.

"Is he dead?" she asked in a low tone of horror. "He—he looks as though he were. Have you sent for a doctor?"

"The taxi-driver saw him fall as though in a fit. He passed away as I got to him." The constable was choosing his words with care. "Is it Mr. John Tait? He said he knew him by sight."

"Yes. It is." The man's insistence on the name made Naylor look at him inquiringly.

"Where's the telephone, sir? I want to use it, please."

"There's one in the library here." Naylor led the way. "Do you want our doctor's number?"

"No, sir. We call in our own doctors in cases like this. Sudden death in the street."

"Rubbish," Naylor replied curtly. "I'm a member of the Bar, constable." The constable's swift eye traveled over the young man, but he did not correct his misstatement as to police procedure.

"Relation, sir?" he asked.

"Cousin," was the curt reply.

"Ah!" And the constable walked over to the instrument. "No, please leave the door open behind you, sir." The peremptory tone made Naylor shoot a long look at him. Standing himself in the doorway, he heard a number called. It meant nothing to him. Came a name equally unknown to the intent, very intent, listener. It was the code name for Superintendent Dartmoor. He happened to be in, and the constable was put through to him at once. Giving his name, number, and the locality of his beat, the man went on:

"Walking along Seymour Place ten minutes ago, sir, just before you get to Upper Berkely Street, I was hailed by a taxi-driver who was supporting a gentleman in his arms. The gentleman died just as I got to him and he was helping lay him down. The taxi-man's well known, and the gentleman's name is Mr. John Tait. Yes, sir. Yes, sir. Mr. John Tait. I'm telephoning from the house." Followed a pause and a couple of Very good, sirs, then, "I haven't sent for the family doctor yet, sir. I thought it better—" The constable left his tentative sentence unfinished. And after listening wound up with another "Very good, sir. It hasn't been moved yet." He hung up, and went to the door. Meantime Lucy, looking up from chafing the hand that refused to grow warm, caught sight of Gillian Dundas on the landing just above. She was looking down at the group below. Her face was ghastly even with her back to the light, even in spite of its paint.

"Don't come down," Lucy said at once, in the tone of an older woman anxious to spare a young one a needless and distressing sight. "Mr. Tait has been taken ill. You can't help us. We're all here."

Gillian made no reply, but she tottered down the stairs and into a room facing the one where the constable was telephoning. Naylor went in after her.

She hardly seemed to see him at first. Then she gave him a sudden frenzied look. It would have startled any man. There was more than the terror of a young girl brought face to face with her first glimpse of death in it. She sank into a chair, or rather crouched there, and closed her eyes. Naylor was obviously dismissed. It was as though she had half-thought of appealing to him—for what? And had decided against it. What had made her change her mind? His impassive face?

"Is there anything I can do for you?" he asked in an odd, muffled, hesitant voice. There was open reluctance in it, as though the words came against his better judgment. She shook her head. There was no sound in the room until the door opened. The constable looked in, a sharp, searching look.

"I'm ready to telephone for your own doctor now, sir." Naylor remembered that he had heard him step to the door a full minute ago. He went on out to him and gave name and number.

Back at Scotland Yard, Superintendent Dartmoor, on hearing the name of the man who had died so suddenly in a street just around one turning from his own house, pressed a button on his desk. Chief Inspector Pointer got the call and came in at once; He listened very closely to the account which had just come in. to them.

"If a crime, sounds like poison," he murmured.

"Fortunately the bobby who saw it happen recognized his name as one of those connected with Lord Mills and phoned up at once for instructions. Drop everything, I see you've practically finished the job you're on, and finished it well, by the way, and have a look into this death. See if there's anything queer there. I'll speak to the D.C. and get a Home Office expert for you."

"It's an odd happening," Pointer agreed thoughtfully.

"Or it wouldn't come our way," Dartmoor added. And the superintendent responsible for the fifth of London in which Tait, like Lord Mills, had died, picked up the telephone, and Pointer hurried away to make a few swift arrangements.

"Here's your impartial witness," Dr. Hardy said good-humoredly, as he stepped in quickly just as Pointer was finishing.

"I don't want one, sir," was the reply as the detective-officer led the way to his car in the great square below, which no car can enter except on direct business with the C.I.D. "I want you to feel absolutely certain that there's been foul play, and determined to find the proof."

"Absolutely convinced yourself, are you?" Hardy asked.

"Oh, no, I've an open mind. You're the one who has no doubts whatever but that a crime has been committed and that you will be able to show it up."

Dr. Hardy, the greatest expert at the Home Office on poisons, and the appearances of deaths from them, shot him an amused glance from veiled but keen eyes.

"I'm poisons," he said oracularly; "the very fact that I was asked to hurry along shows the field of inquiry, but is there any particular kind of poison which I'm so certain has been used?"

Pointer only shook his head and passed on the information received by the constable as to Mr. Tait's last moments on the pavement.

So quickly had all this been done that they drew up at the house in Great Cumberland Place just as Dr. Merridew, the family medico, was jumping out of his car.

CHAPTER SIX

WHILE the chief inspector and the Home Office expert were driving up, Mrs. Burnham at last laid down the hand to which she had held as though to a bulwark.

"I want him taken to the library," she begged, "or into one of the rooms. I can't bear him left here in the hall'. It's, oh, it's too horrible!"

"The body shouldn't be touched any more. It ought not to've been touched at all," the constable said very officially indeed. The butler was just admitting three men.

"*'The body', 'it',*" repeated Mrs. Burnham in a sort of shriek, as though the words had opened reality to her. "John! John!" She let Lady Tait put an arm around her and help her to her feet.

"John gone! Everything gone! All my future—my happy future." She spoke in a sort of desolate monotone that made Lady Tait's tears rise, and she was not given to easy weeping The two doctors—and the man from Scotland Yard waited in respectful silence until the little group of women had passed on upstairs. Then the three of them stepped forward to the body lying on the floor. Pointer had it carried into the nearest large room, which happened to be the dining-room, and the doctors ordered it to be placed on the table. Privately the chief inspector thought of the shock to the feelings of the family who might next be asked to gather about it for some meal, but the medical men had right-of-way here and he raised no objection. He himself had a word with the constable first of all, and then another with the taxi driver.

The latter was crawling along, on the look-out for fares, in the street that ran parallel to this when he noticed Mr. Tait ahead of him. He knew Mr. Tait well by sight, as he had several times driven him away from his step-mother's house. He loitered, hoping to attract his attention, but Mr. Tait seemed to be rushing somewhere deep in thought. Suddenly the taximan saw his legs give way for a second as though some one had struck him across the back of the knees. He kept his balance, but only to stagger blindly across the pavement as though trying to get to a supporting wall. The man was off in an instant, and caught him just as he would have pitched on his face. The face itself was convulsed, with lips drawn back front teeth clenched as though in agony. One hand beat the air, the other grasped at his breast pocket and jerked out a gold trinket which fell on to the pavement. The taxi man shouted to a constable who was already running up, and who helped him to lay Mr. Tait down on the pavement where he died even as they laid him. The trinket the driver picked up and replaced in the gentleman's waistcoat pocket. A few key questions brought no further information. He did not know any other members of the household by sight. He had not seen the dead man, Mr. Tait, in company with any one this morning. The constable's report was practically the same. Pointer went back to the shutoff part of the dining-room where the medical men had finished their, inspection of the dead man's face. The family doctor, was openly impatient. Tait, according to him, "had a heart," and the cause of death would undoubtedly prove to be due to that organ having been overtaxed by hurry, possibly on top of a heavy lunch. The Home Office expert listened in silence. Both were waiting for Pointer to order the body to be stripped. One by one the garments were taken off, after a careful look at each before it was disturbed. The clothes offered no clues of any kind. Pointer then went through the pockets. There was nothing in them of any interest except what the taxi-man had called the "gold trinket." It was the top of a lady's fountain pen. Without initials of any kind, but of rather an uncommon pattern of chasing,

Pointer thought—or rather hoped. The taximan identified it unhesitatingly as the object that had dropped from Tait's hand as he held him up, and the dust in the chasing bore this out. He was now allowed to go after being asked on no account to mention the fact that Mr. Tait had dropped anything whatever, should the pressmen question him on the matter. The taxi driver, who looked a man of his word, promised, adding that it made him laugh the way papers printed every sort of silly little trifle however unimportant. When he was gone the constable also identified the gold object as the one which he had seen picked up. by the driver and dropped into the dead man's waistcoat pocket. He himself had stepped on it, fortunately very lightly, and showed the dent that his glancing boot had made.

"Whoever is the owner is evidently in the habit of biting his or her pen," the constable added, eager to shine before the Scotland Yard officer. Pointer agreed, and put it away in an envelope, but that gold chased top, though a lady's, presumably, from its slender size and ornate work, showed the marks of a man's teeth, he thought, and unusually large and fine teeth they must he even at that. He asked for a wax candle and obtained the prints on, it of all the dead man's teeth. They were not in the least like those on the gold top. Tait had rather small and blunt teeth. The man who valeted Tait was called into the half of the dining. room whose double doors Pointer had had closed so that the doctors could make their, examination in private. All the objects shown to him as found on Tait were identified by him as ones which the dead man usually carried. Pointer had not included the "trinket."

"There's no fountain pen," Pointer said finally. He was told that Mr. Tait never used one. Stooping, Pointer seemed to pick something up from the carpet. It was the little gold top. The man had never seen any pen to which that would fit. All the inmates of the house, if they used fountain pens, had either black or colored ones. He couldn't say for certain about the young lady who had just come to the house—it might belong to Miss Dundas.

Pointer asked him about Mr. Tait's apparent health, which the man thought was quite good. The doctors fancied from his teeth that he had a habit of biting pen or pencil; if so, that would show a certain amount of nerves, Pointer thought. The servant rather indignantly scoffed at the notion of such a habit on Mr. Tait's part. Proof was to be found on his writing-table, where the chief inspector would find pens and pencils in plenty and none of them bitten.

At this moment Dr. Merridew opened the double doors and the man was dismissed.

"Heart failure," he murmured, passing through into the hall where he met Naylor and repeated the two words.

"Strictly speaking, of course, medical etiquette demands that Doctor Hardy should acquaint the family with the cause of death, but"—and here Merridew expressed his sincere sympathy and regret at the terrible loss to every one in that house with great feeling, adding, "Of course, no pronouncement can be made until after the autopsy. Officially, that is. Yes, it's a dreadful necessity, but it'll be quickly over. Just a necessary formality," and with a few more words he hurried away. He was due at an operation.

Naylor's eyes went over his shoulder, through the open door, to the chief inspector, but he said nothing. Pointer stepped back into the shut-off part of the room where the Home Office expert was still bending over the body. Something in the rigidity and intentness of his figure made the other move close to him.

"I want Angelli," Hardy said, without lifting his eyes from the pressure which he had made in the skin with his fingertip. "Angelli of the Italian hospital. Ask him to hurry."

"Doctor Angelli?" Pointer asked. Hardy only nodded. Apparently he assumed that the name would. convey as much to any layman as it did to himself. Pointer got the Italian hospital on the telephone, and in another moment got Dr. Angelli, who, on being told that Dr. Harvey of the Home Office asked him to come at once, assured Pointer that he would be there as fast as his car could carry him.

Pointer returned to the dining-room.

"Dr. Angelli is coming at once. Your suspicions confirmed, sir?"

"Yes. But suspicions only. I wish Angelli would hurry up. See that one rigid eyeball and one loose? See the tint of the pressure pits made by my fingers? Angelli read a paper not many months ago on a poison in use in Mediterranean countries and South America which showed those two symptoms after death. It's rather his specialty. Seen plenty of it when he was medical officer of health on a Brazil coffee plantation."

Pointer had a word with the butler. The man gave a brief account of Mr. Tait's goings and comings that morning. He had had breakfast at half-past nine, and left the house shortly afterwards.

Then he had not returned until about a quarter to two, when he had gone on into the room where lunch was served and had sat on with his cousin, Mr. Naylor, after lunch over their coffee, then he had sent word by him to Mrs. Burnham, who was with the rest of the ladies listening to the broadcasting, that he would like to have a word with her alone. The butler saw him walking up and down the library waiting for her, as though in a great hurry. When Mrs. Burnham came in the door was shut for perhaps five minutes or so, then Mr. Tait opened it, and calling back that he wouldn't be more than a few minutes, was hurrying out, when Mr. Naylor met him in the hall, and insisted on drawing him into the little room by the door "for a word." That seemed to be literal, for, after a couple of minutes at most, Mr. Tait hurried on out. The exact words the butler had heard him call back to Mrs. Burnham were, "Well, darling, I shan't keep you waiting more than a few minutes."

"And the lady, what did she do?"

"She waited a minute or two in the room. I could hear her humming to herself as she moved about, and then she went upstairs, smiling and looking very happy."

Pointer showed him the gold fountain pen top. He had picked it up in the dining-room, he said. The butler had never seen a gold fountain pen used in the house; probably. it belonged to the young lady who had come yesterday afternoon, to stay on as Mrs. Burnham's companion, he believed. Pointer passed on at once to other questions.

He learned that Miss Dundas had gone about half an hour before Mr. Tait early this morning.

The butler had just finished when the front door bell rang. Dr. Angelli was shown in; a big, burly, bearded man with bright, yet impersonal, dark. eyes. After the briefest of introductions, Dr. Hardy drew him to the body and in a few words told how the man had died and when. Then he stood back, as though afraid lest even a thought-wave might affect the other's decision. He was late for a very important engagement and fidgeted from one foot to the other until the Italian stood up and flung over, his shoulder the words *"Amico del Amante* of Naples, and a host of other names in other places."

"Ah!" Dr. Hardy gave the sigh of one who is satisfied. "That's what I rather thought. But I've never seen a case."

"I have! Especially among the Portuguese and my own countrymen. Well, anything more?" Angelli began to look around for a place where he could wash his hands.

"Lots more," Pointer said, promptly. "How was it given?"

"The autopsy will tell. I can't see any cut or puncture on him, but, of course, there may be one in the scalp. This poison is equally deadly when taken with food or when directly administered into the blood. In the one case it's a little slower than the other, that's all, but equally certain and equally without any known antidote."

"And the probable length of time it takes to kill?"

"Ah," the doctor, shrugged his shoulders, "that is just what no one can say, and what makes it so popular. One of the reasons. The other is its difficulty of detection. Looks like unaided heart failure even to most medical eyes."

"But the average length of time between its being taken and death?" Pointer persisted.

"Is one of its mysteries. It varies apparently capriciously, from three minutes—the shortest time recorded, to close on five hours. It seems to depend on the state of nervous excitement of the victim. The more excitement the quicker the death, as rule. But there have been exceptions."

"And the most usual way of giving it?"

"A poisoned cut generally, but often in food."

"What is it made of, Doctor Angelli?"

"The pounded macerated roots of monkshood, aconite and—" He named an ordinary table vegetable which, when combined with the other two, made a terrible trio.

"It's usually in the form of a putty-colored powder which is either given in the food—it has rather a horseradish taste or is steeped like tea in boiling water and the resulting liquid used on a knife or a razor."

The two doctors now began to arrange about the post-mortem, and hurried away together. Pointer reentered the shut-off part of the dining-room.

The body would be taken away any moment. He wanted to look it over again. Something about the right hand fingers lingered in his mind. That detective mind of his that ran and re-ran what he had seen and heard across a strong light of intelligence, as a man might test a strip of film for flaws. Turning down the sheet he picked up the right hand. Yes, on the thumb and first two fingers were black marks such as a man gets who works with machinery or tools. Yet the left hand tips were white and smooth. And then Pointer had a surprise. These, too, felt smooth, in spite of fine black crisscross marks that usually mean roughness and machinery dirt worked into the skin. He used his magnifying glass. Still they looked like marks of work, and still they felt, when touched, as smooth as, the unmarked left hand. Then the marks, whatever they were, must be under the skin. The glass did not show this, but very carefully Pointer tried with a needle as though for a splinter. And he found that he could dig out a tiny speck. And another equally tiny speck. Whatever it was that had run under the skin, was apparently some brittle, substance, though about the thickness of fine hairs. They were straight, and the longest was half an inch.

He had a box of small glass slides with him, but first of all, he had the photographer who had arrived with several other men from the Yard within a few minutes of his own arrival, take careful pictures of the fingers of both hands. That done, he promptly fastened the two specks on a slide, and sent it off post-haste to Dr. Hardy's analyst at the Home Office with a note saying what poison mixture to test for first should the doctor not be in yet. Then he himself stepped out into the hall. On entering he had given orders that no one was to be allowed to leave the house. or use the telephone, but these orders were, if possible, not to be known to the inmates. In reality, be had no right to give them at that stage, one of suspicion only. Now he had been authoritatively informed that Tait's death was not due to natural causes, and could take up the case openly.

He had stepped out of the room quietly, and happened to be half-hidden by a portière that hung over the door, when he saw that three people were in the hall, each of whom stood so motionless that he might have been looking at wax-works figures. One, a slender figure, stood on the landing, grasping the window sill. Something in the rigidity of the position suggested frozen horror. In a doorway near the foot of the stairs stood a Junoesque handsome woman. Her eyes were fixed on the girl with a concentration so intense that Pointer felt as though he could have touched her, and yet she would not have been conscious that he was there. Exactly opposite Pointer was a tall young man with a clever imperturbable face. He, too, was watching the figure on the landing with eyes that looked to the detective officer as though very little would escape them.

But they did not see the man from the Yard for a full minute. When they did he came forward at once.

"You are from Scotland Yard, I understand, though I don't quite know why. Can I be of any use? I'm Claud Naylor, Mr. Tait's cousin. The only man in the family."

Now Naylor had seen Pointer before, had looked full at him when Doctor Merridew had hurried out with those kind soothing words of his. He had not come forward then.

Pointer had a sudden feeling that in some way the young man was coming to the help of the girl on the landing, as if this were a diversion. Or a warning. The woman at the foot of the stairs did not shift her gaze, but the girl on the landing turned her head and looked down into the hall. It was reasonable to suppose that it was the sight of the detective officer that made her shrink back wide-eyed for a moment, then wheel around, and stand as before, quite still, with one hand clutching the window ledge, with her face turned to the glass.

Something in the way she did it suggested a dying person turning her face to the wall. The chief inspector's apparently casual glance strayed to the woman watching. She now looked at him, a very searching, appraising, calculating look. Then Etta Naylor turned,, and went up the stairs to Miss Dundas. But Gillian started away from the window as the other came close to her, and whipped on up the stairs without a glance. They heard a door shut swiftly above, and a key turn in the lock.

Naylor, after a pause, went on into the dining. room. A word from Pointer and he was allowed to pass through the double doors. He halted for a second at the sight of the covered body on the table, then he stepped up to it, and folding back the sheet, stood looking down at the dead face of the cousin from whom he had parted only an hour before. His face was absolutely impassive, but it was that always. Naylor's features formed a shelter behind which he could live all his life and remain totally unknown to his fellowmen should he so choose. Primitive man wasted years trying for the right magic to capture this privilege of invisibility which the man of the world has as his birthright—as regards his real self.

"May I ask the cause of death?" Naylor, said, turning to Pointer. "Old Merridew said heart failure. Rather a safe guess."

"The two doctors who have just left, specialists in their own line, are sure that Mr. Tait was poisoned," Pointer replied.

"Poisoned," Naylor repeated in a low tone of horror, "you mean ptomaine, that sort of thing?"

There had been a couple of food poisoning cases lately, and the papers were full of snippy, comforting articles on *The Truth about our Water Supply, What really happens to the Milk,* and so on.

"No," Pointer said to that, "from the kind used, it looks as though intentional poisoning was the cause of death. The autopsy will tell more, of course."

"You mean that my cousin was murdered?" Naylor said under his breath, and to the keen eyes looking at him so apparently casually, it seemed as though an extra layer of lack of expression covered his face—an extra defense. Then he turned away from the table and followed the other into the room opposite, where he stood, resting his elbow on the mantelshelf, his hand to his forehead, as though plunged in grief —or thought. Then, looking up, he began to ask a few questions, and to answer others put by the detective officer. After the first few words, Pointer was certain of one thing. This man would only tell things that did not matter. Whether in the crime or not, he would not help wholeheartedly. Yet barristers yield the fewest criminals of any profession. A proof of their brains, the chief inspector always thought. This man should be on the side of the law. It was his cousin who had been killed. And yet Pointer had no feeling that here was some one longing to help. He did not think Naylor was ever impulsive. He would always let his head govern his heart. But why should that be necessary here? Possibly some family matter was going to be dragged out by the sudden death of the one cousin. If so, that might account for the impression. No family matter seemed involved in the sudden death of Tait, then the young man before Pointer had some knowledge as yet peculiar to himself.

"If you're right, it's a most terrible and most mysterious affair," Naylor said finally in a very moved voice. "A man less likely to come to a sudden end than my cousin could hardly be imagined. Generous, kind, fair in all his dealings."

"With women as well as men?" Pointer asked, thinking of the gold pen.

Naylor looked him full in the face, and imperturbable though the gaze was, Pointer had a certainty that he had scored a bull's eye in some way—that Naylor was startled, or at least surprised, and wondered how much lay behind the query.

"He was more than fair to women," Naylor said finally, "my cousin was ridiculously chivalrous where they were concerned."

"When did you see him last?"

Naylor explained that after lunch Tait was hurrying out when he stopped him for a last word on a subject they had discussed after lunch

"So that unless some one spoke to him in the street, I was the last person to talk to him," he finished.

The rather chilly, clever eyes of the young man rested on the chief inspector for a second, then dropped to the fire. It was early May and cold.

"Can I ask what the talk was about?"

"The death of Lord Mills. My cousin was in possession of information which would have proved definitely that Lord Mills took his own life because he was afraid of cancer of the throat. He had a brother who died from it, you know, after every sort of operation. Mills, it seems, couldn't face the prospect of going that road"

"Do you happen to know the name of his doctor?"

Naylor did not, but imagined that could be easily learned from Lady Mills. Naylor went on to speak of the dread of cancer which destroys quite as many people as does the disease itself. He spoke well, but Pointer wondered just what it was that Naylor had not told him.

"I wonder Mr. Tait didn't let Scotland Yard know of this dread of Lord Mills," Pointer said finally.

"He intended to, of course. That is why he was so certain of the valet's innocence."

"I wonder why he didn't telephone the information as soon as he knew of Brown's arrest," Pointer repeated thoughtfully. Naylor's thin, flexible lips set in a line that meant temper but he answered easily.

"Perhaps he preferred to do it through Lady Mills. Of one thing you may be certain, he intended to see that the valet was set free at the earliest possible moment."

"But he didn't phone or write to the Yard," Pointer persisted, "by doing which Brown would have at once been released—supposing, of course, that this idea of Mr. Tait's can be substantiated."

"He was probably on his way when he dropped dead," Naylor replied. "At any rate, I shall at once get into touch with Lady Mills."

"The two deaths—following so quickly on each other of two men associated on several large companies—you don't think they are connected then?" Pointer asked. When he asked questions of that kind the chief inspector was solely concerned with the reaction of the person to whom the question was put, not, in the least with his opinions. Opinions, other than his own, played no part in Pointer's investigations.

"The two deaths linked?" Naylor raised a well-shaped, level eyebrow. "Quite impossible. One is a suicide. Oh, I see what you mean—" And Pointer wondered why the other had not seen it at once. "I see what you mean..." Naylor repeated slowly, thoughtfully, "some business gone wrong... If so, you'll find that out... but I don't think so. My cousin seemed in no financial trouble... still, it's an idea of course that I confess hadn't occurred to me. I know Tait was certain that Mills shot himself for the reason I've just given. But of course he might have been wrong, intentionally or unintentionally misled by Mills..." Naylor dropped off into silence. Pointer left him He was in a hurry to see the place where Tait had died, but he had the valet again sent into the dining-room for a moment.

"Didn't your master lose a glove lately? A very thick driving glove?"

"Yes, sir. Kind that can't wear out, they claim. He was trying a. pair. And lost one within the first week. Lost it outside somewhere."

"That was yesterday?"

"Yes, sir."

Have you the one remaining glove?"

The man had. Tait had got them from his usual shop, but he had told the valet that this was the only pair of this new kind in the place. "Peccary skin, he called it. Sort of extra thick pigskin it looked like. I'll show you the glove."

And the man brought back in a minute the mate to the glove that Superintendent Dartmoor had taken from the room where Lord Mills had been found shot. Pointer sent it along at once to the Superintendent at the Yard after the man had initialed it, "in case it should get lost too," as Pointer remarked.

That done, Pointer was free to hurry to the spot where Tait had died. It was a bare three minutes' walk from the house and, as he expected, revealed nothing except that Tait would have had to pass a cab rank and a letter box at the turning. These two facts might or might not mean anything. Four of the men usually on the rank were away. Pointer left word for them to report to him should they have seen Mr. Tait that morning, and then let the constable return to his beat.

So Tait was probably the man who had left those smudges on the marble outside Lord Mills' door. Tait was certain that Mills had killed himself, according to his cousin Naylor, and, still according to that young barrister, knew why. Quite a plausible reason too. Naylor would not have put it forward as the cause of Mills' death unless he had every reason to think he could prove it. But what lay behind all this? Was the one clue so far available, the top of the gold fountain pen, was it a last effort on the part of the dying man to name his murderer? It looked like it.

But the two deaths, so closely following one on the other, seemed, on the face of things, to be linked in some way. Both men, though not business men in the ordinary sense of the word, were co-directors of companies started by Sir John Tait, the poisoned man's dead father. A very good chartered accountant would go over the companies' books... Meanwhile, as he was not capable of following that trail, Pointer would hold to the bitten pen top and see if it led to the City or away from it. Somehow it did not suggest a business woman as its owner. Why had Tait passed on to his cousin only so important a piece of information concerning Mills' death. It looked odd. Pointer would, not feel at all surprised if the one man had killed himself to avoid some financial smash and the other had at first thought that he could pass that death off, as due to morbid terror until he himself was caught in some dark stream that ran into or out of the other—the first death. Yes, Pointer would not be at all surprised if the Yard accountant were not the man to find the right key to unlock the puzzle of the two deaths, but, meanwhile, he must follow up all other possible trails.

CHAPTER SEVEN

POINTER sent up word that he would be much obliged if Mrs. Burnham could give him a few minutes. He did not look forward to the interview.

Lucy's eyes were red rimmed, her face drawn and pale, but she almost ran to meet the chief inspector.

"Is it—true that it's not heart failure?" she stammered. "Scotland Yard being called in—the constable's manner—oh, what has happened to my John?" The last came in a tone of agony.

Pointer thought that truth was the best and the kindest.

"The doctors seem certain that Mr. Tait was poisoned. I'm afraid it's not an accident." He spoke reluctantly. "Now, Mrs. Burnham, if they're right, have you no idea of who the criminal could be?"

"Poisoned! Poisoned!" she repeated in a hoarse whisper. She covered her blanched face with her hands for a moment. Then she looked up, pale still but resolute.

"He had received a threat of some kind, I think a couple of days ago, but evidently he found out more about it, or received another threat today... But I'm afraid I'm incoherent, and I do so want to be clear and to the point. He sent up word after lunch today that he wanted a word with me. When I ran down he walked up and down in the bay window—we were in the library—without saying anything. I asked him of course what was wrong. He told me that he had received a threatening letter that included me too in its threat. And that for that reason he felt he must tell me all about it. He put his hand in his breast-pocket and felt a moment. He looked surprised and said would I wait a moment, he'd be back very quickly, and rushed off. That's all I know." She broke off to say in a tone of agony—"Not a word of good-by between us! He in a rush to get something, I all excited to hear what it was. And that was our parting for ever!"

She fought down the hysteria which threatened to swamp her.

"Could you tell me more about what you mean by his having received a threat of some kind?" Pointer was listening very carefully, and showed it.

"The first time was the day before yesterday. Something came up about one's character having a good deal to do with one's fate—I'm not a fatalist, he was—and be said very slowly and as though. thinking aloud, 'Yes, but what if one deliberately makes a decision that inevitably entails fatal-consequences? What then? Is that fate or is it character?' And I replied that if one feared any consequence enough, one wouldn't do whatever it was that would bring the consequence down on one. He seemed to turn that over in his mind and still speaking as though in a sort of deep reverie he shook his head and said:

'No. One might dread very much some consequence that would be inevitable if one continued a certain line of conduct, and yet be unable to change, because to change would mean to change one's character, one's whole outlook on life, one's sense of right and wrong. And death would be preferable to that.' Then he added something about threats not always coming true, and that death would be preferable to allowing oneself to be intimidated. He was turning a letter over in his hands as he spoke, but he put it away in his letter-case without showing it me. I did ask him, of course, what he meant, what was worrying him, but he seemed to realize that he had been talking on things that might frighten me, for he changed the subject."

"When did he say this to you?"

"Night before last, we were alone, walking back from a night-club into which we had dropped for half an hour or so."

"That would be the night that Lord Mills shot himself?"

She looked startled. But after a moment's thought she shook her head decidedly. "That's not possible! I mean that there should be any connection. We talked of Lord Mills' dreadful end, and Mr. Tait didn't link it with this other—this talk of a threat. From something he muttered, as he thrust the letter into his pocket, I have a very fixed idea—only an idea, of course, as I can't even give you the exact words—that the threats were in some way connected with his family. Or to do with his family."

"Of whom does his family consist?"

"Oh, I don't mean the Naylors his cousins, or his step-mother Lady Tait. I have an idea it was connected with some discharged servant—that sort of thing..."

"Could you describe the letter at all, that you saw in his hands?"

"It was bright violet in color, with rather sprawly spidery writing on it, very large and scroll like, and written apparently with a very fine nib and violet ink I thought after lunch that he meant to show me that letter, but, of course, on thinking his words over, I realize that he must have had another, a fresh one, which, as he said, included me?"

Pointer asked her other questions. He learned nothing more. He thanked her, seemed about to open the door for her, and, stooping, picked up—or seemed to pick up—the gold pen-top from the carpet. She evidently had never seen it before, or at least did not recognize it. Certainly she did not associate it with Tait, and therefore it did not interest her. But he had one more question.

"Your companion, Miss Dundas, has she been with you long?"

Mrs. Burnham said that, strictly speaking, Miss Dundas was not her companion. Very briefly and clearly she gave in outline what she had already told Lady Tait in full.

"And you don't think there's anything odd about this young lady having arrived—in just that way—the day before Mr. Tait died?"

She looked at him in pitying horror.

"I think I should go mad if such a thought occurred to me," she replied simply. "Miss Dundas and Mr. Tait had never met, chief Inspector, except at Vichy. Where I doubt if either was more than just aware of the other's existence. What could have put such a ghastly idea into your head?" she asked with a sort of horrified curiosity.

"The man charged with investigating a crime, Mrs. Burnham, has to have all sorts of ideas," Pointer replied a trifle dryly. "Frankly I think some one ought to point out to you two facts. Miss Dundas arrived the same day as that on which Lord Mills shot himself. And the day after, Mr. Tait dies. However horrible the thought, if I were you, I should bear those two facts in mind—for your own sake." He spoke very gravely. Lucy turned white.

"I shan't be able to get it out of my mind. But simply because it's so utterly horribly impossible."

There was impatience now in tone and look. "Lady Tait has been talking to you!" she said accusingly, and yet as though this partly excused him. "She dislikes Miss Dundas. And, finding that to be so, I shouldn't have allowed the girl to stop on here at all. But it's not easy, when one's busy with one's own affairs, to make time for other people's. I thought a few days one way or another wouldn't matter. But if she talks like this about that poor girl, it would have been much better for Miss Dundas to have turned to some other acquaintance rather than to me."

"And just why *did* she turn you?" Pointer asked meaningly. He wanted Mrs. Burnham to appreciate a little of the dark possibilities which she seemed so to ignore.

"Because I was happy, I think." Mrs. Burnham's lip quivered for a moment, but she went on steadily. "Like all girls who have to earn their living, I think Miss Dundas is a good judge of character as far as it concerns herself. I mean, I think she feels who would be kind to her and who wouldn't. She's so lovely that a good many women aren't kind to her. Not that that is Lady Tait's reason. I can't think why, she dislikes her so! Or rather, she has explained it all to me, but I don't agree with her. But to go back to the reason for Miss Dundas turning to me. I should like to think that she knew I would want to help her anyway, in such an impossible position as she was in, but I'm afraid it's partly because. she doesn't know many people in town just now, except Mrs. de Souza's own circle. I was out of that circle, and, as I say, I think she banked on the fact that any one as lucky as I was — then—would be kind to those less lucky."

"Did Mr. Tait object?"

"Why should he? But, in point of fact, I had not yet had time to tell him of her being with me."

Then why is Miss Dundas so shaken by his death? was what Pointer thought.

"And was Mr. Tail attached to his family? I understand that his only relatives are here in the house, staying for the moment with Lady Tait?"

Lucy, said that this was so, and added that there existed a very genuine and warm attachment between John Tait and his step-mother, and that, as far as she knew, he was as fond of his cousins as people usually are, and they of him.

She looked very pale and done. Pointer did not keep her longer answering harrowing questions. He let her go with his sincere sympathy. He stood a moment, thinking things over. Apart from Tait's death, the only odd thing in the house seemed to be the sudden appearance in it of Miss Dundas. Naylor had given this quite a light and airy touch in passing, as it were, but it struck the chief inspector as very singular, which was why he had given those straight words of warning to Mrs. Burnham just now. He decided to see Miss Dundas last, and learn meanwhile as much as possible about her from the other members of the household.

He asked for Lady Tait. She had him brought up at once to her sitting-room. He found her not as much shaken by the tragedy as a more imaginative, softer character would have been. If really as attached to her step-son as Mrs. Burnham thought, and as she herself immediately represented herself to be, then he thought that things had moved too swiftly for her to grasp them yet. She answered all his questions very helpfully, and yet he had a sudden conviction of reservations somewhere, of something withheld that might well be important, but which the woman before him, masterful, dominant, did not wish to tell. Obviously it must concern John Tait, but it did not seem to concern any one else in the house. About them all Lady Tait answered with what he thought was genuine candor.

"And where did Mr. Tait lunch today, do you know?" he asked towards the end.

"You mean —oh, of course!" Horror made her dose her eyes for a moment.

"We know nothing as to how the poison got into the body—as yet," Pointer reminded her. "But, of course, we want to get our facts as quickly as possible."

"I don't know where he lunched," she said, speaking as though lost in thought. But her eyes wavered. There was a silence after the short sentence, which was full of trouble, so Pointer, felt. Finally Lady. Tait looked up. "I don't know where my son"—she generally called John that—"lunched this morning, except that—I—well—I wonder if it could have been with—" Again she broke off and seemed very unwilling to proceed.

Pointer did not help her out with a question. This was not the kind of nature that needed supporting or sustaining.

"It's a terrible predicament," she began again. "I hope I'm not unjust—led away by personal dislike—but I shouldn't be very much surprised, Chief Inspector, if you learned that my son had lunched with Miss Dundas. Have you been told who she is?"

Apparently Pointer had not. Lady Tait gave him a brief but far more detailed account of that young lady than had Naylor. She made the young woman's presence in this house of death a very inexplicable business. She began with the note dropped into her cabin at Vichy, and finished with her maid's account of the meeting between the girl and the dead man the night before. A meeting on which Naylor had intruded.

"Of course I ought not to have tolerated her for a moment in the house, nor would I have, but for Mrs. Burnham's sake. If this old affair of Mr. Tait's really should prove to be at the bottom of his death it will break her heart. I had half decided to say nothing about my suspicions," she went on, "just because of the pain it will give if I'm right, but I owe it to my son to tell you all I suspect."

"I think you do," Pointer agreed. "Your idea then is, that whatever it was between them was being renewed?"

"Oh, no! My son was entirely and deeply in love with Mrs. Burnham, as you would have known had you heard the tone of his voice, as well as his words, when he left her a little over an hour ago!" Emotion then nearly overcame her, but she steadied her lips and went on after a pause. "No. He was trying to get out of some old affair— some escapade—that sort of thing." There fell a short silence.

Pointer asked her if she had ever seen the pen to which the gold top in his hand belonged. He had picked it up, he told her too, off the dining-room floor. Lady Tait looked at it without interest, said she had never seen one like it to her knowledge, and suggested therefore Mrs. Burnham as the possible owner. "Though it would be quite in keeping with the preposterous belongings of Miss Dundas, if it were hers."

Cleverly concealed but very skilful questions had led to no confidences about threatening letters having been received by the dead man, so Pointer put the question finally point blank. Had her step-son received any such?

"Of course not!" she said to that in a tone of sharp, almost terrified indignation. "What a wild and romantic idea, Chief Inspector!"

So now he knew what she had been keeping back. Lady Tait knew of such a letter, or letters, or the possibility of their having been received, and for some reason wished to withhold the information from the police... He thanked her, closed the interview on that, and next saw Miss. Naylor. He learned nothing from Alysia. He did not think that she was in possession of any knowledge that would help him. Her interests in the tragedy were entirely as to how it concerned herself, so he read her. He might be all wrong, of course, but for the. present, he put her down as a talker, not a doer.

But her sister Etta, who came next, was an entirely different proposition, apart from the strange glimpse that he had had of her watching Gillian Dundas so intently.

Here was a strong character, he thought. It was not the kind of face that he, the chief inspector, cared to see in the family of one who had died by poison. Not that it was an evil face, but it was the face of one who thought her own thoughts, would go her own way. Something about the handsomely-cut, full lips suggested intense repression. The cheek bones were high, the neck short rather than long. A woman of swift action when roused, one would expect. Not the face of one to quietly endure. And yet something about those lips suggested a woman who had endured much. Unlike Lady Tait, there was a singular tone of insincerity about all that she said to him. But Pointer did not think her fundamentally insincere. She affected him more as a woman who might be very sincere indeed, but who, for some reason, chose to assume a character, play a part quite at variance with her natural one.

These smug sentences with which she referred to the inevitability of death and our duty to so live that we, could at any time be called away, struck him as so many gags used by an actress, yet he felt that she was far more interested in the tragedy than she showed Or rather, he felt that her interest was quite removed from anything to do with the emotions, with grief, or with horror. He had felt the same about her brother There was a look in the eyes of both that spoke of some active, engrossing preoccupation arising from Tait's death Pointer's habit, in a murder case, was always to ask the person to whom he was talking who that person thought might have committed the crime, unless they had already, suggested a criminal. His question was put entirely with a view to obtaining information as to the relationships among themselves of the circle around the dead man. Many a time, unsuspected mistrusts, enmities of which he would never have otherwise heard, rustled and showed themselves in answer to that query, like snakes coming to the charmer's flute.

Etta, like Alysia, told him that she had no idea where to look for the criminal or the motive. So she would not name the girl on the landing. Yet, if her fixed stare at that shrinking figure had not meant suspicion, what did account for it? Strange currents flow into and out of murder. If John Tait's death proved to be, as seemed certain, a planned murder, they would surely be here too. He asked her to describe the scene in the hall when the body was brought in. He learned nothing, except that she confined herself rigidly to facts.

"Who profits by Mr. Tait's death?" he asked, after a pause.

"If you mean in a money sense, all three of us, his cousins, profit. But the only real profit, Chief Inspector, are the things that cannot be set down in a will."

"True," he agreed placidly, "yet of the things that can be so set down and handed on, you, your sister, and your brother are the sole inheritors?"

"We're his only relatives. Yes. It is at times like this that one realizes how little money means, how passing its possession."

A question as to where Tait had lunched today met with an absolute inability even to guess.

"What exactly is the position of the young lady whom I saw standing for a moment on the landing?" Pointer asked.

Gillian Dundas was explained briefly but very accurately by Miss Etta.

"She hardly knew Mr. Tait, then?"

Etta further explained about Vichy.

"So they had met at Vichy?"

She nodded. "Yes, but she knew him very slightly indeed. She certainly did not know him well enough to poison him." She said this with a certain gleam of the eye that made him feel sure that here was a bit of the real Etta Naylor. Pointer, finding that there was nothing to be learned from Miss Naylor without her will, and nothing with it, passed on for the moment, as he had done in the case of her aunt.

She, like her elder sister, claimed not to recognize the pen-top.

"I wonder if you would kindly arrange for Miss Dundas to come in for a word?" he said as he went to the door. "I think she may be of great help."

For a second a curious look passed over Etta Naylor's handsome face. A very singular look made up of more than one emotion.

She shot a most penetrating look at Pointer.

"Can you ride in this race and win?" was in her eye. But she only said "Indeed? On the principle that outsiders see more than insiders?"

"Something of that sort," he agreed. As he opened the door for her Gillian Dundas came in very indifferently, very listless in look and bearing She sank into a chair without a word, and, resting her forehead on her white hand with its mandarine-colored nails, looked dumbly down at the table. Then she raised her eyes and Pointer was genuinely startled. Terror and dread stared from her white, delicately painted face And looking into his clear, calm, very fine gray eyes, the terror showed yet more plainly as guilty fear, abject and absolute.

"Who was she herself?" he asked first. Her father was a Major invalided out of the war. Her mother had to look after him in every way. They were traveling abroad at the moment. Travel was the only thing that seemed to help him. She did not know where to reach them. She had not heard from them, nor written, since Christmas, when they were in Switzerland. They had then intended to go to Malta. As for Mr. Tait, she had first met him in Vichy. She had come to Mrs. Burnham because she had to go somewhere in a hurry, and she had an idea that Mrs. Burnham would help her if she could, and was not a friend of Mrs. de Souza's.

Pointer did not believe one word of all this. Any more than he believed her when she said that her talk with Mr. Tait last night had been merely the idle talk of being found by him in his step-mother's house when he thought—if he thought of her at all—as somewhere in France with her employer. He asked her various questions and obtained replies of the same color.

But when he stopped, and seemed to pick up the top of a gold fountain pen, and she gave it one indifferent, careless glance before saying that she had no idea whose it was, he did believe her. It meant nothing to Miss Dundas—that, he thought, really was true.

When he let her go, she passed out and up the stairs like an automaton whose spring was set in some dreadful terror. Almost it seemed to him that he felt a chill as she brushed by him.

When he closed the door behind her, he stood a long moment staring at his shoe tips, hands deep in his pockets, head bent on his breast.

This terror of Gillian Dundas's, it seemed to linger in the room where she had been. Guilty fear of the police investigation might be part of it; he felt sure that it was, but it was by no means the whole. That fear was, as it were, on the surface of something even deeper yet. Gillian Dundas was afraid for her life, not from anything that he could do, but from another cause. Even supposing her to be guilty of Tait's death, she would know that she might hope to escape the extreme penalty, or indeed get off entirely, but whatever it was that lay beneath that fear of him was something which Pointer believed she thought to be inescapable and imminent.

A murder had been committed, a girl was afraid for her life. Surely it must be the same hand that she dreaded, unless, guilty of Tait's murder, she dreaded vengeance. Pointer dallied with this last idea for a second or two, but if Gillian Dundas were guilty, then there was another potential life-taker in the same circle. This was most unlikely. It seemed much more likely that she was afraid of the same hand that had struck down John Taft. Why? Why should she fear his fate with such helpless certitude of her doom? It could not be that she had seen something, or knew something, which, if made known to the police, would lead to the detection of the criminal or criminals. Or one would think she would have been prevented from seeing Pointer. She had been allowed to return to the house unmolested. She had worked and lunched at the studio, she had told him, alone. Also, against this idea that she might be in danger because of some knowledge of the criminal, was the fact that she was the only person in the house who showed any terror. Yet if she were in possession of any incriminating fact, the criminal would indeed have cause for alarm, for Gillian Dundas looked to Pointer both stupid and entirely self-centered.

Had she received a threatening letter too? This seemed a possible explanation. That she knew that Tait had had one also—that he had told her as much in that talk last night—and that when he died today she knew that she would not escape either. That would mean that they both were linked in the past. Pointer turned the case this way and that to try and catch some gleam of light from its dark surface. Tait, by his position and his record, was a man of high intelligence. Gillian Dundas, from the point of brains, did not exist at all. Then how could the two be in such equal danger that the death of the one meant the death of the other? He gave it up for the present; all he did know was that she was waiting, dumbly, for the end. So certain was she of this end that she was not struggling against her fate. Though he did not think her a fighter ever. She had not turned to him. She had not made the slightest effort to obtain protection. He felt that as far as her greater terror was concerned, he was out of it. Altogether she was a strange fact in the case. Two clues and two alone he had so far. The gold fountain-pen top, and this terror of Miss Dundas's. And they were not linked, as far as he knew...

He was called to the telephone. The Home Office analyst was speaking. The two specks sent him on the slides were particles of spun glass, dyed a light green with the usual British commercial light green dye, just as the manufacture of the glass was British. As for the poison, for which he was requested to test especially, he had found it on both specks but not equally applied. This looked as though the specks had been part of some spun glass object which had been dipped, or sprayed, with the poison after it was made. The object of which these specks had formed a portion was something very brittle, and therefore small. Nothing for use. Something ornamental probably. More the analyst could not say. Pointer told him that he had not hoped to learn so soon.

So those marks in the thumb and first and second fingers of John Tait's right hand were thin filaments of green dyed poisoned glass...Had something burst that he was holding? Something so fragile that a touch would shatter it and drive its spun walls into the hand that held it? He went up now to Tait's rooms, where he had at once sent one of his men to stay on guard. There were three rooms in all. He went rapidly through the dead man's writing table. Most of his belongings would be sifted and sifted again, but he might at once come on some outstanding feature of interest. First of all, he picked up a book of engagements from beside the large inkstand, where lay an assortment of pens and pencils. All unbitten, as the servant had said.

He looked, the book through very carefully indeed. This morning he found marked with an asterisk in pencil and the figure eleven beside it. Now, eleven was the number of Miss Dundas's studio in the Fulham building The other entries seemed all straight forward enough, with the exception of exactly a week ago. On that day was an entry "*Letter from*—" and then came a space where a name had been erased. Then came the words "*that of course I would. Next Tuesday.*" Today was 'next Tuesday.' Pointer studied the erasure through his glass. It was rather a long name beginning with a capital letter that was as broad at the bottom as the top. He decided that it had been either an *H* or a *W* or an *M*. There were absences of marks that ruled out other letters. There was one or possibly two tall letters in the middle, and quite clearly two tall letters to finish It suggested some such name as *Weatherell* offhand. Pointer also thought that following it had been the words "*I replied*," and that they had been rubbed out with the name. Certainly it was a simple proceeding which suggested some one not afraid lest the deletion be noticed. Just as the book had lain out on the table for any one to see. It rather looked—so far— as though Tait himself had rubbed out that name, Pointer thought. But why? He looked next at the dead man's check book, a very recent one. There was a comfortable balance scribbled on the back of the last counterfoil. Pointer looked at the pile of old counterfoils fastened together with a rubber band which, he found in a locked drawer. Two things interested him. Some five months ago was a check to *Self* for five hundred pounds followed the next week by one for fifty pounds. The same thing happened exactly six months before. Here too a check for five hundred to *Self* was followed by another to *Self* of fifty. There was nothing else of interest. Nowhere did any name occur that might fit the erased blank in the engagement book. Pointer took the check book and the old block of counterfoils. Then he looked once more through the engagement book. There were no other erasures nor any other name that seemed to properly fit the blank. The valet professed an absolute ignorance concerning what was, or was not, in the book. An ignorance that, seeing the book lay out on the table, struck the chief inspector as overdone. Did Mr. Tait keep his old engagement books? Pointer expected a negative, but to his joy the man pointed to a locked cupboard. "Full of stuff of that sort. Brought over from a cupboard they're altering in his house."

Pointer found inside it all he would have desired—a pile of personal hooks of all kinds. But he had to go back nearly a year in an engagement book before he found an entry. "Letter from W. Wants me to go there. Made an appointment over the phone for tomorrow," and on the following day was an asterisk. So the erased initial was probably *W*. There was no other helpful entry in the book. After some fruitless, further searches, he came on an old game book nearly six years old. In it be found several entries that showed that Tait had often shot at a place called Pilgrim's Halt, and that on each of these occasions there was always one name among his fellow guns that did not vary, the name of Westmacott. Probably, therefore, the host. Pointer saw that by trying the letters on tissue paper over the erasure, the name would exactly fit in.

Westmacott of Pilgrim's Halt... sounded familiar...But why the erasure, and the guarded entry today at eleven? He went to the nearest telephone outside the house and rang up a young man about town who acted as one of the Yard's voluntary assistants in matters of this kind. Ward-Thynne worked in the Ascot Office at St. James' when it was a question of admission to the Royal Enclosure. His mind was a perfect card-index of people in society, though he could not have earned threepence a week as far as the rest of his attainments went.

Who was a Westmacott? Apparently the owner of a place called Pilgrim's Halt some five to six years ago?

"You mean Westmacott, the multi-millionaire, Westmacott of Pilgrim's Halt and Park Pinnacles and Mariners and two hunting boxes in the Highlands, and a huge house in town—11 Palace Green? Sort of Second Lord Shaftesbury. He's been out in China for the last three years or so, carrying on a relief mission of his own."

Pointer asked if he was known to be a friend of a Mr. John Tait, who was a co-director with Lord Mills on some Companies.

"Very great friend indeed. They regularly have gone fishing together in Norway for years. I should say Tait is Westmacott's particular pal. And besides that, Tait's Miss Henrietta Naylor's cousin, you know. What does that signify? Dear me, how little you chaps at the Yard really know, when it comes to important things! Westmacott was going to marry her, and then suddenly turned and whizzed off to help the Honduras Earthquake victims on the spot. Left the lady high and dry. Nice girl too. Rather a bit out of his line—a hard riding, hard swearing, and probably hard drinking young amazon then. She's turned herself into the equivalent of a Salvation. Army lass since, and it doesn't suit her."

The man at the other end was warming up. "And then of course Lady Ida! Lady Ida! Westmacott's widowed sister-in-law who acts as his hostess and keeps his houses. open now he's away. Yes, John Tait and Lady Ida were at one time rather bracketed together. Oh, not as Westmacott and Etta Naylor were. The last had the banns all but read out. No, but people rather expected something would come of it in due time with regard to the other two. Only nothing did. When was this talk? About two years ago more or, less. Since then, Tait seems to've dropped out of Lady Ida's circle. Anything else?"

He was warmly thanked, and Pointer rang through to his own rooms at the Yard. Had any fresh information come in? Very much so. The first test of the blood of the dead man had proved, the existence of a deadly dose of the poison mixture named by Dr. Angelli. It had been administered directly into the blood. By a cut, a prick, an injection of some kind a splinter," Pointer mentally added

Pointer's next step was to drive to Palace Green. It looked as though the eleven referred to that, and not to Miss Dundas's studio.

Palace Green is one of the few unspoiled streets of large houses still left in town. As yet no buses roar through it, and it remains broad and stately, facing Kensington Palace and the Gardens. Westmacott's was one of the largest of the houses, and an end one. Along its side ran a passage way into Church Street. A very high wall with a. door in it protected the garden from being overlooked. He rang tile bell, sent in his name only, and asked to see Lady Ida on "a matter concerning Mr. John Tait."

CHAPTER EIGHT

HE was shown into a fiercely modern room where the chairs and tables seemed better suited to a submarine in their metallic economy of line and space than to a London town house. The usual flashing cushions were piled everywhere, a heap of them in one corner around a steel radiator. The lighting was concealed, the ceiling colored, the floor metallic looking. Altogether Pointer was quite prepared for the ultra smart-looking woman who came in a moment later with the inevitable long jade cigarette-holder stuck at an angle from pillar-box red lips. In age the woman was perhaps forty. Very handsome, and a more resolute jaw and eye he had not often met. "Thou shalt want e'er I will" should have been the lady's motto, whatever her family. But she looked at him very keenly, and she had come in very quickly in answer to his message.

"From Mr. Tait?" she asked.

Pointer hesitated to allow her to make some further remark. That might be enlightening, for he thought she was disturbed by his visit.

But as Lady Ida said nothing, he explained that Mr. Tait had been picked up dying near his house, that his dead body had been carried into his step-mother's house, and that, believing that Mr. Tait had been in to see. Lady Ida that morning around eleven, he, Pointer, had wondered if she had noticed anything odd, whether he had looked ill, or if she had heard him complain of feeling ill.

Lady Ida dropped her cigarette in apparent shock and stupefaction. She expressed both emotions too in no stinted measure.

"Yes, you're quite right. He dropped in for a chat—
about his engagement. My brother-in-law is quite a pal of
his, you know, and of course John's coming marriage
interested me enormously. I saw his fiancée and Lady
Tait at the theater the other night. Charming woman she
looks. Poor, poor thing!" Sympathy spoke in the voice, but
none looked from the bold, hard blue eyes. "And how
awfully sudden," she went on. "Of course, his father
dropped dead, didn't he? But Mr. Tait looked so fit and
well and happy this morning—" and again Lady Ida gave
vent to a flow of amazed and shocked murmurs. Again
she eyed him closely. "Let me see, I think you said your
name was—?" She apparently groped in her memory.

"Pointer. Chief Inspector Pointer, of New, Scotland
Yard," the visitor explained pleasantly. Her jaw dropped.
This time the holder fell as well as a new cigarette that
she had just started. Her shining finger nails quivered for
a second as though she had been shaken with a tremor,
but her face showed nothing of this.

"Of Scotland Yard," she murmured. "Really? Pray,
what has poor Mr. Tait been doing to get you interested
in him?"

"It looks as though he had let himself be poisoned,"
was the rather grim reply. "The doctors think there is no
doubt but that some virulent poison was the cause of his
death, and that being so, of course everything connected
with him this morning must be gone into."

Pointer thought that sheer horror held her dumb for a
moment. And he was rather surprised at it. This woman
would be hard as nails, he thought, except where it
concerned herself or her own family. But the fact that
Tait had died by poison would not, one would think,
directly concern her. Yet he believed her to be deeply
shaken, and anxious not to show how great her
perturbation was. True, he had just learned that she was
credited with a willingness at one time to marry, the dead
man, and both these emotions might be due, to her
knowledge of this gossip, but—well, his quiet, casual-

seeming glance had placed her as a masterful, resolute woman, not at all squeamish in the choice of the path by which to reach any objective on which she, might have set her heart. A nature which, if he was right in reading it, might or might not mean a good deal in this case. She seemed now intensely curious as to every detail of Tait's death which could suggest the criminal, but not at all curious, or concerned as to his actual end, or any suffering that he had endured. In short, she conveyed the idea to the keen observer talking to her that in some odd, secret, hidden way she was on the alert for danger to herself. But, try as he would, he could not make up his mind as to whether she expected this danger to come from him—the law—or from another source, the same source possibly as that which seemed so to terrify Gillian Dundas. If the latter, Lady Ida was only on the look-out, not in the least terrified. Pointer spoke of Miss Dundas when alluding to the Tait household, and at once something watchful crept into Lady Ida's brilliant, hard eyes, but she made no reference to the girl herself.

"How awful it all is!" she said finally, after a deep breath or two. "How incredibly sudden and awful!"

Pointer agreed. "Can you suggest where to look for the criminal?"

Lady Ida bit her, lip and stared at the floor for a full minute before saying "Will what I say be strictly confidential?"

Pointer explained that if it was merely her opinion, it would be so, but that any facts told him might have to come out at the inquest or the trial, though, if possible, the source of police information would be held back from public knowledge.

"It's only my opinion," Lady Ida said to that, "and of course you've thought of it for yourself. Mr. Tait's cousins are the only people who profit by his death. I happen to know that one of them borrowed more than once from him for her so-called charity works among the poor."

"You mean Miss Henrietta Naylor?" Pointer looked his interest. "I wonder if we shall find details of the borrowings among his papers?"

"I'm sure you won't. But Mr. Tait to my knowledge advanced her some five hundred pounds towards a woman's model lodging house, or the alteration of one, something of that sort. Miss Etta Naylor promised to repay him as soon as some shares or other of hers would rise and could he sold without throwing them away. I told him at the time—I heard of it through another mutual friend—that he'd never get a penny back, but he insisted that he'd see to it that he was repaid all right. He had no intention whatever of letting her keep the money as a gift."

"What shares were they, do you know?"

She named some of the coal and iron heavies that were enjoying a sudden rise at the moment. "Had Mr. Tait lived another week," she went on, "those shares would have had to be sold and the loan repaid."

"But if there is nothing in writing, and supposing Miss Etta Naylor had chosen to—?" Pointer asked vaguely.

"She'd have had to pay up," Lady Ida said with conviction. "You forget that she was living in Mr. Tait's house, or with his step-mother, and Lady Tait lets no one off in a money question."

There was a short silence. Pointer now knew one more fact. This woman hated Etta Naylor with an active, virulent hatred.

He brought in the name of Mrs. Burnham next.

"Charming woman, I understand," she said sweetly, "but how the two Naylor women loathe her! Natural, of course."

"They spoke of her to me most affectionately," Pointer murmured as though perplexed.

"They would. But with Miss Etta Naylor, Chief Inspector, it's a very safe rule to go by the opposite of what she says." She laughed with an ill-natured distension of her painted lips that showed two gold-cased teeth on one side, and what Pointer felt sure was a bridge on the other. Her teeth were not her best point.

"We found part of a lady's gold fountain pen in Mr. Tait's pocket," he now said lightly. "I wonder if you can suggest the owner? We intend to have it photographed and reproduced in the papers if we can't get any other identification of it."

Just for a second something startled and wary showed in her eye, as she held out her hand with a smile that spoke more of effort than reality.

"Can I see it? Yes—" as he laid it in her thin, narrow, rose-tinted palm. "This is the top of one of my pens. I have a frightful habit of biting the ends, and he was so shocked by the appearance of this this morning, that he insisted on taking it away to have it put right."

Pointer dropped the little object back in its envelope as though of no importance. "That's saved us a great deal of trouble. As soon as the case is over we'll send it back to you."

She smiled again, and again Pointer noticed teeth whose rounded edges could no more have made those savage marks than a kitten could leave a tiger's scoring on a piece of bark. A young man burst in at that moment with the air, of one running in to save a family heirloom in a fire. Flinging open a bookcase, he seized a volume and would have dashed out again, but Lady Ida stopped him.

"Luttrell, put that down a minute. We've just had an awful piece of news. This is a Chief Inspector from Scotland Yard—my son, Luttrell Westmacott."

The young man in question turned a pleasant, freckled face on the visitor.

"Is myrmidon spelled with a 'y' or an 'i'? If it's 'i'—"

"Mr. Tait has just died, Luttrell," his mother went on. The expert in crosswords dropped a book, and stood without picking it up, staring blankly at his mother.

"But I thought he was here only this morning," he expostulated, and by the remark gave the apparent measure of his brains, in appearance borne out by his weak, good-natured, silly face and weak, wide, good natured, silly, smile, a smile, however, that showed quite a useful double row of ivory. Pointer eyed them as intently, as a dentist. They did not come up to his standard as regards size.

Luttrell made other horrified, inane remarks and asked for details. Pointer left it to his mother to pass on all the information she had obtained.

"Can you tell me where Mr. Tait was lunching today?" he asked, when this was done.

Luttrell said that he had not seen Mr. Tait this morning. "He only came for a talk, with my mother," he explained Lady Ida professed to have no idea what Mr. Tait's engagements were, they had only talked of his coming marriage. How long had Mr. Tait been at the house? She gave eleven exactly to a quarter past as the time. Pointer apologized for the next questions which were as to their own movements until three today. Not that it really mattered, but he learned that neither, had left the house. The day was bad and had kept most people indoors until well past the hour when Tait had stumbled, flung the deeply-bitten gold top of a fountain pen out of his pocket, and then died.

There were plenty of artificial flowers in the room where they were. Tall lilies coiled on their own greenstems rising from black Chinese bowls. A couple were at Pointer's elbow—he had chosen his seat to be near them. As he talked, he fingered them absentmindedly, but though of glass, they were blown, and firm, and waxen, smooth to the touch. Would that be true, however, of any other artificial flowers that might be found in the other rooms?

He left with the certainty that Lady Ida was deeply perturbed, but that her son did not share this feeling. As to her explanation for the reason for Taft's call, it certainly failed to convince. But it was difficult to imagine what reason there could be which called for a lie on her part and an erasure in Tait's engagement book. Business it would hardly seem to be...

Apart from other things, she was not a business woman, nor had any fortune of her own. It was not political, one would think... though this was possible... But that caution on Tait's part that no chance curiosity should know that he was going to see Lady Ida had, to Pointer, rather the look of his being the bearer of a message from the brother-in-law.

An ultimatum of some sort? Why had not the absent millionaire sent it himself? Apparently the call had been in response to a request of Westmacott's, not one of whose letters had been found, so far, among Tait's papers. Was it possible that the blank space was not due to Tait himself, but to some one else? At any rate, the deletion had been made, so had the call, and now Lady Ida was alarmed, not merely grieved, if grieved at all, by the news of the caller's sudden end.

A second woman was afraid when she heard that John Tait was dead. And though there was no comparison in the degree of fright, therefore, quite probably, none in its origin, the fact remained, and the chief inspector brooded on its origin or origins, as he got into his small swift car. At the Yard Superintendent Dartmoor was out, and had not yet therefore learned that a mate had been found to the glove left in Lord Mills' room, but one of his men had a piece of information for the chief inspector. Among Lord Mills' papers were some dealing with the letting to a Mrs. de Souza of a villa at Capri about two years ago, at a price which was remarkably high. The house in question had come to Lord Mills from a relative.

Judging by the letters, a personal acquaintance between himself and the lady had come about as the outcome of the transaction, though, apparently, but of the usual invitation-to-dinner-now-and-then kind.

So Gillian Dundas was linked, through Mrs. de Souza, with Lord Mills, and through her own action, or chance, with John Tait. Her studio was on Pointer's list of ports of call, but he decided to see Mrs. de Souza first, as he did not wish to ask for a description of her from any inmate of Great Cumberland Place.

He had got her address from Gillian, and now drove there. She was in, and he sent in his own personal card with a word to the effect that he "called about Miss Dundas's references."

He was shown into a most expensive room, where Mrs. de Souza, with a look of sleepy good nature on her face, was petting an overfed Pekinese—also expensive. She was still on the young side of forty, but her face looked as though it had suffered from over-steaming, or over-massage in the past, or else too many late hours and cocktails.

"Miss Dundas has nothing to do with me now," she began at once, in an excited, high-pitched voice, but the voice of an Englishwoman none the less. "She left me without any notice, and is companion now to another lady. And I never give two references."

Pointer wondered why she troubled to see him in that case. But it was possible that it was only a woman's curiosity that had procured him the interview.

He did not wish to be detained by giving an account of Mr. Tait's death, so he merely bowed and said that he apologized for having disturbed Mrs. de Souza for nothing. But she would not be content. "But why have you come to me? How did you hear of me? Miss Dundas left me days ago...Has she applied for a job with you? A Mrs. Burnham whom we met at Vichy took her on..."

Pointer was in a hurry. He apologized again, and fairly tore himself away from the lady, who seemed extraordinarily unwilling to let him go. When she heard of Tait's death, supposing she did not already know of it, she would understand why a Mr. Pointer was interested in Miss Dundas's more recent past, and Pointer intended to have a long talk with her in the near future. But for the moment all he wanted was to see the lady who had rented Lord Mills' villa. This being done, he drove rapidly off in the opposite direction, to turn back on his tracks and make for Miss Dundas's studio. He found that you turned off Knightsbridge proper, down a little alley, and into a square surrounded by dingy old houses, all of them used as offices. The house in which was the room that Miss Dundas claimed to use as a studio had a back entrance as well, approached from the direction of what will always remain in the mind of old Londoners as Tattersall's. Here, too, as it happened, was an almost unobserved little alley and several shops. It might be merely chance, but certainly no fortune-teller anxious not to come to grips with the law could have chosen a better little dive. The studio itself, as Pointer found on unlocking it with one of his keys—he had a search warrant, if needed—proved to be an unexpectedly large and pleasant room. Yellow walls, deep blue linoleum, and very thick blue curtains which, when drawn, would allow no glimpse of the interior to be caught from any overlooking windows. A gas stove stood in a neat fireplace. On a long green-painted table stood some china, each piece carefully labeled with directions and addresses. In the drawers of the table were various tools and implements for mending china. Altogether a most innocent, workmanlike looking place—with no green spun glass ornaments. The bureau was open, in its pigeon holes were neatly stacked accounts. Yet all the cupboards and drawers in the room showed slovenliness. It looked to Pointer as though the accounts had to be kept up-to-date and ready for inspection by some backer. They showed that so far the business did not pay for the rent of the room, let alone for heating and lighting, or any living expenses. Yet, from the look of the linoleum, when he moved away bureau and potters' bench, the room had been fitted out as it was at present for at least two or three years.

On the mantel was the dottle out of a pipe. The whole room badly needed dusting. There was a tin of Turkish cigarettes on the shelf which corresponded with some ash dropped near the bureau, and with some stubs on a shelf over a fitted basin. Expensive scented cigarettes, these. They suited Miss Dundas's appearance, but the dottle? Pointer retrieved that too very carefully and put it away for analysis. He tested the room quickly for finger prints, especially the green painted wooden arms of a smoker's chair that stood just beside the end of the mantel where he had found the dottle. On it he found quite a collection, recently made apparently, and made by the same hands. Unusually big hands of a man, but with slender fingers. And there was one place on the side where he had evidently drummed. Pointer stared hard at the prints, which his powder brought up sharp and clear. For though the marks showed that he had drummed with curved-in fingers on their very tips, there were no marks of rounded or pointed nails, only a jagged notch here and there. The man apparently either bit his nails, or had worn them roughly down by some form of work. Yet the dottle was of a very good tobacco.

The telephone buzzed. Pointer took down the receiver.

"Is Miss Dundas there?" It was a man's voice, rather a thick voice, but suggestive of a big frame and youth.

"Yes," Pointer said quickly.

"Can I speak to her, please?" In a tone of great relief.

"Dare say you can," Pointer said in cockney accents, after which he laid down the receiver and walked noisily into a kitchenette off the studio proper.

"Here, miss. Yer wanted on the phone," he called as he went. A minute later he picked up the mouthpiece again. "She must've just gone out. Can't be gone for long from the way she spoke."

"Who are you?" came the question, sharply put.

"I'm the plumber," came the reply. "Something wrong with the hot-water pipe. Well, are you coming round, or shall I give the lady a message, or what?" Pointer spoke in weary tones.

There was nothing weary in the voice that replied rapidly: "I'll be round at once. Ask Miss Dundas to wait for me, will you, if she comes back before I get there."

"What name?" Pointer asked listlessly.

"Strange. Say. I'll be round as soon as I can, and want to see her very particularly. If she can't wait, will she leave a message for me."

Pointer murmured "Right ho!" and hung up. The next instant he was telephoning in code to a man at the Yard. He had a wardrobe room full of disguises, all ready packed. In a minute a man on a motor bicycle was hurrying to him, a bag tagged with a number that meant a plumber's outfit. Pointer meanwhile waited on the landing outside, in case Mr. Strange should get there before his man, but the latter was first by a good ten minutes. It took Pointer just four to turn into a round-shouldered, be-spectacled man with graying hair, who had evidently not shaved this morning. A pair of greasy overalls protected well-worn, much rained-on clothes. A bag of plumber's tools also showed signs of hard wear. He lit a candle and stuck it in true professional style under the washbasin so as to dribble as much tallow on the floor as possible, and smoke as much of the surrounding wall as possible, then he strewed his tools around him, and waited. He did not make the mistake of looking out of the window. Presently he heard steps taking the stairs two at a time. There came long pressure on the bell. Pointer waited. Had the visitor a latch-key, and were his finger-nails bitten to the quicks? As for Miss Dundas, a message to the house—in code—had assured him that she was still locked in her room far from any telephone. The ring came again. A long ring and two short ones. Still Pointer waited. Again and for a third time the long and two short rings came. Finally a key was inserted, and some one stepped in hastily and as hastily shut the door. Next moment the door of the studio was jerked wide. A tall

figure of a man hurried in. At sight of the plumber. it
stopped dead.

"I thought the place must be empty. I've been ringing
for ten minutes."

Pointer looked up from under the sink. "Sorry, I'm
sure," he said civilly. "I heard a bell but I never thought
of it being in this flat. Ye see, whot with the water
running and my ear to this pipe I can't hear clear—"

"Where's Miss Dundas?" the other broke in
impatiently.

"Not back yet," Pointer replied, working away with a
spanner which he carefully did not screw home on a nut.
He peered up once at the man as he answered, then
seemed engrossed with his work. That one glance had
shown him a man looking around thirty, dressed in the
very smartest of clothes, but worn without the right air of
complacent strut demanded, for the garments in question
had been chosen and made with a view to creating an
impression. But the man wearing them was not thinking
of making an impression just at the moment. His face
intrigued the chief inspector. Pointer classified it as a
ravaged one. By what? Drug? Drink?. Neither quite
fitted, though Pointer thought that the last was one of the
habits of the man now standing irresolutely in front of
the fireplace. But there were lines on the face turned first
this way to the window, then that way to the door, which
even Pointer could not quite classify. He saw some of
them for the first time. Odd lines in odd places, or else
odd lines in usual places. The face looked to him as
though an earthquake had at some time or other taken
place in it, and the features still bore the mark of their
violent distortion. Was the man an epileptic? He thought
that this explanation might be the right one. The man
now set his teeth and worked his lips, now pursed to
cover them, now drawn far back. He was evidently quite
unconscious of the grimaces as, deep in what looked like
anxious thought, he stood staring at the unlit gas fire. He
had very large and strong yellow, teeth, deeply serrated,

apparently all intact. Just such teeth, in fact, as Pointer would expect to leave just such marks as he had seen on the gold fountain-pen top that Tait had flung out of his pocket as he fell into the arms of the   taximan,   the pen top which the dying man might have meant as a guide to his murderer. This man wore gloves, he fidgeted now with the buttons, and Pointer hoped he would discard them.

Pointer did something with what looked like a cold blow-pipe, in reality he was snapshotting the man who stood in an extremely good light by the large window.

"Lucky she slipped her latch-key under the mat outside, or I couldn't have got in at all," the visitor now said suddenly.

Pointer agreed that that habit was useful. There was no key under the mat, and he had heard the jingle of a key-ring as the lock was turned.

"Did she say how long she would be?" the man now went on.

Pointer shook his head. "Absent-minded lady, ain't she? She didn't seem to rightly know what was wrong with this basin, yet she had asked us to come in and look at it. Ladies of that age are apt to forget."

"Of that age? Of what age?" The visitor had spun round and was staring fixedly, at Pointer, and with evident excitement.

"Why—well—" Pointer looked embarrassed.

"Sort of fortyish, I mean."

The man tore off his gloves and flung them on the mantel, then he lit a cigarette with hands, big but slender fingered, with nails bitten and broken to the quicks. "Look here, that wasn't Miss Dundas; what was the lady like?"

Pointer described—not too closely—Mrs. de Souza. He might want to modify the likeness later, for this young man might have just been with Mrs. de Souza and know that she could not have been here. Strange, if that really was his name, looked uneasy, he was listening with really extraordinary closeness to what the plumber was saying.

"Reddish fair hair combed down in a wave on this side and rolled up. from her neck?" he asked, illustrating what he meant with remarkable deftness. Now Mrs. de Souza's most noticeable characteristic was the way she wore her hair. Just in that fashion. So the man did know her and was, though intensely interested, not incredulous at hearing that she had been to Gillian Dundas's studio. Pointer said he had not noticed her hair.

"Must have been a friend of Miss Dundas's," Strange finally said. "What did you say she was doing?"

"I thought she was sitting at that there writing-table," Pointer suggested, "but I didn't notice pertikler."

"She didn't say why she had come? She left no message?" Strange seemed puzzled. Pointer would have liked to put a message about some green spun glass into the imaginary lady's mouth, but he did not dare let his fancy roam. He had an idea that Strange's next move in any case would be to have a word with Mrs. de Souza. So instead of replying, Pointer breathed heavily as he "wiped" an already welded joint and said, "Must be a handicap being deaf."

"Deaf?" Apparently Mr. Strange was slightly afflicted that way himself.

"Used one of these electrical ear things," Pointer went on. Strange looked utterly at sea.

"Come to make some new curtains I thought myself," the plumber now explained. "I thought she was just a-jotting down of measurements at that there writing-table."

Strange's face cleared. "Oh, that's very likely!" And there was an amazing amount of relief in the tone and eye. "Very likely indeed. I thought, for a moment, you meant a lady I know too, but it doesn't fit."

The plumber began to search his greasy old carpet bag and then his pockets. "I suppose I couldn't ask yer for a pinch of tobacco, sir? I ain't cadging, but I've left me pouch at home. And seeing as the lady isn't here —I can't work proper without a pipe."

Hardly listening to him, Strange shook some out on to the table. "Help yourself," he muttered, turning to stare out of the window again.

Pointer thanked him, filled his clay pipe and swept the remainder into his pocket apparently carelessly, in reality into an envelope opened in it. It was the same tobacco as that of the dottle. It confirmed the idea that the man, who evidently had a latch-key, knew the studio well. The question was, among many others, did he know it as a friend of Miss Dundas's or not. Obviously he was the man who had sat and drummed on the wooden arms of the chair just by the fire, and even as Pointer thought it, the other dropped into the seat and began tapping his finger ends impatiently on the sides of the arms. Pointer would have taken the man for an exceedingly affluent actor, judging by his clothes, or—more likely, a man who made his living by grimaces, in film work, but why those broken nails? They were not bitten, he saw now, or not only bitten, they were also ragged and jagged from other causes. What causes? The man's hair, too, showed signs of neglect, the back of the neck was badly in need of a barber's clippers. Yet the hair was smartly waved. The man was a curious problem. He certainly was ill at ease. Though whether for himself or not, Pointer could not make out. Was he afraid of Gillian Dundas's knowledge or was he afraid for her? His uneasiness was certainly connected with her. If she knew something that made this man nervous, that made Lady Ida nervous, was it something for knowledge of which John Tait had been murdered?—and Lord Mills shot himself?

Starting up from his chair, the visitor hurriedly said he would come back again in a little while, and strode off. Pointer hurried after him, reaching him just as he got to the front door.

"You haven't left no message," he said, as though one were a necessity. Strange looked irresolute. "If the young

lady comes to whom the studio belongs, tell her I'll ring
up again shortly and find if she can spare me a minute,"
and so saying he hurried off. The plumber returned
without another glance after him. The man who had
brought the tools and outfit would see to that. Which was
why Pointer had spoken to Strange in the doorway. He
himself went upstairs again, put his tools together,
changed, removed all traces of his presence in the flat,
and was just about to leave, when again the telephone
rang.

"Is the plumber there?" asked the voice of his own
man.

"Speaking," and Pointer gave a code word.

"Reporting from a police station, sir," came the reply.
"Kensington High Street Police Station. I followed the
man to a house close by here, where I've left a constable
to watch the doors till I get back—the house of Mr.
Westmacott in Palace Green, sir. He let himself in by the
side door into the garden. Looked right and left first—the
door opens into a little short cut from Church Street
which passes the corner of the house. The door key
turned and the door opened and shut without a sound."

"He paused to look up and down the street before. he
unlocked the door, you say. Did he pause again. and seem
to listen before opening the door and going through it?"

"No, sir. Put his key in, opened the door, slipped in
and closed the door all in one swift silent motion. Highly
trained burglar couldn't have bettered it, supposing he
isn't one. For he'd made sure—as he thought—that he
wasn't being followed. Went through the whole bag of
tricks. Underground passage out of Barkers—he went
there first—then two railway stations—but he was quick
with it all."

"You are sure that he has no idea that he was
followed?"

"Certain, sir. Struck me from the sort of way he never
tried to see who was behind him that he was just
following some usual rule of his.. It seemed to me that he

was that absent-minded really that he was sort of walking in his sleep. Another thing, sir, there's a sergeant here at the station who's a great pal of the Westmacott chauffeur, but he won't be on duty for another three hours. But the officer in charge here, he says he knows the household fairly well, he can't place any such man as I've described, says he's never seen any one like him coming or going—the constables here say the same. Yet he certainly had come and gone by that little side door before, sir. At least once, if not much oftener. The constable thinks they've changed a footman there lately. It may be him, of course." This ended the report. The man hurried back to a place where he could watch the house again.

It might be a footman, which, supposing his duties were more of a houseman's type, might account, for his fingernails and dusty hair. His clothes might be his own exuberant fancy or some gift from a late theatrical employer. In speech and bearing he belonged to another class than a servant's, but that might mean nothing except misfortune. The fact remained that the man who knew Gillian Dundas and Mrs. de Souza, also knew Lady Ida Westmacott... the owner of the gold fountain pen marked with those strong teeth... Like everything else, so far linked to Gillian Dundas, it was odd and puzzling. That personal terror of hers, the alarm of Lady Ida, the acute interest of Mrs. de Souza... Those poisoned filaments of green glass... a poison much in use among the natives of the Mediterranean countries, that villa bought by Mrs. de Souza from Lord Mills at Capri... It was a tight coil this. Those poisoned filaments of green spun glass... of what had they been part? What had become of the whole? Pointer still saw them probably as something that would crush or burst if subjected to any pressure. Something small, if so, since only the first two fingers and thumb of the one hand, the right, showed the glass splinters. What had become of the article? However exploded, some fragments must surely be in existence...

Seeing that death could follow so quickly Pointer would
expect him to have been given the dangerous article to
carry away with him outside the house or room of the
poisoner. But if so it had not been wrapped up, or some
microscopic fragments of paper would have been driven in
with the splinters. That was not the case. But how would
he be induced to carry away an object not wrapped up?
Made of green spun glass. And what had become of it?
Was it possible that some suspicions had been roused and
that he posted the—whatever it was—dropping it in the
pillar-box? Pointer had asked the postal officials to let one
of his men search the box for a possible poisoned glass
article, and, seeing the nature of it, for once the postal
authorities had hastened to give permission. A postman
and one of Pointer's men would be at it now. But still
remained the puzzle of what it was that, unwrapped, the
doomed man had carried with him. He was not known to
have flung anything away—unless that gold fountain-pen
top—he had not been seen carrying any object by the tax-
driver who had held him as he died. Negative evidence all
this... not like the presence of a man who had access to
both Miss Dundas's studio and the house where lived the
owner of that gold fountain pen.

Suddenly Pointer's eyes sparkled. He had been
thinking over Strange's appearance, an appearance that
fitted his name so well. Pointer saw again the pretty little
buttonhole he was wearing, a sprig of lily-of-the-valley
half enwrapped in its own leaf.

It had looked natural, this was early May, the sprig
had been tiny, so had been its leaf... but was it natural?
Could such things be imitated in spun glass? An artificial
buttonhole made of spun glass, if such a thing existed,
could be handled and taken away by Tait without any
wrapping, worn in his buttonhole, though Pointer had
rather a memory of an unstretched little slit in the dead
man's coat. He was just passing a big shop and strolled
in. He asked for artificial flowers, had they any made of
glass? He was promptly, shown some splendid tulips,

nothing of spun glass about these. What about leaves for them? He was shown some tall upstanding or bent over leaves, astonishingly like nature, but brittle as only glass can be. "Spun glass these," the assistant told him, and a recollection came suddenly to Pointer of the window-boxes in Westmacott's house in Palace Green, where a row of tulips, with their leaves, had stood in a handsome double row, quite easy to reach from inside the room or from the steps. A word about them, a suggestion to the guest to just rumple one of the leaves... it could have been done that way, supposing the leaves to have been, like these, made of glass. He remembered them as looking the same, but were they? But first of all, he asked the assistant in the shop whether smaller flowers, buttonholes say, were ever made of glass The young woman did not think so She had never seen any. Pointer thanked her and hurried out, to make for Palace Green at once. Yes, the window boxes did come close up to the front door steps. True, he had the long arms of a six foot four man, but even a smaller man, such as Tait was, would not have had the slightest difficulty in reaching them. Slipping quietly, but not suspiciously so, up to the front door, with one gloved hand, and in one swift motion he transferred the green tulip leaf nearest him into his pocket, went through the appearance of pressing the bell, and then walked away again On the quiet little strip that joins Palace Green to Kensington Gardens he looked at the leaf.

As his touch had told him, it was artificial and made of spun glass; he now found that it crumbled easily at the edge and was of a kind that, on running a careless, hand up and down it, or even handling it thoughtlessly, would easily send fine splinters into the fingers He was very careful not to do this It was quite possible, knowing no one had any cause to, touch that well-ordered double row of flowers, that some one had poured poison over all the leaves, trusting to the next rain to wash it away, and to the fact that Tait's death would be considered a natural one, or that even if poison were suspected, the means by which it was administered would never be discovered.

It would have been quite a simple matter for Lady Ida to find a dozen pretexts to get Tait to handle one of the leaves. If so, her attitude of alarm or wariness would be explained, supposing she thought herself safe from actual detection but had hoped Tait's death would pass as due to heart failure.

Yet there seemed no reason for Lady Ida to wish to remove John Tait, except the old idea that hell hath no fury like a woman scorned, with which Pointer did not in the least agree Certainly she struck him as the last woman to risk her neck for the sake of thwarted passion. Now, if it had been a question of money... some message from her rich brother-in-law that affected her income... those were the lines where Lady Ida's character would be at its weakest, he thought. However, obviously the first thing to do was to rush the leaf to the same Home Office analyst to whom the specks from the dead man's fingers had been sent. And here Pointer had a check. Mr. Harrowby saw him at once, glanced at his precious leaf, and shook his head, pulling forward a color chart on which he had marked a pale green.

"That's the color of your spun glass specks, Chief Inspector. All exactly the same shade, so it looks as though the. object had been uniform in die. And they're finer spun than this, by far." He tweaked off a piece and examined it under one of his microscopes. But only for a second. "Not in the least like your specks. These are foreign dye and of a totally different color and composition—and not poisoned."

Pointer was looking at the color chart. The shade was exactly the color of a lily of the valley leaf... a tiny little sprig like that would be finer spun... the man who wore a buttonhole that might have been made of glass, though it looked so natural, had let himself into a side door, of the Westmacott house.

... But what about Gillian Dundas's studio where china, and therefore, presumably, glass was mended? Was his step-mother right in believing that John Tait and she had met today at lunch? One thing was certain, Pointer thought, as he drove back to Great Cumberland Place, motive would play an enormous part in deciding this case.

CHAPTER NINE

AT Great Cumberland Place Pointer was met by Naylor. That young man had a dinner engagement, that he did not wish to break. Pointer assured him that every one in the house was free to go and come as they pleased. By the way, could Mr. Naylor suggest what his cousin had written in his engagement-book and then erased?

Pointer and he were alone in a morning-room, and the chief inspector took the little book in question out of his pocket. Naylor stretched out his hand for it with almost overdone slowness, as though he wanted to be quite sure not to grab it. Reading the entry, he shook his head as though in complete mystification. "Not an earthly idea of who this could be—and the odd caution about the whole entry—" He stood with bent head as though musing. "You know," he said finally, "there was something rather odd once before about an engagement of my cousin's. It, too, was in the morning" he added with a note of vivacity. "A dog of his was run over outside his house in Chelsea Gardens; my cousin was devoted to the beast, but he caught sight of the clock and said he must rush off. His car was outside but he walked away, either to take a taxi or to go on foot. He was away nearly half an hour, and when he got back the dog was dead. Something about him on his return suggested that he wished to hear no mention of his being unable to be there. Nor did he ever refer to it, let alone explain it, as far as I know. One thing I feel sure of. It wasn't a love affair, or if so, it was an old, irksome one. He went because he felt that he must—not because he wanted to."

"What date was this?"

"Last Lord Mayor's Show."

That was the first week in November. In the latter
part of November Tait had gone on a sort of official-
unofficial mission to Rome. Then on to Vienna. He had
only returned to town shortly before Lady Tait's accident
in Vichy, somewhere around the middle of March.

"And another thing about that errand of his, or, that
engagement of his," Naylor went on, "when I went out to
meet him in the front hall to tell him the dog was dead, it
struck me that he was wrapped in some tragedy of his
own, or had just had a very painful experience. He looked
a bit shaken. Even the dog's death seemed—for the
moment—to be something trivial."

The talk went back to the erasure in the engagement-
book.

"Could it by any chance stand for Westmacott?"
Pointer asked, as though grateful for a little light.

Naylor seemed to consider that suggestion.

"Apparently he does know a man of that name,"
Pointer added.

Naylor nodded. "Oh, very much so. Great friend of his.
Now off in China running a relief camp of his own.
Millionaire bloke. But there obviously can't be any reason
why my cousin, or any one else, should have deleted the
name, if it's Westmacott," and he seemed to ponder again.

Pointer left him to it—supposing him to be frank on
the matter. He wanted to go over the house, and took
Rainer, Lady Tait's maid, with him. Pointer hoped that
she would chat about the latest addition to the household,
Miss Dundas, but she was silent about her and her
arrival. He found Lady Tait's rooms comfortable and
quiet, and on her shelves the kind of books he would have
expected to find. Mrs. Burnham's rooms could obviously
not be much help as to character, except that her toilet-
table, like her luggage, showed her taste to be for the best
and simplest-looking articles. Her own books were of the
Barrie type, with some translations of Selma Lagerlöf,
much marked at the side, and here and there a marginal
note of "How true!" "Beautifully said," and so on. Naylor's

belongings were very up-to-date, with the most recent of scurrilous novels on his bed-table, and some rather stiff law books well hidden behind a piece of Persian weaving. But there were hints of a complex personality on his shelves too. The books of a man of no fixed ideas, Pointer would have said, but great activity of mind.

Miss Dundas was asked to go down to the library for a word with one of Pointer's men. Her room was really a maid's room. Her belongings overflowed it in shocking disorder. Rainer's lips tightened as they stood among a sea of filmiest underwear, dainty shoes and expensive boxes of bath salts and face lotions. Miss Dundas, when she rushed from Mrs. de Souza's flat, appeared to have first waited to pack all her belongings, though Rainer now mentioned that Miss Dundas had explained that Mrs. de Souza's maid had packed and sent on her clothes. Mrs. de Souza had told Pointer as much already. Certainly nothing seemed to have been forgotten, and certainly Miss Dundas was a young woman of expensive tastes and the means with which to gratify them. The other rooms were of no interest. The only photographs were in Lady Tait's room. Pointer had Rainer tell him who they were. There was the late Sir John Tait, some members of her own family, all dead, and a handsome boy with the eyes of Sir John but a self-willed mouth entirely his own.

"That's Mr. Hudson Tait, sir. Sir John and her Ladyship's only son. Mr. John, as you know, was the son of a first marriage of Sir John's."

"Dead?" Pointer asked, looking at the unusually "alive" young face of Hudson.

"Died about twenty years ago now, or nearer twenty-five it soon will be. Hit by a falling chimney-pot and never the same afterwards. Oh, it was a dreadful grief to her Ladyship."

"Were you with her at the time?"

As her tone had suggested, the maid had been.

"How old was Mr. Hudson Tait when he died?"

"Twenty-three. Only twenty-three."

"Married?"

"To an Italian." The maid's tone suggested doubt as to whether such a union could be called a marriage.

But Pointer looked interested.

"She was the daughter of an Italian grocer in Soho. Mr. Hudson was knocked down just in front of the shop. They carried him in, and she—his daughter—nursed him. And then he married her, our Mr. Hudson did. Just married her in a registry office and telephoned it to his mother and father afterwards. Nearly broke their hearts."

"What happened then? I want to get the history of the family clearly in my head."

"Well, they couldn't find at first where they'd gone to for the honeymoon. Then they came back, Mr. Hudson and that Italian girl—we saw very little of them. Sir John died a few years later—and you couldn't expect her Ladyship to be a mother to that piece. Insolent thing! And their Mr. Hudson died of pneumonia, and that's all there is to it. Her Ladyship never refers to him now. It broke her heart. But she always keeps this photo in her room."

"Any children?"

"Mr. Hudson had no children, sir," the maid said promptly, and as though answering Pointer's question frankly.

"And what became of Mrs. Hudson Tait?"

"She married again, sir. Only waited a couple of months. She married her cousin, an Italian waiter. We never hear or see anything of her nowadays, which is a blessing."

The remaining swift glance over the house showed nothing of interest. On hearing of the cause of death, Pointer had at once telephoned in code to his men to hunt very carefully, though unobtrusively, for anything made of green spun glass, or for any fragment, however small, of that brittle stuff, warning them to handle it only with gloves if found.

He was coming out of Miss Dundas's room where he had gone back alone, coming empty-handed, when he heard below in the hall what, in that quiet house, could well be described as a hubbub. Against the background of the butler's subdued tones something strident and brassy could be heard shouting:

"I willa see her! I willa see her! She shalla see me, al fino!" As Pointer bent over the staircase railing, he saw the butler's plump figure, a still plumper woman's figure, and a youth who apparently did not belong to either, but who, with an air of complete detachment, was petting the house cat. He might have been a customer waiting to be served in a shop.

"Did you ever! "Miss Rainer appeared on the landing above Pointer. "Not that I should have recognized her if I'd met her in a cup of tea." A door below must have opened noiselessly, for Lady Tait's quiet, clear-cut tones came.

"What is the matter?"

"It's Mrs. Ricci, my lady" The butler's tone implied that by giving that name, a full and complete explanation of any disturbance had been furnished

What Lady Tait would have said, if indeed she would have said anything, will never be known, for, with a rush, the woman was up the stairs and on to the first floor landing, facing the elder woman For a second they stood like that. To Pointer, the finest piece of sculpture in the world is Nike, and something of the amazing rush and triumph of that immortal masterpiece was in the stout woman's figure now. Pointer saw that she might be around forty-five or a little less. If not handsome, she had a look of tremendous vitality and energy. Stout though she was, she carried her head beautifully, like a stag's. Her bold, dark eyes surveyed the woman before her contemptuously. Lady Tait did not turn away. Eye to eye the two stood, the elder woman's face was faintly paler than usual; her expression was absolutely unreadable. Not so the other's.

"Aha! My fine lady! What do you think of my words now? Eh? Do you now regretta that you turn away like a stone? It was a mistake, eh?" There was something so malignant in tone, and in the face that she thrust forward, close against the other woman's, that the butler below took a step forward. So did the maid above. Pointer was poised on his toes, but otherwise he did not move. The woman fell back a pace and suddenly extended her arms full length, drooping as though something heavy lay across them, something inert, that all but dragged them down. For a second, Pointer had a most vivid impression that across her outstretched arms hung something long and heavy, like a dead body. She stiffened her arms, and by what looked like sheer will-power lifted them higher, and then an inch higher yet, coming another step forward towards the silent woman facing her, and such a sudden tremor passed across the face, so riveted were Lady Tait's eyes on the Italian's outstretched arms, that Pointer felt his breath come quicker. He was certain that Lady Tait, too, saw her, step-son's body held out and up to her in that dreadful dragging yet exultant gesture. Then the Italian dropped her arms, and it was as though she, flung what they had supported with such difficulty down at the other woman's feet, she stretched her elbows for a second as though to ease some terrific strain and then took another step forward, right up against Lady Tait.

"You thought I was justa talking?" Her English was fluent enough, but she separated two consonants as a rule by a vowel, like all her half-educated type. "Justa talking when I told you that John Tait should nota have thata money, while my son and your son's son goesa without one penny of what shoulda be his. I told you you woulda regretta not listening to me. I—I—" she struck her breast savagely—"was turned from thisa door"—she pointed down the stairs—"the door of my husband's mother. I told you to beware. That you woulda suffer! Have I nota kept my word? Have I nota made you suffer by taking John Tait afrom you? The man you put in the place of your own son. The man you loved as you never loved your son. The man to whom you give the money you refuse to your own son. Ah, now do you thinka I was talking nonsense?" She flung back her head with its short curls and smiled, a cruel smile that showed magnificent teeth clenched tight together, her eyes mere slits of glitter. She was now like a statue of gloating evil, and yet, true evil, like good, is impersonal. This woman was quite the opposite. Suddenly she snapped her fingers. "Aha!" she cried again in a voice that rang like a brass trumpet through that house of death, "who is righta now? Who is the winner, eh? Hudson!" She called into the hall.

"Oh, don't!" It was Mrs. Burnham who now spoke in a pained, horrified voice. She had appeared from close. beside Lady Tait, and I stood with one hand pressed to her heart. "I don't understand what you are saying, but you sound dreadfully cruel. Not in this house. Not now. Not here!"

The Italian woman turned and stared at her. Something of the fury then died out of her dark face as she looked into the gentle, fair one.

"Who are you, eh?"

"I was to have married Mr. Tait next month."

For a second it looked as though the Italian would burst out afresh at that, but meeting Lucy Burnham's eyes, she said more gently, "I am sorry you had to suffer. Buta she had to be taughta her lesson. What I say, I mean. What I threaten, I do. I tolda her if she would give all that money to John Tait and none to her own son's son, John Taita would never live to have it. Did I not, eh?"

She whirled on Lady Tait who was staring at her with a look of horrible apprehension on her features. At last, even her mask was beaten down. "And him the same— that I woulda preventa his ever getting it."

"How did you prevent Mr. Tait getting the money?" Pointer asked. "I am a detective officer in charge of the inquiry into his murder."

She turned to him, exultant fury still in her face, her eyes like a madwoman's. "How? Finda that out! If you can. But you never will be able to! Never! Again I tell you the truth. You can find out whata killed him—possibly— but never, no never, how I killed him!"

"Mama!" came a voice from the floor below. The young man had detached himself from the cat and was now coming up the stairs in his turn. The butler hurried after him Pointer could have told him not to worry. No young man in so tight fitting a coat, with so high a collar, could be dangerous until he shed or burst his bonds. The young man, moreover, had an effeminate face and smelled heavily of scent. "But, mama, why are you so?" he asked in weary exasperation. Why are you always so?" The tone was plaintive.

"Mouse!" his mother hurled at him. "Sparrow! Chicken! I have avenged us both. As I told my mother in law, my dear mother-in-law, that I surely would. Aha!" Apparently Mrs. Ricci used that exclamation as a war-whoop, for she turned again to Lady Tait.

"How did you hear of Mr. Tait's death?" Pointer asked before she could speak.

"From Miss Naylor. His cousin. She has always been kind to me. She told me over the telephone at once."

"Where is Miss Naylor?" Pointer asked, raising his voice.

"I'm here." Etta was in the drawing-room and now came out.. "I'm more sorry than I can say for this dreadful scene. Knowing how John had always. been to Mrs. Ricci, I thought she would like to send some flowers."

Etta certainly looked appalled at the outcome of her action.

"But why telephone her at once?" Pointer insisted,

"It is a comfort sometimes to be able to send flowers." Etta eyed the Italian with anything but a friendly look. But Mrs. Ricci still paid no attention to her.

"You want to be arrested, I wonder why?" Pointer, said casually, looking at her with a skeptical, bored eye.

As he knew it would, it roused her to a still more reckless passion.

"You, too, mocka me?" she asked, "you, too, think I cana do nothing? That I have done nothing? You cannot arresta me withouta proof. There is no proof. If you arresta me I shall say, I am given to saying mad things. You cannot arresta me without proof, and you cannota find any proof, and you will nevaire find any proof."

"Oh, please—" It was Mrs. Burnham's voice.

"Are you going to arrest her?" she asked under her breath, "or is the poor thing quite mad?"

"How did you do it?" Pointer asked the woman. A routine question, but something might slip out which would show whether she had any knowledge of what had killed Tait.

"You willa nevaire find out!" gloated the Italian woman, hugging her arms across her breast as though to hug a secret against her very heart. "Nevaire!"

"Oh, mama, why are you so?" her son expostulated, trying to take one of her arms. She flung his hand off, and did not take her eyes off the apparently petrified figure of Lady Tait, who, every vestige of color drained from her face, still stood where she had been standing.

"It's not possible!" came now in a sort of strangled gasp of horror, "it's not possible— " Lady Tait could not finish; she stared hollowly at the other woman, who again showed her strong, clenched teeth in half-mad elation and triumph.

"You understand that I'm the detective officer from Scotland Yard in charge of the inquiry; are you making a confession, which you are willing to have taken down and signed, that you murdered Mr. Tait, presumably with the assistance of this son of yours?"

She cast a glance of most unmaternal scorn at the moon-faced youth whose collar seemed to have grown higher at the inspector's words.

"No, no! I am a hairdresser," came in a quick voice of terror from him. "I am not like mama. None of us are like mama. She told me to come with her. I have left several good customers waiting in my shop—I must return. I have nothing to do with what mama does," he fairly squeaked.

"Look at him!" the signora commanded Pointer, "at Hudson Giacomo Tait. This woman here"—she pointed to Lady Tait—"says he is not her son's son. She lies. But there are times when I could thinka him no son of my own." She advanced on the young man as though to shake him. Hudson Giacomo Tait beat a hasty retreat down the stairs. His mother followed. Pointer went after them on to the pavement. He lifted his finger to a taxi, a Yard taxi, that was hovering near on purpose.

"Where is this shop of yours?" he asked the young man who showed the whites of his eyes as he shot a frightened glance, first at him, then at his mother.

Pointer could not say which of his two companions he feared the more. On the whole, he thought the mother...

"Rupert Street, Soho Square," he twittered, "but why are you coming?"   .

"After what your mother has just said I want to see your shop, and where she lives."

Hudson Giacomo seemed to cower in his corner, his mother swelled out in hers.

"You willa finda nothing," she asserted, cocking her head proudly, "nothing. You cannota prove one thing And until you cana prove things you cannot arresta me" She spoke as might his Lordship on the Bench "Hudson, your tie is crookeda, put it straight." As the young man seemed unable to do it, she leant forward and wrenched the tie violently under his chin. Then, folding her hands with a satisfied smile on her lips, she closed her eyes.

When the taxi stopped at a small but neat looking barber's, she prepared to get out, but Pointer stopped her.

"I want to see the place alone, with your son."

For a second she looked as though she would froth up, but after a look into the meditative eyes on her own, she subsided "Do nota be long. I cannota wait long," she called after the two men.

There was no doubt as to the hasty relief with which Hudson Giacomo stepped into his little shop and closed the door. There he sank limply into a chair.

"It is the weather," said a stout gentleman in Italian who was being lathered.

"No, it is my mama," wailed the hairdresser. The customer laughed. The assistant shaving him laughed too. The young man turned to Pointer. "Come into my private room. We can talk there."

Pointer nodded. His eyes were on two trays of buttonholes under a glass case. Among them were some lilies of the valley. Each sprig half enveloped in its own tiny leaf. A long look at them and he was prepared to swear that they were the same as those which he had seen in Strange's buttonhole. He stepped out again, up to the driver, one of his own men, and told him in a low tone, apparently concerned with something about the rear lights, to go into the shop, and buy a packet of razor blades, and then one of the little artificial lily-of-the-valley buttonholes which he would find in the glass case to his right as he entered. He was to get it put up for him in a box bearing the shop's name, or failing that, wrapped in paper, with name and bill enclosed. That done, Pointer returned to Hudson Giacomo, who fairly pulled him into a stuffy little back room and fumbled for a bottle of Chianti, muttering Ciao at intervals in distraught tones of self-pity.

"What do you want with me?" he asked wildly; "what is the use of asking me? Ask mama. I know nothing. Ask mama!"

"She helps you here in the shop?" Pointer asked sympathetically.

Hudson Giacomo nodded mournfully.

"Nearly every day she comes and finds this and then that wrong. She generally takes the till. The customers

like her. They find her funny." Hudson Giacomo's tone
suggested that their sense of humor must be unusual.

The Chianti seemed to put heart into Hudson
Giacomo.

"It was the papers saying that Lady Tait was going to
give all that money to Mr. Tait. They made mama angry.
When Miss Naylor came to see us last week my mama
thought she came from her. Perhaps she did, but not to
bring any money. Why should she? Mama always talks
about Lady Tait owing us her son's money. But no one
likes to give money away mama certainly does not. Mr.
Tait used to send us some every quarter. It was with it
that my papa bought me this shop. It is a nice shop. I am
a very good hairdresser. Trade is good. What do I care for
the Tait family? Nothing at all."

Pointer had one rule in capital cases, or inquiries that
could involve capital charges. He never questioned a child
about its parents, or a parent about their children, nor a
husband about his wife, nor wife regarding her husband.
There was always some other way of getting at the truth
than by trapping a garrubus tongue into some admission
which might darken all their days. But he could question
Hudson Giacomo about Miss Naylor. It was Etta Naylor,
the one who interested Pointer, who had been coming
regularly to see the signora, he now learned.

"This feeling your mother seems to have against Lady
Tait," Pointer said cautiously, "has it shown itself any,
stronger since Miss Naylor's last visit?" "Possibly. I
thought the, papers..."

"But she might have heard about it from some one
else, Miss Dundas or Mme. de Souza."

"Miss Dundas, who is she? I have never heard mama
speak of her; as for Madame de Souza, she comes here,
mama sees to the tinting of her hair; she has it
brightened now, and then. But how would she know
about Lady Tait's money? Is she a friend of Lady Tait's?"

Pointer said that he did not know. So Mrs. de Souza
was in the habit of coming to this shop... He went out into

the shop. He now, produced his freshly made little snapshot of Strange. "Seen anything of him lately? I know he comes here."

Hudson Giacomo did not know the face and said so, but at Pointer's request he showed it to his two assistants. One of these at once identified it as that of a gentleman, previously unknown to him, who had come in in a great hurry yesterday morning and had bought three buttonholes—lily-of-the-valley.

He was quite sure of the man, he said; the gentleman wore gloves and had rather a difficulty in consequence, in separating two notes which stuck together; the salesman wondered why he didn't pull a glove off, rather than fumble as he did. "

"When was this?"

"Exactly at twelve. He, the salesman, was in a hurry to go to his dinner."

"Did the man look around the shop before choosing the buttonholes? Anything that helps to fix date and identity," Pointer said to Hudson Giacomo, "we're making some inquiries as to the man's actions—"

No, the salesman said that he was just going out himself when the man jumped out of a taxi, kept it, hurried in on foot, he thought he looked at the name over the door as though he had not been there before, looked about him as though for something, stepped over to the glass case and bought the buttonholes, taking them away with him, and being very quick about the whole transaction. Neither Hudson Giacomo or his mother were in the shop at that moment.

"I saw one today and thought it very well done. I took it for natural."

Hudson Giacomo beamed "Are they not pretty? My sisters make them There are no others like them But they are too fragile We are not going to make any more. These camellias here are much liked, too, see."

But Pointer took up a lily-of-the-valley sprig. "They, don't look fragile," he said, examining it carelessly.

"It is the leaves, the spun glass is too fine, it breaks if you but touch it. And the lily bells drop off. But these camellias—"

Pointer put a lily-of-the-valley buttonhole into his coat and insisted on paying for it. He did not care to have it as a gift. Signora Ricci was a dangerous woman, whether a guilty one or not. And she knew Mrs. de Souza.

"And how many sprigs did Miss Naylor buy?" Pointer wanted to know next. He still trifled with his own as though chatting idly now.

"I do not think she bought any. I do not know. I was not here. But there seemed to be none gone when I returned."

Back in the taxi, he took his seat again. Signora Ricci did not open her eyes. He had the address of where she lived, a small hotel, from Hudson Giacomo. As the cab stopped, she opened her eyes, stared at his buttonhole, but said nothing, as she sailed into the dingy, garlic-smelling, but apparently crowded old house, the *Città de Milano*.

"Where is the *padrone*?" she asked a waiter who was flicking dust off the bread in the dining-room. On being told that he was out, she seemed to lose all interest in Pointer.

"Whata do you want of me?" she asked, as though he had forced his company on a lady.

"Just a talk over things in general," he said vaguely. "Can we talk in here?"

Signora Ricci led the way into a tiny room where a round table nearly touched the four walls and a stuffed canary hung from the chandelier.

"Now, what is it?" she asked, sitting down facing him. She looked by no means a fool, he thought. Education might not have come her way, but her native wits would be keen and sharp. Violent she was, and, he thought, vindictive. Courage, too, was in that face, or rather, recklessness.

"I want you to tell me about your son and Mr. Tait,"
Pointer said, gravely. "It's a painful thing to have to ask a
mother, but we can't help that. Why did your son kill his
father's half-brother?"

The Signora jumped up. Out came a flood of words.
Imbecile was the mildest of them. Pointer waited until
her fury had spent itself for a moment.

"Come, come, Mrs. Ricci," he said then, very officially,
"certain facts, facts, Mrs. Ricci, link, your son—not you—
with Mr. Tait's death. I'm sorry for you, of course, but
didn't you directly incite him?"

"Incite?" she queried.

He explained, She seemed to swell again with fury
and contempt.

"Look at me and then at him! Would I needa Hudson
Giacomo to acta for me in any matter?"

There was a step on the stairs. In came a large, fat,
but still very handsome man with his Trilby set askew on
his curly thick black hair.

"Giacomo!" his wife fairly snapped at him, "this is a
police officer. He has come abouta the death of John Tait.
He knows I did it, but he cannot arresta me because he
cannota prove that I did it. Oh, I am clever! Clever! Too
clever to be caught But do not forgeta, Giacomo mio"—she
thrust her face almost against his, her fine teeth bared—
"do not forgeta, my husband, that when I threaten I do.
And what I threaten I do."

Giacomo Ricci was pale as he turned to Pointer.
"What does this mean? My wife must be drunk!"

"But drunk or sober, she carries out her threats,
piccolo mio. Make no mistake about that—"

"In this case I think she is screening her son," Pointer
said slowly. "He is probably the real criminal."

"Eh, what is that? What do you mean?" Ricci spun
round in horror. "What are you saying about Giacomo?"

"It looks as if he had murdered his father's half-
brother, Mr. John Tait" Pointer spoke very gravely.

Both the Italians went up into the air. Both raved together, in their own tongue for a few minutes. Like two cats they spat and swore at each other. Finally the man roared in English, which he spoke as well as Hudson Giacomo:

"Giacomo would not hurt any one. He does not know this man John Tait. Why should he kill him? This woman here, what has she been saying that has led to the arrest of my son."

"Our son," she said in a tone of quite unexpected gentleness.

He thrust her aside and faced Pointer.

"Listen. Giacomo is my son. He knows it. We all know it. The Tait family is nothing to us. Nothing, you understand. We have no grudge against any one. Maria here has tried to make the Taits believe differently. It was natural. But it was no good. Nothing doing eh? With the old lady at any rate. And she is the only one where much money is. As to Giacomo killing this Mr. John Tait, why should he? Mr. John Tait paid my wife a hundred pounds every year which I set aside for Giacomo. Miss Naylor brought it every quarter in pound notes. It was useful, the money, but it came from a stranger, not from a relation Giacomo knows. And would Giacomo hurt this kind stranger who sends his mother twenty-five pounds every thirteen weeks for him? It is ridiculous"

"Mrs. Ricci threatened to be revenged when Lady Tait said she would make a gift of thirty thousand pounds to Mr. Tait on his approaching marriage," Pointer said to that.

"Oh, my wife and her threats!" Ricci snapped his fingers under the nose and looked dangerously like tweaking it. That acted like a match to a squib. Up into the air went the signora. Up into the air went the husband. "It is nota true! They cannota touch him. What I say I do. Remember that!" she screamed amid her more fluent Italian.

"Come, Inspector, let me have a word with you. As man to man, eh? We shall soon understand one another." And by sheer force Giacomo pushed Mrs. Ricci out of the room, locked the door, and with a smile produced a cobwebby bottle of Asti Spumante.

"Not easy to match this. Just a little glass, eh?" But Pointer stayed his hand and corkscrew.

"Listen, then," Ricci said, pressing a thin Italian cheroot on him, "this wife of mine, a good wife, mind you, and a good mother, but just a little—well—jealous. He smirked at his own reflection in the glass and twisted his mustaches till they looked, like black darts. "Yes, jealous indeed!" he sighed. "We had a cashier. A really sympathetic girl. Quite young. And so pretty! She has a sad home life. I talk to her a little and give her good advice. My wife comes upon us as I am giving her the advice. And misunderstands. There is a scene. She tells me that if I ever see the young lady again she will poison both of us with a poison that no one can detect. I laugh. Though I am not happy. She swears that she has such a poison handed down in her mother's family. And—well, her grandmother was a well-known witch. Many things are possible. But I laugh. Now I think my wife thought this would be a splendid opportunity to make me tremble, eh? She would claim to have killed John Tait. She has so often tried to frighten his stepmother into giving her money. Which the old lady refuses to do. She has brains, that old lady. She knows the truth about Giacomo. Oh, at once! Is it likely that my handsome boy was the son of that son of hers? No, indeed. Does he look like him? My wife's father was at Scotland Yard—"

"What was his rank?"

"Interpreter. He spoke every language. He was always talking to her of Scotland Yard. She knows, we know, that you won't arrest except you have proof of guilt. And she is not guilty. So she is safe. Why, she did not know that he was dead until a little while ago when Miss Naylor rang up to say that he had dropped dead in the street and that the police feared he had been poisoned. She would like Lady Tait to think she did that, and she would like me to think she did it. To get even with both of us, and to—well—keep me away from Eleonora. As to why you should want to come here and fasten it on my son Giacomo, unless you want to frighten her, to give her a lesson, eh? In that case it is clever. I can understand your wanting to frighten her," he repeated enviously.

Pointer was non-committal. The shop of Hudson Giacomo would be carefully watched, so would this little hotel. But truth has a way of shining out of things, and Pointer, an acute observer with a very penetrating intelligence, believed that the man before him was telling him the truth. He had felt the same about the son. It was only Signora Ricci who perplexed him. There truth and falsehood were mingled very cunningly. As he made for the door she bounced out of some dark stairway and stood before him.

"He has been telling you not to pay any attention to what I say, eh?" she said, eyeing her handsome husband out of the corner of her eye. "He has been telling you that I threaten and only wordsa come? Aha! Well, you can believe him if you like. I tell you both thata what I threaten I do. And that I am clever enough to do as I say and yetta not be found out.

"As for trying to frighten us by arresting Hudson Giacomo—" struck in Ricci.

"Hudson Giacomo," she amended, "that, of course, was bluffa." And before Pointer could speak, she turned on her heel and seemed to vanish down the dark little stairs that led to the basement.

Pointer walked away, deep in thought. No one could say of Signora Ricci what was truth and what was false. Her husband might think she only wanted to frighten Lady Tait and himself, but... Pointer had taken from a pigeon-hole in the little inner room. some papers, grocery lists, and such, apparently, written on purple note paper, in purple ink, with a thin nib, so that the writing was florid and ornate and spidery... There had been malignant hatred in her face, voice, and manner when she spoke to Lady Tait just now... She was an Italian, she claimed to have a recipe for, an undetectable poison. The buttonholes would perhaps help. If the leaf around the spray proved to be the same as the specks dug out of Tail's finger tips, another step would have been made.

A detective must be ready to suspect any one, but Pointer put the husband and the son of Signora Ricci among his list of unsuspected-till-the last. Pointer was due back at the Yard now for an interview with his superiors. But first of all, the chief inspector once again made for the Home Office analyst, who received him with scant favor this time. He was busy weighing what looked like a rat's whisker. At Pointer's abject entreaty, he turned, snapped a fragment of the lily-of-the-valley leaf that the chief inspector was wearing between two slides, examined it, and then looked at the labeled specks

Then he nodded. "This is the same. I have found, since I saw you, that there is a slight, very slight mixture of turps. in the dye. Probably it was poured into a bottle that had held turpentine. This green dye shows it too. And the glass is identical in manufacture." With that he pushed the slide towards Pointer, drew the balance again towards himself, and seemed to drop into a shut-off recess on the instant.

Pointer hurried away.

CHAPTER TEN

POINTER showed Mrs. Burnham the purple sheets of note-paper and the writing. Both, she said, resembled exactly the paper and the writing of the letter which she believed that Mr. Tait meant to show her at noon that day.

Pointer then asked for Lady Tait. He knew, from the interview between her and Signora Ricci, that threatening letters, one or more, had been received by her, and he guessed that that was the something held back which he had felt when talking to her before. That John Tait's murder might be due to her severity would be a terrible fact to face, supposing her to have loved her step-son as she said she had, and as Pointer believed that she had. For she struck him as too proud and too fine a character to be a liar, let alone a criminal.

She received him this time lying on a couch in her room. Her eyes, deep sunk in her head, flickered as they rested on what he held out to her.

"Yes," she said tonelessly, "yes, that is Mrs. Ricci's writing and paper. I have a letter from her, one of several, but I destroyed the others. I kept this to show to my solicitors if I had any more of the same kind." Out of a locked dispatch-box she took the one that she had shown to her step-son only the morning before. As Pointer took charge of it she said, still in that lifeless, battered voice:

"I don't, and won't, believe It! That John was killed because of anything to do with my refusal to let this dreadful woman sponge on me as she did on my son. It's not the money, Chief Inspector, it's—" Lady Taft did not finish. There were too many bitter words thronging to her lips. "I cannot and will not believe it," she repeated.

Pointer read the letter through again after he had left her. It was an unpleasant letter to have reached Lady Tait the day before her step-son was poisoned. But it led to no fresh fields. The Riccis' were now a no-thoroughfare, possibly he need go no further, but that young man who came to and left Miss Dundas's studio wearing one of the little buttonholes, led to a house where the chief inspector had already paused, where the gold pen top belonged, that bitten top which might well have been jerked out by the dying man as all that he could do to name the criminal. And the man had not left the house, his watchers were certain of that.

Pointer drove back to Kensington High Street, and up to the police station, where, as he hoped, the sergeant who knew the Westmacotts' chauffeur was waiting for him.

"I've just had a word with Osler—that's the chauffeur," the sergeant said, hurrying to conduct Pointer into a private room. "I was very careful, of course, though he's a chap you can trust to any extent. I only spoke of a bloke who was 'wanted,' and said that we heard that such a man had been seen letting himself into the side door of Mr. Westmacott's house. I described him. Ogler said there must be a mistake. That door is never used. Never unlocked even. The garden house is shut up and has been for years. There's a covered passage-way from it to the back part of the house, to what was the old study, but all that part, garden-house, passage and back of the big house, is all shut up and empty. Even millionaires have to economize nowadays. apparently, and, apart from that, he's never seen a man answering to the description I gave him, which we had from you, sir, at the house."

"Has he been in Mr. Westmacott's service long?"

"Going on for six years, sir."

"Does he live in?"

Pointer learned that none of the servants lived in except Lady Ida's two personal maids, her son's valet, and an elderly manservant called Craven who used to be Mr. Westmacott's valet.

"When Mr. Westmacott went to China, he left him behind to make himself generally useful in any way he liked, at the house. Major something or other, I once heard the chief constable of my part of the country call a man like that. Major Omo, that was it! Though a Major doesn't usually make himself useful," the sergeant added with a grin.

"Have you met this man Craven?"

The sergeant had, and a very good impression the ex - valet had made on him Not clever, but reliable and do what he was told type

"Not likely to be allowing the shut-off portion of the house to be used in some way his employers know nothing about?" Pointer asked.

The sergeant replied that no man with eyes in his head would make a proposal of that kind to the elderly valet any more than they would to Lady Ida's butler. In fact, he considered all the servants of the house to be an exceedingly respectable, trustworthy lot.

"But none of them very quick or clever?" Pointer suggested.

The sergeant had to think that over. Then he agreed, and the more he thought it over the more he agreed. "Not even the two maids of her ladyship. They too are uncommon slow, but steady like the rest."

Pointer was looking at a map of Palace Green.

"What about these flats directly behind the gardens of the Palace Green houses—do you know anyone there?"

As he expected, the head porter was quite an old friend of the sergeant's. The police simplify their work a great deal by cultivating constant chats with porters of big blocks. The sergeant jumped in beside Pointer now, and the two drove off up to the building in question. A word from the sergeant, and the porter on duty at the corner block took the two of them up to a room at the very top, his own. It was dark by now, but the lights from the landings of the building in which Pointer was, shone on something in Mr. Westmacott's garden that dully reflected their gleams. It was the roof of the zinc-covered way, that led, he was told, from the disused summerhouse to the disused rear of the house itself.

The porter was told that a man who looked like the man wanted by the police had been seen late that afternoon letting himself into the side door of the end house.

"I've once or twice from up here seen a man go in and out of that door," the porter volunteered. "Very cautious he is about going in. I watched him once walk three times past that door because people were passing, and when he did go in—why, it was like a rabbit bolting into its burrow. One moment he was in the alley, the next there was no one there—as you might say. If you ask me, he's one of the servants slipping round the corner into the Churchill Arms."

Both men listening laughed and agreed that that was likely. But they asked for a description of the man all the same. They got only an impression of a youngish chap, very big, who always wore his hat brim turned well down, and always wore gloves. More than this the porter had not noticed. He felt certain that it was always the same man, but at that distance that could only be guesswork on his part. He could not swear to it.

"What makes me think that he's one of the servants is that the back part of that house ain't used," he added.

Both the men, Pointer and the sergeant, looked suitably surprised.

"Yet the windows don't look dirty," Pointer observed. The moon was kind enough to show quite a glittering row of oblongs in the high house wall facing them some distance away.

"Stoutish party cleans them every month. Red hair— what there is of it. Takes a shocking time over it too. Yet the rest of the house is done by the same firm of window cleaners as we use. You wouldn't expect a millionaire's household to save window-money, would you?"

A few more questions that led to no results, and, Pointer, followed by the sergeant, thanked the man and made for his car.

"The man who cleans the windows must be Craven," the sergeant said. "Only man in the house who's stout, bald and red-haired."

Pointer drove hack with him to the police station. A message was waiting for him there, from the very man told off to watch the Westmacott house, while doing some telephone repairs ostensibly, a little further down. The man—Strange—had not left the house, but a car had driven up, and Mrs. de Souza had gone into the house. That was exactly twenty minutes after the chief inspector had left it. Just the time in fact that it would take that lady to get there had. she been urgently telephoned for. Mrs. de Souza had stayed just thirteen minutes and driven off. She looked worried, both when she passed him going to, and when she passed him leaving the house, the watcher thought.

Pointer himself got through on the telephone at once to his own rooms at the Yard. Watts, his detective sergeant, was given very detailed instructions as to make-up and the line that he was to follow in a call at Mr. Westmacott's house as soon as he could reach it. Pointer dared not go himself. A certain time always had to elapse, he had found, to make even a perfect disguise pass muster with a keen-witted woman, and he thought that Lady Ida's wits were razor-sharp.

And yet the house was growing odder and odder. That an elderly valet should be left behind as a major domo and allowed to choose his work more or less was understandable—fairly. But why the man should choose to clean the windows of the unoccupied part was not so easy to grasp. Servants are very careful not to lose caste, and Pointer could not see why Craven should labor over

work done expertly enough for the rest of the house...
That shut-off half-house. Was it being used in some way
quite unknown to the owners? All very well for the
sergeant to be so sure of Craven's character and of the
characters of the other servants. Pointer felt that he must
have a more unbiased report. For the identity of the man
who had called in at Gillian Dundas's studio had become
very important, once the chief inspector had had those
glass buttonholes tested. Granted that the criminal
thought that the means by which Tait had been poisoned
would be impossible to detect, and he might well have felt
confident of this, then the wearing of the vehicle by which
the other, had been poisoned might be the safest way of
disposing of it for the time being. Or had it a more
terrible meaning? Gillian Dundas went in terror of her
life, of that Pointer was certain. Was it possible that this
man who had called at her studio, who had evidently
often been at her studio, was not a friend but an enemy—
a destroyer, wearing the same kind of buttonhole as
might have killed Tait?

It would be so easy, for a man who always wore
gloves, to make a remark on his lily-of-the-valley spray,
which defied the sharpest eyesight to detect as artificial.
A handing of it over to the person with whom the wearer
was chatting, the inevitable tiny slivers of glass run into
the fingers that touched it to verify the wearer's
statement that it was not a real flower, and the thing was
done... yes, decidedly he must know all that there was to
be known about that man with the strangely wrinkled
face, the powerful yellow teeth, and the nails worn down
to the quicks. Well, he could depend on Watts.

Watts was a youngish man, slight of build, who
possessed a face that could be made to resemble almost
any other face at a few minutes' notice.

It was rather a scholarly looking young man, dressed
in very well-cut clothes who rang the bell of the
Westmacott house just half an hour after Pointer sent his
instructions through to the Yard. He, too, had had a word

with the Yard's observer. Mr. Strange had still not left by either door. A tall flunkey with powdered hair opened it. Lady Ida still went in for powdered footmen.

"I say, I'm awfully sorry, but I'm afraid a very poisonous little snake that I was taking to Lord Wilbraham's reptile house has escaped. I've been hunting for it, and by some marks on these steps it looks as though it must have whipped in here when the door was open. I'm awfully sorry. It's only the size of a small pencil, and swift as light. Ah, that's its track!" Not Pointer could have pounced with more appearance of truth than did Watts on a shiny mark on the marble square inside the door. The footman muttered something, and incontinently fled. A second later the butler, looking distinctly perturbed for once in his life, hurried to where Watts, on his knees, was feeling gingerly with gloved hand under the edge of a carved bench in the hall. To him Watts gave his name as Dorrington, Assistant Keeper of the Reptile House at Whipsnade, on his- way to bring a spare snake to Lord Wilbraham for the latter's famous collection of deadly reptiles. He told a swift story of some one knocking against him in the street, of the little box flying out of his hand and breaking—he showed the box ruefully—and of the escape of what was inside it, one of the deadliest small snakes known.

"I have traced him up these steps and into your hall," he wound up firmly. "The question is, where has he got to? Is any member of the family at home to whom I can explain matters?" He spoke swiftly and urgently, as a man should, who knows that the brother of a fer-de-lance has entered a house.

"Mr. Luttrell Westmacott is in, sir. He'll see you," stammered the butler, scanning the floor with bulging eyes.

"I'll come with you and see if I can catch sight of the little brute on the way."

The butler was grateful for company. Together they hurried along a passage, carpeted thickly enough to suggest a jungle to any tropical snake. Throwing open a door, after a. swift scanning of the handle, the butler in quavering tones ushered Watts into a smoke room where sat young Westmacott, the nephew of the house's owner, hard at work on a crossword puzzle.

"Mr. Dorrington of the Zoo to see you, sir. He thinks a snake has got in here."

This was rather too condensed a way of breaking the news, Watts thought, who, enjoying himself, elaborated, and explained, while he looked around him, over and under the rugs.

"He's not in here," he said, after a few seconds.

"He leaves faint traces of his passage—when you know enough to recognize them—rather like a snail's marks, but drier and fainter. And only here and there where he's doubled back on himself." Watts trusted to natural history not being one of Luttrell's hobbies. That young man was helping with a will after putting gloves on. The butler, similarly protected, was helping too. So were the two footmen.

Lady Ida was informed of what had happened and came down into the drawing-room, where the hunt had been proceeding, almost at a run.

"I never heard of anything so disgracefully careless," she said in quite justified indignation. "Of course the creature must be found and at once! It may bite at any minute—from anywhere."

Watts murmured abject contrition.

"Some one must have come in or gone out—I mean, the door must have been opened for him to slip in—it's possible the snake might have slipped into any rug or package—"

"When did it escape? I thought it had only happened this minute," Lady Ida asked peremptorily. Watts, acting on instructions, named the moment when Mrs de Souza's car had stopped at the house.

"Mrs. de Souza!" the butler, murmured, drawing a deep breath of horror. "That would be the only time the door was opened... That and to let her out, of course"

Watts had attained one of the objects that had been set him, to get the household to name the lady in his hearing, so that he could have an excuse for calling on her next But the man seen entering by the little side door into the garden house, he had not yet found, and that, and a careful survey of the inside of the house, were his main objectives If possible he was to get into the disused portion of the house But that, Pointer had told him, might be impossible

Lady Ida showed that firmness of character that Pointer had read in her, face She was no slacker herself I and she allowed no inefficiency. All the servants, except the cook and a maid who was out, were called in to help, and for awhile nothing was heard but frightened breathing and moving furniture.

"You didn't leave the door open behind you?" he heard the butler ask another servant in a suppressed voice. Watts had already put him down as Craven, the man described to him over the phone just now by the chief inspector. The reply was a quick look in Lady Ida's direction and a quicker shake of the head. Another minute and Lady Ida herself took the same man aside into a room. They were alone but for a few seconds, but when Lady Ida came out again she looked very relieved.

"I think we've hunted everywhere now," she said after a little longer search. "Below stairs has been done by the cook, my maid has gone through my cupboards, and we've accounted for the rest of the house."

"But surely we haven't searched all the rooms?" Watts asked as though in surprise. "The house looks a lot bigger from the outside."

"Mr. Westmacott's own part is shut up and never entered," she explained, and on that Watts, who had been given very careful orders not to arouse any suspicions, suddenly caught sight of marks on the outside of the

window sill which proved that the snake had slipped out
that way. He rushed down the stairs. "It can't live an
hour in this chill," he explained, "nor can it climb a
perpendicular wall of any height over two feet. By
morning it will be dead, you may be sure." He ended in a
mass of apologies, and unshriven, took his leave.

So the shut off portion of the house, was really
closed... and, though Watts had seen the whole household
with the exception of one maid, he had not seen Strange.
He was to try Mrs. de Souza next, and find out if she
would. let drop any remark about the house—or the
mysterious man.

A car rushed him to Mrs. de Souza's flat. Evidently
some sort of an entertainment was on, but a message that
he had just left Lady Ida and would like to speak to Mrs.
de Souza for a moment, had him at once taken into an
empty room of mirrors and stucco walls that struck him
as about the most vulgar thing of its kind that he had
ever seen. He perched himself on a scarlet and purple
divan, and meditated on a great heap of crystal oranges
piled at his feet, when Mrs. de Souza hurried in. A
middle-aged woman with a crafty face followed her.

"You come from Lady Ida Westmacott?" Mrs. de Souza
said, and fixed a pair of eyes on Watts that looked him,
over from head to foot, and found, he was sure, nothing
wrong with his appearance.

He explained what had happened, or rather what he
wanted her and Lady Ida to think had happened.

"The point is this, as you called there this afternoon,
the snake might have got into your handbag had you laid
it down anywhere."...

"Or up my stockings," shrieked Mrs. de Souza,
swirling her skirts around what looked like a couple of
inverted champagne bottles, and jumping up and down on
the floor—shrieking with each jump. Her maid shrieked
too.

"No, no!" Watts managed to shout above the noise the
two made, "that's impossible. I pledge you my word it

couldn't, and wouldn't climb a stocking. And probably you've opened your handbag since you went to the house."

They, calmed down at that. The bag in question, a tiny affair, was brought on the end of a pair of tongs, and Watts, gloves on, and with the look of a man prepared at any second to pounce on a deadly reptile, opened it, examined it, and pronounced it safe.

"There is a mark on a window sill of the Palace Green house which looks as though he had slithered out that way. If so, he can't survive a night of this temperature and all is well. But I was afraid you might have inadvertently carried him off with you, or else that he might have crept into the unoccupied part of the house."

A look of utter consternation showed in Mrs. de Souza's face at his last words. Again she jumped to her feet and hurried into another room, whence in a moment came the sound of a telephone bell's tinkle, but with all her hurry she had closed the door behind her. A few minutes later she came in smiling.

"Lady Ida says that fortunately that wouldn't matter, as no one ever goes in there. The rooms are quite shut off."

Watts found she refused to be drawn into any remarks about the house, or the household, in Palace Green.

The maid had taken no part in the conversation whatever, which was natural, but not so natural was the fixed, unwinking stare that Watts found fastened on him whenever he glanced in her direction. Watts now, took his leave, again apologizing humbly for the "dreadful accident" and its inconveniences. Mrs. de Souza, like Lady Ida, refused to be gracious, and a quite abject Watts was shown out, to recover himself in his car and look the picture of pleased success. But he stopped the car some distance from the Westmacott house, and taking something from the watcher —to whom he had handed it on his arrival—once more, rang the bell and dangled

before the at fist frosty—then delighted—eye of the butler
what looked like a piece of bootlace.

"Got him! Numbed with cold, it was easy. Tell your
mistress that it's all right now."

The butler thawed into human thankfulness. Watts,
chatting happily, as a man does who has escaped a
calamity, told how he had even rushed to the house of the
lady they had said called, to ask her to make sure she
hadn't unwittingly taken it away with her.

"That mark on the window sill wasn't as clear about
the snake not having crawled in again as it might have
been," he confided. "However, all's well that ends well,"
and he passed a handsome tip into the palm nearest him.
The, butler, promised to let Lady Ida and Mr. Luttrell
Westmacott know on their return, and the incident was
closed pleasantly. Watts gave a sigh of relief. After
reporting, he would be free to go to bed. He had now
carried out his instructions to the letter. Pointer heard
what he had to say, and then, as Watts hoped, let him go
to his home, but for the chief inspector bed was yet quite
a distance off. So many things had to be hunted out by
day, that all that was possible must be done by night. The
shut-off portion of the house puzzled him. Watts had told
him that each of the passages upstairs ended in a wall
mirror, enclosed in plain or gilt pilasters. All were at least
six or seven years old. At least. That, meant that the
alterations must have been done, the part of the house
shut off, with Mr. Westmacott's knowledge, by his
directions. Why? Any idea of a Jekyll and Hyde existence
was ruled out by the man's years of absence on
philanthropic missions that really were a blessing to the
countries he visited. This, Pointer had been told, was
undisputed, and his presence abroad impossible to
question. Then why had he blocked off that portion of his
home, in the remaining part of which his sister-in-law
and her son lived? It would have seemed simpler to have
shut the house up, putting a trustworthy caretaker in.
Mr. Westmacott was no collector, he had no known

treasures which he might consider it safer to hide away. Pointer had been telephoning to the police at the places where his other houses were. None of them presented any such peculiarity. That half shut-up house, in which nevertheless, Lady Ida lived, intrigued the chief inspector. John Tait had scratched out the name of the owner before he went there this morning. He had not mentioned where he was going to any one. Why this double caution? And the secret entry into the house and apparent disappearance there of a man who might easily have made those marks on the pen top. Pointer had hoped to see Strange biting something, pencil or pen, as he stood waiting for Miss Dundas in her studio, but he had been disappointed. The chief inspector had with him, however, a piece of paper on which were several dark smudges. While waiting for Strange, he had substituted for the thick cocoanut fibre mat inside the door a very thin little rug that had lain in front of the divan, and under this he had put a sheet of white paper, with a blue carbon paper on top, which had been brought him with his outfit. These smudges showed the very approximate size of big shoes. They were useless for identification, for the soles that had stood on them had no marks, but they did give a very clear idea of length and breadth, point of toe, and size of heel. Armed with a duplicate, Pointer once more made his way to the house in Palace Green. He was making for the side door, where, after but a second's work, he let himself in. The lock was a good one, harder to pick than any Yale except for such an implement as Pointer carried in what looked like a fountain pen. It had also been well oiled, and much used, he fancied, from its ease of working and noiselessness. The same was true of the hinges which, as he carefully inspected them from the inside, showed bright marks of use.

Facing him, as he closed the door behind him without latching it, was an unswept passage that stretched to some equally black steps leading to a door into the house, In the inch-thick dust were many marks of feet. All the

same size, coming and going. The last made were
entering the house. Compared with his blue prints they
fitted exactly. So Strange was in the habit of using this
passage constantly, and yet no one swept it or cleaned it...
the steps told the same tale of neglect and usage. The
door had another Chubbs lock, black with lack of
attention, yet showing a sort of bright star where many
times a careless key had been thrust into the little slit..
So many were the marks around it that Pointer deduced
a hand quite unusually unsteady. Indeed, there was one
that suggested a drunkard's random thrust. Just as
Strange's face had suggested drink. Very carefully he
tried his tool. He expected bolts on the other side, and
found that he was right. Top and bottom the door resisted
pressure. He did not try further but turned his attention
to the wall of the, house. Halfway round the unused part
he found what he hoped to feel—warmth. This part of the
house was heated. He located some pipes that looked like
waste water and again he felt the unmistakable
difference that meant that warm water had passed down
one not long ago, from a bathroom, he judged. All the
windows showed dark and without any hint of lights. He
did not dare climb up. However agile and light on his feet,
six-foot four weighs more than these staples were meant
to support. He had learned quite enough to satisfy him,
and caution was the greatest need here. With infinite
care he let himself out and made his way swiftly to his
car.

Ward Thynne was at a kinswoman's ball. A message,
and he joined Pointer in the latter's car.

"I rather expected to be arrested—" the young man
said cheerfully, "and stuffed myself with Westmacott
facts until I could hardly get into my dress clothes."

"I'll take everything over that you've found out,"
Pointer assured him gratefully, "and Westmacott's life
was swiftly detailed to him. Finally Ward-Thynne
reached his marriage. "Westmacott married Lady
Blanche Bohun. Then came his tragedy. She died a year

later, when her child was born, and the child—a boy—
turned out an idiot. Mercifully, he too died some years
later, while undergoing treatment abroad, it's said, and
Westmacott was free of an awful load. Since then he has
been the target of more marriage aims than a prince of
the blood royal. I told you about Miss Etta Naylor—" and
the story continued. Pointer asked many questions.

When Ward-Thynne had poured out the last word
that he knew about the absent millionaire, he was set
down at the house where he had been picked up, and
Pointer blessed him for his hard work,

"Should you find any gaps, apply to your own A.C. for
the filling. Major Pelham is one of Westmacott's friends
though not so close a one as Tait was," and with that
Ward-Thynne returned to his dancing.

Pointer drove on to the Yard, thinking hard. He saw,
if not light, then at least something that might lead to the
light.

Late though it was, the Assistant Commissioner and
Superintendent Dartmoor were both still at the Yard.
There were some very big affairs on just now. But they
gave the chief inspector an immediate interview, and
listened with absorbed attention to what he had to say.

Dartmoor, naturally, was most interested in the case
as it concerned Lord Mills.

"I thought Tait might be the caller of the morning—if
so, I wonder what lies back of it... " He went on to tell the
chief inspector that the keenest man at the task had
been. going through the affairs of all those companies on
whose board both men figured, and had so far come on no
trace of difficulty, let alone obscurity. "Solvent, all of
them Straight-forward, too, is what he says, and he
couldn't be two seconds in face of a crooked balance sheet
and not smell a rat," Dartmoor said with one of his
frequent double metaphors. "So Mr. Naylor thinks it's
suicide, and that Tait intended to tell us all about it.
Suicide for fear of cancer... I wonder! We've had a letter
about Mills—" The superintendent turned more directly

to Pointer. The assistant commissioner already knew about it. "From another friend. Enclosing a letter, Mills must have posted just before he shot himself. Oh, yes, the letter says he intends doing so. And is undoubtedly genuine. Mills gives no reason except that he's tired of life. Not worth the candle, he says. It's brief. Here it is." He drew it from some papers he had with him and passed it over.

It was, as he said, brief and firm enough. In it Mills wrote that he had decided to go out of life, as he disliked the thought of middle-age, let alone of the years still further ahead. It was a letter that told absolutely nothing of the man's real reasons.

Pointer handed it back without a comment. "Even Lady Mills can't go against that," Dartmoor went on. "Influenza effects is what she calls it and intends the coroner to call it. Why not? But it means, of course, that Brown is now at liberty, released without a stain upon his character."

Pointer was looking at some brief notes on the banking accounts of Tait and Lord Mills. Both showed certain similarities. Both had lately developed a habit of drawing out sums of five hundred pounds followed by fifty, and both were traced to money exchanges where the sums so drawn were changed into French thousand franc notes, untraceable therefore.

Dartmoor looked over, his. shoulder and nodded.

"And Brown remembers that his master, Lord Mills, was distinctly worried round about each of these times. Quite unlike himself, he says... pretty clearly blackmail, I fancy, with Miss Dundas holding the threads in the middle as Mrs. de Souza's companion. Can't find out anything about the lady. Says she was a Miss Edwards. Says father was a curate in Huddersfield. Well, there was an Edwards there, a curate, around the right time ago, had a large family too, but beyond that..." Dartmoor give a faint frown.

"At any rate," the assistant commissioner put in, "we know that both these women were known to both the men. It looks as though Tait had been having a sort of secret conference with Lord Mills, perhaps on some way to escape the clutches of the two harpies. Mills shoots himself..."

"And Tait apparently is poisoned by Signora Ricci, old Compieri's daughter," the superintendent finished. "I've looked him up for you," he went on to Pointer. "He was pensioned off. Rather in a hurry. Did good work but had the temper of the devil, and a way of getting even with those who vexed him that we didn't like. Looks as if you had a straight run there. Though, of course, you're right to round up all the other possibilities too—as you always do."

"How did she spend. this morning, by the way?" Pelham asked.

"She was out shopping for an unusually long time. Owing to not finding a tender enough chicken for their own dinner, she told her daughters on her return."

"Of course, that's the sort of explanation she might be expected to give," Pelham said.

"So she remarked to the man I sent to question them," Pointer agreed grimly.

"Did. she seem worked up at all on her return?" The assistant commissioner wondered.

"Very much so. Her husband hinted that that was due to her having tried to follow him and failed, but of course, Mrs. Ricci insists now that it was only the excitement of having poisoned Mr. Tait."

Pelham laughed outright. Pointer gave rather a one-sided smile as he went on:

"That poisoned buttonhole is also connected with Lady Ida Westmacott. I think there's some odd story there. That divided house... "

Pointer looked at Major Pelham, who in his turn stared back at him thoughtfully.

"What does that house suggest to you?" the assistant commissioner asked finally.

"Well, I was wondering whether Mr. Westmacott's son was really dead. That part seemed to me a bit vague, and all Mr. Ward-Thynne could tell me came to a rumor of his death on Westmacott's yacht in the Mediterranean while under his aunt, Lady Ida's, care. He thinks there was a funeral at sea... Now Mrs. de Souza's villa was in Capri. I wondered, whether, by any chance, Lord Westmacott's idiot son wasn't really dead, but is being kept in the one-half of the quiet house here in town?"

There was a short pause, then the assistant commissioner said:

"You're right in your guess. I've just told the superintendent, and was going to tell you. Only four people besides Westmacott up till now, have known it, barring the Lunacy Commissioners. Lady Ida, Tait, Miss Etta Naylor, and myself. I was told it in my official capacity. And Tait didn't know that Etta Naylor knew. By her request. Horrible story for poor Westmacott. One of the best of fellows. Luckily he's a deeply religious man and bears it like a stained-glass-window saint. But it's pretty ghastly just the same. That's why he doesn't marry. He as good as told me the night before he left England that, however deeply his heart was engaged, his conscience wouldn't let him marry once he had to give up all hope of his son ever being cured.

"They say he's just like an animal. Good-natured enough, but spends his time biting and scratching at wooden balls. Terrible. For years Westmacott refused to believe it was hopeless. There was one specialist in particular he himself was so certain that his gland treatment would do the trick, that Westmacott accepted the promised cure as a certainty. That was around the time when he hoped to marry Miss Naylor. But nothing came of it—the cure. And then even Westmacott realized that there was no hope.

"Westmacott had to get out of England. Away from the woman he loved, and from the son he couldn't save. But evidently he left his old valet to look after the son. Apparently this fellow, Strange, is some sort of attendant under him. Lady Ida, too, sees to it that he is well cared for. The boy, was always deeply attached to her. And she's awfully good to him, Westmacott told me. But, even so, he has Tait, who was a special pal of his, look in on him every few months if he's in England."

"So that's why Mr. Tait erased the name from his engagement book, and wouldn't explain where he'd been... and probably had been to see him when his dog died, and was still under the influence of the sight..." Pointer was thinking aloud.

Pelham nodded.

"Shocking story. I hope to God we can keep it dark."

"What does the son look like, sir?"

Pelham had no notion. He said that even the Lunacy Commissioner only saw bright eyes gleaming from a heap of straw.

"Was he supposed to be like his father or his mother as a child?"

"His mother."

"And what was she like, sir?"

Pelham's wonderful memory did not fail him. "Like a gipsy. Blue-black hair, blue-black eyes. Thin hawk face. Scarlet, thin lips, and magnificent teeth."

"And his age now, sir?"

Pelham thought back-. "Let us see. Westmacott was barely twenty-one when he married. I suppose the boy would be around twenty-two or three."

Pelham glanced at the clock. Even for the Yard it was late.

His two subordinates rose. Outside, the superintendent had one more word.

"The A.C. wouldn't forgive it if Mr. Westmacott's story were dragged into this case needlessly.` Pointer was quite aware of that, but neither would Pointer have forgiven himself if he had made such a dreadful blunder which, to him, was of vastly more importance. He didn't have to live with an irate superior, whereas he had probably quite a number of years yet to live with Alfred Pointer, and his standards. But he only said he would make, very sure of each step.

"You're evidently going on the plan of excluding first all the innocents," Dartmoor said approvingly. "That lets you settle down finally to the guilty residue, which you can rout out of their holes then with double energy," and they parted on that fine mixed metaphor.

CHAPTER ELEVEN

AGAIN Lady Ida was in, when, early next morning, Pointer sent in his official card. She was dressed as though to go out, but she sat down again and a pair of resolute, watchful eyes fastened themselves on him.

"Lady Ida," he began at once, "as you know, a man in whom the police are very much interested, was seen to enter the side door of this house, a door which I have since learned connects directly with the so-called unused part of this house, the part where Mr. George Westmacott is kept. He may be in danger. Would you permit me to have a look at him—now —to convince myself that all is well?"

"Certainly not, Chief Inspector. I refuse absolutely." She spoke firmly.

"I can get a Commissioner in Lunacy to accompany me. I can also get the necessary authority from the Home Secretary—if need be." Steel showed in Pointer's tone and eye. "If his attendant could be with me to verify the fact that it really is Mr. George Westmacott, I should be quite satisfied not to make either application. Apart from the man seen entering, a very dangerous little snake is said to have escaped in this neighborhood last night."

Lady Ida looked profoundly disturbed. Then she rang for Craven.

"Craven, this detective officer wants to see Mr. George. To be certain that he hasn't been attacked or killed by that snake or by some housebreaker. I am taking him now to see Mr. George, and I want you to come too."

"Very good, my lady." Craven looked bleak indignation.

Lady Ida led the way to the second floor—on which her own rooms were. Passing down the broad main corridor, she moved a little switchbox beside the mirror that closed one end. Opening the flap, she inserted a key into the keyhole inside, turned it, and then opened the mirror door by merely pressing it away, from her. It was a private door, but hardly a secret one.

Following her, Pointer stepped into a large, bare, but clean room. Craven shut the mirror door behind himself as the last of the three. After that the further door of the room was unlocked.

"All this is terrible, but necessary," Lady Ida said quietly. "Not that Jacky—we call him Jacky—is ever dangerous, but he's as curious as an animal. He might escape, and that would mean unbearable grief for all of us." Craven now gave a little whistle, and, after a second, turned the handle of the door.

"There's a sort of cage built round the door on the other side," he explained, still holding the door closed, "so that he can't run out, as he might otherwise."

He flung the door open and stepped aside. All entered a wired-off portion of the room which, Pointer saw, would serve just the purpose Craven had mentioned. Craven now unlocked the grating door leading on into the room proper, but Lady Ida stayed him.

"All the detective wants is to see that Jacky is alive and well." Which was precisely what Pointer could not see. The room was bare of furniture. The floor was piled in places with straw. A stack of it was built against the opposite wall. Around the one large window another cage, similar to the one in which they stood, had been made. The room was very airy, and warm, and light. Something rustled in the straw, but nothing showed itself.

"Jacky!" Lady Ida coaxed. "It's all right, Jacky! He is terrified of strangers." She turned to Pointer reproachfully. "When the doctors come and have a look at him he's like a mad thing for hours afterwards, hiding and shivering."

"Sorry," Pointer said, "but I must have at least a glimpse of him." She nodded to Craven, who now opened the cage door and stepped on into the room.

"Now then, Master Jacky," he said in a cheery, kindly voice. "I've got some bananas for you."

Out was thrust a wild matted head of hair, and a pair of rat-like eyes peered at the visitor above a perfect bush of a beard. He gave a sound like a yelp and clutched at the banana.

"Now are you satisfied?" Lady Ida asked bitterly, turning to Pointer.

"Can I offer him a banana too?" The chief inspector had already taken one from Craven as he spoke, and was now holding it out by its extreme end as though he feared that Jacky would bite his fingers.

A large hand darted out with ape-like speed and clutched the fruit, but Pointer held on.

"Come out, Mr. Jacky," he said, as one might wheedle a shy animal. But Jacky let go the fruit and retreated further into his heap.

"I'll try him with a ball," Craven said, picking up something that looked as though it might once have been an old-fashioned small, wooden croquet ball.

"He'll bite and scratch at it like a kitten," he murmured to Pointer as he rolled it with friendly cluckings towards the heap of straw, but Jacky did not show himself.

"He'll come for me," Lady Ida said confidently. "Come on, Jacky, come on and play. There's nothing to be afraid of."

In reply, something on all fours shambled out of the heap and sat a moment on the floor, its knees against its chest, its long arms hugging them till it looked like a human ball itself. The man, for it was one, was dressed in leather shorts and vest, and looked like some medieval gnome of vast size. Suddenly he made a dive for the ball and began to lie on his side on the floor, knees still up, but biting and scratching at the bail. In another minute he let it fall and caught at Lady Ida's hand as she bent gently over him, pointing to the stranger and bursting into a string of gibberish.

"Have you seen enough?" she asked over her shoulder, patting Jacky affectionately as he clung to her.

Pointer said that he had. He had just bent down a moment ago as though to pick up something and had measured against his forearm the length of the unshod feet so close to him.

They now left as they had come. Lady Ida and Craven showed their indignation at the needless humiliation to which the family had been subjected. Pointer was officially apologetic, but when he stood alone with Lady Ida for a moment he said suddenly:

"It was Mr. Jacky who bit the top of your fountain. pen, wasn't it?"

She nodded. "It was in my hand and I let him play with it for a moment. Mr. Tait thought people might notice the dents made by his teeth, and insisted on taking it off to have them straightened out. It was quite impossible for me to tell you how the marks were made, without telling you what does not in the least concern you, the story of that wretched man in there."

"And Mr. Tait came occasionally to see him while Mr. Westmacott is away?"

"Yes. At Mr. Westmacott's request. Just a glance at him to see he wants for nothing. On the quiet, of course. Every one in my service knows the truth, but no strangers so far." The last came half-brokenly, half-savagely.

Pointer hurried from the house. In a rubber-lined pocket of his coat was the banana that had been clutched by those long fingers, with their nails worn to the quick by scratching and clawing at a wooden ball. A few minutes more, and the Yard expert was comparing the fingerprints on it with those found on the arms of the chair in Miss Dundas's studio. Yet another few minutes, and Pointer knew that he was right in his idea that the dreadful figure peering from its heap of straw was the same as the dandified man who had hurried in, wearing a buttonhole made of the same glass as that which had poisoned John Tait. One of. the chief inspector's men had been round to the Ricci household posing as a buyer of artificial buttonholes. He liked the material of the lily-of-the-valley leaf, but did not care for the leaf itself, he said. Perhaps they made other objects of the same glass? He was told that they had never used it except for that particular buttonhole, and, even so, were not using it any longer owing to its tendency to break, and worse yet to splinter. Customers had complained of the glass getting into their fingers. Signora Ricci said she always warned customers of this who felt inclined to buy the sprays. She liked them to buy the violets instead, which were more profitable.

So now Pointer knew, that, as he had guessed, it was an artificial lily-of-the-valley buttonhole which had been used as a vehicle to convey the deadly poison to Tait. A buttonhole suggested a certain intimacy... suggested as first choice a woman giver...

Major Pelham sat with clenched hands as Pointer told him of the long step just taken. "You mean that poor old Westmacott has been deceived; is being deceived? Or do you mean that his son has more lucid intervals than he lets people suspect?"

"I'm sure Jacky is a fraud, sir."

"How can you be sure?"

"Wig, sir, shows that. No one could tell Jacky's hair isn't his own, it's too wild and tangled. But, as I had seen him smartly shorn and smooth-shaven a few hours ago, I knew those plumes hadn't grown since then. Suppose Jacky to have sane intervals and be able to go into the outside world, it's quite conceivable that he might wear a wig then, but not during his fits of—whatever they would be called—reversion to the primitive and so on. Well done stunt his, I am certain that we shall find he worked for the films. At least I'm going to start inquiries in that field."

Pelham's jaw worked. It was a vile story.

"How long do you think it's been going on, this deception?".

"That illness he had on Lady Ida's yacht looks like the time as a guess. Say, when he fell ill, she deplored her position to some friend should Jacky die, and Westmacott marry again and have a family? Suppose this some one suggests getting hold of some one who could play the part perfectly during the very few times that Jacky is inspected? It seems, to be around that very time that Mrs. de Souza took Lord Mills's villa by the sea. Just along the stretch of the coast where the yacht was lying, and where it often put in. Lady Ida would need help in getting hold of a substitute. Strange is much older than Jacky would be, I think, but no one could tell that who sees him with his face all screwed up, and twisted into ball shapes on the floor. Lady Ida could hardly, have searched for him, I think, herself. It would have been too risky."

"Do you think this valet,. Craven, knows the real truth?"

'I feel sure he doesn't. Which is probably why Jacky keeps up his old fondness for biting and clawing at wooden balls, and for bananas, and so on...

I don't think Lady Ida's son is in it either, but that notion is simply founded on the fact that no one but a fool trusts a fool with a secret."

"Lady Ida's certainly not that! By Jove!" Pelham rose and lit a cigar with kindling eye. "By Jove, that accounts for her virulent hatred of Miss Henrietta Naylor. It's positively indecent. But natural if she had prevented Etta from marrying the man who loved her. There's a title coming some day, and every inch of land Westmacott has is entailed by his father. Gad, if you're right, and I don't doubt you are, what a pity rope-ending at the tail of a cart has gone out of fashion." Then Pelham's eyes widened. He saw where Pointer was driving his ball.

"You think that this—this secret, this infamous secret, was suspected or stumbled on by Tait, and that that was why he was poisoned?"

"It looks like it, sir. He talks to his cousin about believing in a devil. To a friend of Westmacott's the trick being played on him would seem devilish indeed."

Pelham nodded fiercely.

"If I'm right, Tait must have been suspicious of the truth when he went to see this Jacky yesterday morning. And must have shown his suspicion, perhaps in a talk with Lady Ida, or the poisoned buttonhole wouldn't have been got ready for him. It's possible that the real boy had some mark on him to which Craven may have innocently referred, or of which Westmacott may have written... Anyway, Tait goes to Palace Green determined to find out the truth. But in some way they hoodwink him there, or manage to postpone the real test. At any rate all this is still quite foggy yet, sir, I think he thought of something when, just on the point of telling his fiancée about it, he dashed off for a few minutes—possibly to go back to Palace Green—and dropped dead on the way."

"If this yarn is. anywhere near the truth," Pelham said slowly,. "Lady Ida would know that her explanations would only satisfy him for the time being. For, do you know, I had a talk this morning with a business friend of Tait's. And he happened to mention a peculiarity, of, his. Said you had to give him time to reflect on things. That any infant could hoodwink Tait while he talked to him— the man was extraordinarily susceptible to plausible suggestions for the moment, but give him time, and no fraud, however clever, could blind him. But he had to be able to look it over again, mentally, by himself. But, now to go back, the poison used, makes one, of course think of Mrs. de Souza, who has spent many a winter along the Mediterranean, apart from being the widow of a

Portuguese. At least I suppose he was that, if he ever existed."

Pelham paused for Pointer to continue the tale of possibilities.

"My idea is, sir, that Strange bought some of these artificial buttonholes down at the Ricci's hair shop. I don't think the choice was accidental Nothing in a murder is, as a rule That would mean that he, or Lady Ida, or some one associated with him, knew all about the Ricci's and their feeling towards John Tait, and knew therefore that they would be safe suspects."

"I wonder if this whole deception is Strange's?" Pelham said... Pointer thought this highly improbable... "Nor do I see what Strange has to gain, except by being a paid actor doing a permanent part in which he's been engaged," he objected. "Without good pay the task would be too loathsome. It's anything but an easy job, and he threw himself into it splendidly. No, sir, I feel sure that he's a party to a regular business proposition from which they all draw, handsome profits. So much to whoever procured him. So much to Jacky—"

"And the rest to Lady Ida!" Pelham nodded. "Well, after Strange buys the buttonholes, what next?"

"Then my guess is, sir, that he takes them to Miss Dundas's studio. And that either there, or at her own house, some one—Mrs. de Souza say—dips one in poison and dries it. I doubt if any poison entered the house in Palace Green. But there's no openly known connection between Mrs.de Souza and Tait. We shall search both places, of course, but my belief is that it will be in the flat we find it. I don't believe any of them think they're suspected, in which case, I should expect to find the poison still in existence. It must be very difficult to get in England. It doesn't alter, the doctors say, however long its kept. Certainly I think Miss Dundas feels sure there is more where it came from. If the poisoning was done at the studio itself, and if the poison is kept there, my men have failed to find any traces. They've been at work there, and have reported a total blank."

"And this Miss Dundas, is she in the poisoning of Tait?" Pelham pondered.

"I don't think so, sir," Pointer replied slowly. "I think his death was a terrible shock, a real shock to her. But she's pretty certainly mixed up in the blackmail business both of him and of Lord Mills. That being so, as I read it, she's threatened with being shown up and sent to prison by her confederates if she tries to speak to us about Tait. As I read her," Pointer went on, "she's about as much pluck as she has morals—which is to say not a speck of either in her whole make-up. For such a coward, she turned down a terrible road when she let them use her as a decoy."

"We've learned," Pelham glanced at a paper, "that she and the de Souza woman stopped either at the same place or I at the same hotel with both those men—Mills and Tait. By the way, as you thought, that pitiful tale of dependent parents is a myth. We've learned from the people who let the studio to her mother, or rather who sold her the lease, that that good lady is dead. She was an artist's model who married the artist. He took to pottery, and died when the one child—this Gillian—was about fifteen. The mother struggled along for another three years supporting them both by china painting, mending pottery, making gloves, doing small decorative repairs. She seems to've worked for some good houses. When she died, Gillian was taken as companion by Mrs. de Souza. The studio was generally let to artists, but there's been no complaint about the rent, it's been paid regularly by Miss Dundas."

"Worked for good houses..." Pointer repeated thoughtfully, "the daughter would accompany her mother probably... I wonder... My first idea was that blackmail was at the root of Mr. Tait's murder. Blackmail that was afraid of being shown up. He was so determined to clear Brown from any question of being implicated in a murder.

But I couldn't see why Miss Dundas bolted, as she did, from Mrs. de Souza. Now it looks as though she had overheard something, which gave her an inkling as to what was on foot at Westmacott's house."

"And tried to warn Tait without its being known." Pelham found the death of John Tait a fascinating problem. "That would explain why she thrust herself on the only member, of the household there who wouldn't refuse to take her in, however thin her story. Yes, that would explain that, and also why it took place after the suicide of one man and so shortly before the murder of another. She might well be terrified, implicated as she was in blackmail but not standing to win anything from a murder."

There was a short silence. Pointer was thinking of Naylor who was so certain that his cousin's death was not linked with that of Lord Mills. Naylor's whole manner bore out, to Pointer, the idea that he knew Gillian Dundas was the blackmailer, but felt sure she was not in any murder plot. At any rate, he believed that Naylor was attracted by Gillian Dundas's beauty, but struggled between that attraction and the repulsion to what lay beneath the beauty. That meeting the first night in the library between Miss Dundas and Tait, of which Lady Tait had told him, was, Pointer now thought, very possibly not connected with Mills at all, but with Westmacott. It was possible that she was even then warning him, yet altruism and Gillian Dundas's face seemed a most unlikely combination. Suddenly he saw a far more likely supposition.

"I don't think she went to warn Tait, sir. But I should think it quite possible she told him all she knew, and offered to get proofs for him about the Westmacott fraud. Or possibly she had some papers proving it... She was some four years with Mrs. de Souza. If I'm right, she might have got hold of something which she was willing to sell to Tait. I wonder if Tait had anything on him which she had handed him, any paper which she alone could have got at to give him? And that the poisoner got hold of those? Oh, before he left Lady Ida's, of course got them by a trick... to look at, claimed they were forgeries... that sort of thing." Pointer's mind was groping. "If she knew that he had had them, and that they were, not on him when he died, it might account for her certainty that her number is up. You know, sir, bad lot though she is, I'm sorry for her" —he was speaking with a perplexed frown—"but I don't see any way to help her. In my opinion, she's so certain she's for it, that she thinks that even prison for a stretch of years, as she would get if convicted of blackmail, can't save her."

"You think she's certain it would be prison first and then poison when she got out?" Pelham arched his eyebrows. "Well, certainly Lady Ida has everything at stake. Glad to think that, if she's in it, she's going to lose everything too. This Westmacott fraud is about the limit in heartlessness, and has been practised for years on a chap who has been generosity itself to her and her son. I always did know she was as sharp as a needle, and as unscrupulous as they're made. I bar her at Bridge. Nothing proven, of course, but her placing of cards is a bit too good to be true. But all the same this sort of a charge... We must have cast-iron proofs." Again there was a shortsilence. Each man mentally tested the links so far. All seemed to stand the pull—so far.

"And that buttonhole the fellow Strange was wearing when he came to the studio—" Here Pelham had the same terrible suspicion of that decoration as Pointer had had. "We might have come upon Miss Dundas dead too, only in her case a letter would probably have accompanied the corpse, supposed to be from her, relating to an old story between herself and Tait, for which reason she had first poisoned him, and then taken her own life... There was an old affair between them, Lady Tait thought." Pelham put the papers together.

"What are you working at now?"

"Trying to trace any taxis taken by Tait yesterday morning. He arrived in one for his belated lunch, I know."

"Perhaps he left his buttonhole in one," Pelham. suggested.

"You make, my mouth water, sir. But it's possible. Anyway, I want to find out if he was wearing gloves, or not. The butler says not when he came in to lunch. But he might have stripped them off as he entered. As long as he wore gloves he was safe, even if he handled that poisoned spray. And it's possible he tossed it into the street."

"I suppose your idea is that it was handed him with some sweet word of 'wear this to show me you've no longer any suspicions of me' by Lady Ida?"

Pointer grinned an assent. Some such words would, he thought, have accompanied the little sprig.

"And the poison? How will you find out if there's any more?"

Pointer looked bland. "Bit of routine work may do it, sir. My fear is, lest Mrs. de Souza, or whoever has it, carries it about with her in a phial or powder form. But I doubt it. She seems to've used it very freely, according to the analyst, which suggests that she has plenty more."

"Ah, yes, you think Miss Dundas knows that too." And Pelham let Pointer go.

Gillian Dundas was being discussed at the same moment at Great Cumberland Place. Early that morning, around ten, Alysia Naylor came into the library, where her brother was reading the paper. He looked up sharply. He made no show of effusive greetings, either to her, or to Claridge who had come in with her. Etta was writing at a table in a corner. She turned round to hear better.

"It's about that companion of Mrs. Burnham's," Alysia began. "I've brought Reggie along because he knows something we think the police ought to be told. But because it's the police well, I induced him to tell it you, and abide by your judgment."

"Unusually flattering," Claud murmured, with something like a veil dropped over his eyes.

Claridge cocked his sleek little head on one side and wetted a cigarette with a look of relish on his face.

"It's about Miss Dundas, as Alysia says. I happened to be passing her studio yesterday morning, when I saw Tait come out. I thought, of course, the police knew of this visit of his, that you all would know of it, or I should have come round at once. But I had an engagement in the country which I couldn't avoid and now, when I do rush round, Alysia tells me she hasn't heard a word of it."

"He told me," Claud said negligently, "but, as you say, it's of no importance." He looked slightly bored.

"Told you!" Alysia's voice came in surprise. As for Etta, she shot a long, rather odd look at her brother, but said nothing. Claud nodded and permitted his eyes to stray to some papers on the table with an unmistakable interested look.

"But why didn't you tell the police?" Alysia asked sharply. "They want very much to find out every place where John was yesterday morning."

"The police don't tell you all they've heard," Claud said to that.

"Rubbish!" she retorted "they don't know anything about where he went nor whom he saw yesterday, and are simply wild to find out."

Nalyor looked as though considering a knotty. point. "Then in strict confidence," he said finally, "I thought it as well not to tell them about this interview Tait had with Miss Dundas because it concerned you, Alysia."

"Me! With Miss Dundas!" Incredulity was in her voice and eye.

He nodded regretfully. "It's rather a private matter. Perhaps you'd rather Claridge left us?"

Claridge rose—very slowly. Alysia stopped him. "Of course Reggie can stay. I can't think what you mean, Claud."

"John had got a funny idea in his head that you wanted to separate him from Mrs. Burnham," Naylor said to that, speaking very quietly and objectively. "He got an idea, further, that Claridge was sent by you to Vichy with some idea of coming between him and the lady in question—Lucy. I ridiculed the notion. He went to Miss Dundas as to an impartial umpire to decide the question. She was to be asked in some indirect way whether she too had noticed how hard Claridge tried, to pay his court to Mrs. Burnham."

Alysia, for once, was speechless. A wave of scarlet flamed in her, thin face.

"Oh, but—oh, how—" she faltered, then stopped, biting her lip.

"He got the idea partly from Claridge's very sudden gallantry " Naylor's lip curled, "partly from the fact that on his return he seemed more in. your pocket than ever." The barrister's cold, clever eyes, with their finely cut lids, looked once at sister and sister's finance—for Claridge and she had become engaged the evening before—and said nothing. Alysia looked genuinely shocked and humiliated. "As a matter of fact, Miss Dundas had no idea of what he was talking," Naylor went on. "She scouted the idea. And on that, Tait hurried away. Now you see why I didn't mention it to the police? It is of no use whatever."

"Oh, none! None!" came hurriedly from Alysia and from Claridge in unison..

"And it would look—odd," Claud went on slowly, "very odd. For, of course, we none of us must forget that as immediate beneficiaries under John's will, and probable beneficiaries under Aunt Norah's will—we're all just a bit suspect. Distinctly so. So now you see still more reason why the unimportant talk that John had with Miss Dundas should not be mentioned. At any rate by us. I can only hope the police will remain in ignorance of it. It had nothing to do with John's murder."

"What had?" Claridge asked suddenly, looking very closely at the other man Naylor adjusted his blotting-pad more closely in line with the table edge.

"Some form of spite, I fancy. Apparently the Ricci woman has confessed to having done it from hatred of Aunt Norah, and dared the police to prove it. Interesting problem."

"As one who has had the pleasure of seeing some of the friends that Miss Dundas keeps, I wonder," Claridge said meaningly. Claud gave him a swift inquiring look that brooked no denial.

"It was at Victoria—" Claridge gave a version of what he had seen of Gillian's strange friend. "The man was mad—really mad," Claridge wound up "And dangerous There was no mistaking it."

Naylor listened with an attention so close that Claridge was flattered. As a rule he only got half or a quarter of an ear from the young man.

Some sad little story, probably," Naylor said rather abruptly when the other had done, "but nothing to do with John's murder. Miss Dundas does not—like we three -benefit by that crime. No, but for Mrs. Ricci's confession, if it was a confession, I should be inclined to see the poisoner as some one who wanted to injure Lucy..." he finished meditatively.

"Lucy! Mrs. Burnham!" Alysia opened her eyes and then closed them tightly. "Oh, I see," she finished faintly.

"Which was an additional reason for being silent," Claud added.

"Oh, very much so!" Alysia said fervently. She gave Claridge a look, and the two went off together. Etta left her chair for a second to come and lay a hand on her brother's arm. Rather unusual for Etta. She was chary of personal contacts.

"Damned clever—and unkind—of you Claud," she murmured with a half derisive, half admiring laugh. "I mean," she corrected herself swiftly, "I think it was so clever, of you. From beginning to end." And without waiting for a reply she took up her writing again. There was absolute silence in the room.

Which was not the case in the lounge to which Claridge and Alysia bad gone.

"I don't believe it," Claridge was saying spitefully. "Claud's in love with the girl. When I saw your cousin he was tearing out of the house as though he'd seen the devil. Of course, if Claud chooses to give that explanation, we can't say anything But it doesn't fit the expression I saw on Tait's face"

"Why didn't you say so to Claud?" Alysia asked with her usual shrewdness. Claridge humped his shoulders.

"What can One say when the other chap takes up that kind of an attitude? Nothing. I don't believe it, that's all. But he's done what he meant to do and that's put us where we have to let it go. Oh, yes, he's in love with that young woman all right. Hope you'll like her as a sister-in-law," he added nastily.

But Alysia only laughed. "Claud is not the kind to fling his career away," she said confidently. "Nor do I believe he's struck with the Dundas girl," and she began to talk of their own future, now so rosy.

In the library Claud sat with shut eyes, behind his paper. Etta, too, only made a pretense of writing. Suddenly the door opened again. Claud's jaw set, but it was Mrs. Burnham who slipped in, rather breathlessly. She closed the door carefully behind her before she spoke.

"Will you come and talk to Miss Dundas, Claud? She's beyond my doing anything with. I'm—well, she positively frightens me..."

"Frightens you?" Naylor gave her a very intent look.

"For herself only, of course." Mrs. Burnham seemed surprised by the misunderstanding.

"She wants to go away—now. At once. Secretly. She wants me to let her have the money to slip off to the continent and stay there till all this terrible affair has been cleared up. But how can I? Of course, it is terrible for her. Oh, more than for me, my dear Claud, for he belongs to me. Anything that has happened to him is just as though it had happened to me, and one can't run away from one's sorrows. But he's nothing to Gillian. The poor child is near a nervous breakdown with the shock of this dreadful, dreadful business. I'm very sorry for her. I. don't want to be selfish. It's not for my sake, or for the looks of it, that I want her to stay. I think she should stop, don't you? Surely every one, even if like Gillian they have nothing to do with my dear John, should stay? Don't you think so too?" She ended on a note of surprise to Etta, as though Claud's silence perplexed her. But Etta said nothing.

"She wants to go away, does she?" he asked heavily, in a very level voice. "Well, Lucy, I don't see how I can talk to her on the matter. It lies with herself, I suppose. At any rate, not with me." He spoke in a very aloof, rigid voice.

She stared at him again.

"Claud, what's the matter with you? You act as though you disliked Gillian. I thought you—-?" she hesitated. "What makes you act so oddly?" She finished.

"Oddly?" Naylor did not seem to like the word. "I fail to see anything odd in my not talking over her plans with Miss Dundas."

"But your face—your whole manner to her since —it— it happened," she persisted, eyeing him very closely, and yet with a frown of bewilderment on her face. "I can't understand it. My own belief, or rather certainty, is that his death is due to some dreadful accident, but even so, she had nothing to do with it. Why did you look at Gillian in the hall yesterday as though—when they brought him in—as though, well I don't know how to put it into words. If it weren't so monstrous I should say you suspected her of having —having had a hand in whatever happened to him You must be reasonable, Claud."

Naylor said nothing, he was looking at the wall behind Mrs. Burnham with a steady, unblinking stare.

"I insist on your talking to her," she continued "You're a barrister. You must know that I'm right, that she oughtn't to go—that she can't go, in fact."

"I don't feel myself in a position to decide for Miss Dundas," he said as stiffly as ever. "The responsibility is too great."

"If only John—" She put her hand to her, eyes for a second. "Do you know, Claud," she said in a whisper, "that I actually ran to his library just now to ask him to help. I can't make him seem dead"

"Don't try, my dear," he said gently "Don't try, Lucy. It's heaven's help to those hurt, like you."

She nodded. "I don't feel anything here." She touched her heart "I'm told—the terrible fact that lie's gone—that never—never—never—" Her voice seemed to fail her on that, but she went on, her back to Naylor, "that I shall, not see him again, but I can't seem to realize it. It's like knowing that some terrible disaster has happened on the other side of the world."

He nodded. There was a little silence. "But Gillian," she resumed, "does realize it. She's a very sensitive nature. I guessed as much when I first saw her at Vichy. And all that she went through with that dreadful nephew of Mrs. dc Souza's... alone in the flat... it broke her nerve, I think. That's why I wanted you to talk to her. Sensibly—as you can talk." The young barrister did not stir. She made a hopeless little gesture.

"I'll see what Lady Tait can do." But Lady Tait was out.

Upstairs in her bedroom, or rather the bedroom now assigned her for a very short time, Gillian Dundas was lying, more than sitting, in an armchair. Without moving she had listened to Mrs. Burnham's words. Even now, when some. one came in and stood beside her, she did not stir, nor lift her weary lids. But at the touch of a hand on her shoulder, she started up with a cry.

CHAPTER TWELVE

"GILLIAN." Etta had never called her that before. "I would like to help you. Mrs. Burnham said you want to get away for a little quiet. But she doesn't think you should, or can, go just now. I don't agree. Suppose we slip away together, and I'll help you to get some little place where you can rest—and be at ease. Come! Don't wait for anything. That dreadful chief inspector is off the premises for the moment. Come along, Gillian!" She almost pulled the girl to her feet. "I can't help you if you won't help yourself. Like Heaven! And I do want to help you. I'm sorry for you."

Etta Naylor was talking in an odd hurried splutter. As though haste and some other emotion were both at work.

Just for a second Gillian hesitated, a look of something like wild hope shot across her features, then she shook her head and sank down again.

"I want to go by myself," she repeated, "I want to get away by myself. To Brussels."

Etta shook her.

"Gillian! Don't be a fool! There's a chance now. Quick! Follow me!" She herself rushed to the threshold, but she was not followed. Gillian had risen, but was staring at her with a white, distorted face, suspicion and terror in her eyes. Her hand clutched the back of her chair as though she were giddy, and overhung an abyss.

"I won't stir," she said finally.

There was something almost menacing in the step towards her that Etta took. Then she stopped. Mrs. Burnham turned the handle and came in. On her face was a look of surprise as she stared from one to the other.

Then she went to Gillian, with a little cluck, half-impatient, half-sympathetic.

"I said I wanted you to talk to her, not to scold her!"

"I can't stand people who shilly-shally." Etta's tone was of intense anger, and she shot a look at Gillian as though she could have struck her. "You said she wanted to get away. She doesn't. She refuses to budge with me."

"I want to go away alone—to Brussels," Gillian repeated dully.

"But she mustn't go! She can't go!" Mrs. Burnham protested. "Etta, why don't you help to make her understand. I can't put it into words. But if she goes now, the police may think, will think—" She did not finish the sentence.

"We all know what the police are," Etta agreed. "Nothing but red tape and routine. Even that clever looking chief inspector talks of routine. It's in their blood. Of course, Brussels is out of the question, but if Gillian and I go now, together, at once, we shall be far away in some quiet nook before they know it. And then, it'll be too late to find us."

Mrs. Burnham shook her head.

"But I don't think she ought to go," she murmured helplessly, "I don't think Gillian, won't you be sensible and stay on here—just a little while with me, until all this sadness lifts—for you. I know it's terrible just now. But we must bear things sometimes for others. Won't you stay?"

She looked pleadingly down into Gillian's face. The girl did not lift her head.

"I want to go—to Brussels, if possible, but at any rate, I want to leave here," she repeated like an automaton.

Etta spoke up briskly.

"Then let me have my way, Lucy. I think she ought to go, if she feels like that. I'll take her to—but no, better not tell you. At any rate, it's somewhere where she'll be quite quiet. I'll put my things on." She hurried off. First she went back to the room where her brother still stood. He did not seem to have moved since she had left him.

"Claud, I want fifty pounds. Can you let me have it, and in pound notes?"

"For what reason?"

"In strict confidence, I'm going to take Gillian Dundas for a rest cure before she breaks down. She's very near it."

Still Claud did not stir. Then swiftly he came very close and spoke in a low, level voice.

"I can give you the fifty in a moment, but to hand to her to use. You yourself are to have nothing to do with Miss Dundas, Etta. Neither to help nor to hinder."

"My dear Claud! How like the legal mind! But inasmuch, and forasmuch as I am sorry for her, I certainly shall try and help her."

"This is no case where you should help," he went on harshly. "Leave Miss Dundas alone, Etta. I'm the head of the family, now poor. John's gone, and I warn you most seriously to have nothing whatever to do with her. I know what I'm saying, and why I'm saying it." He spoke solemnly. For a moment she stood as though trying to read his tone and manner more than his words. Then she shook her head. Without another word, he let her have the notes from his bureau.

"Thank you, Claud. I wish you'd be frank—I haven't time now, but—"

He turned away, bleakly but definitely.

Upstairs she found a white-faced but more collected Gillian just pulling her hat on.   .

"My bag. You can't take a hag. Come as you are. Remember, we're off to Selfridge's florist department at once."

"But, my dear," protested Mrs. Burnham, looking harassed and upset, "you can't! You mustn't! Gillian, I won't allow it! Why should you act as though you were deaf to everything I say to you? After all, I am your employer. I'm responsible for you."

"Not now!" laughed Etta, a curious triumphant laugh. "She's my companion now."

"I want to get away," was all Gillian said, in a thick, choked voice.

Mrs. Burnham made a gesture of surrender, and went to her writing-table.

"You must have money." But Etta would not wait. She fairly dragged Gillian after her out of the room. A maid on the stairs stepped back to the landing to let them pass.

"Do you want one of the cars, miss?"

But Etta told her that she and Miss Dundas would walk. "It's only to Selfridge's for some flowers," she added in a tone that the man on duty in the hall below could hear.

"And certainly that's the truth," she added to her companion when they stood outside. Gillian seemed to shrink away from her. She shot a strange, swift look up and down the street as though meditating taking to her heels.

Etta instantly laid a very firm hand on her arm. A very tight grip indeed.

"Now, don't do anything foolish."

Gillian trembled, but she said nothing.

"No one's following us. We're safe. Now, then, Gillian, I want you to trust me. I'm your friend, remember. No matter what the trouble is into which you've got yourself, I want to help you." But the grip on the arm did not relax.

Gillian suddenly quickened her step. Just round a corner hung a sign. "Public telephone." It was a grocery shop and post-office combined. "I must telephone." Gillian wrenched her arm free and darted inside. Etta followed, looking darkly angry. But Gillian was inside the single telephone booth. Etta stood in the doorway biting her lip. A man passed in with a civil apology. He stepped to the counter.

"May I use your desk telephone for a minute? I'm in a fearful rush." He spoke fluently, and the damsel across the counter pushed the instrument over, in exchange for a sixpence and a "keep the change, miss." Down the phone went the number of an ordinary office in Piccadilly. When he got the connection, as he did instantly, he said one word which meant Scotland Yard, and then went on: "I'm speaking from 193 Upper Berkeley Street. Is Mr. Pip in?" Apparently he was not, for with a disappointed, "I'll ring again later, then," the man hung up and pushed back the instrument before he went on out.

His inquiry had meant that any message now being sent from the same office would be instantly duplicated to Scotland Yard as well The message was to a house near Victoria Station and was, as follows, in a swift rush of Gillian Dundas's voice:

"Are you there? Are you there? Thursday."

"Speaking," came in an almost equally swift reply.

"May ninth."

One was the day of the week, the other the date. Evidently a protective signal. Then came again in the hard clear treble:

"Likely girl is a dead cert."

There came a sharp exclamation from the man and then in a rush, "At once!" in tones both urgent and reassuring, not at all the voice in which the name of even the most certain winner is usually received.

This was a request for assistance of some kind, a plea for help on her part, which was instantly responded to by him.

Meanwhile the girl telephoning from the public booth peered out at her companion. She saw that for a second Etta's attention was distracted by a little cocker who had just rolled in with his mistress, and she slipped like a shadow out of the booth, behind the counter, and out of the door. But swift as she was, a young woman waiting in a taxi a little farther along, got out, motioning to the driver to follow her. Pointer's orders were that Gillian Dundas should not be left alone.

Gillian doubled back down a side street and got a taxi just as Etta Naylor was looking incredulously into an empty booth. For a few seconds Etta stood waiting, thinking Gillian must be consulting a directory somewhere, but after a while, a question or two told her that the only one hung inside the kiosk. She went to the door and looked up and down the street. No sign of the girl. A taxi-driver told her that he had seen a young lady nip out and down the next street "like billy-oh." Etta Naylor went first white, then red, then with a flame in her eye told him to drive her to Gillian's studio.

At the studio she found no one in. She spent another fifteen minutes waiting at the door. Surely Gillian Dundas would come on here, even supposing she mistrusted her—Etta's—offer of help. Where else could she go?

The young woman who had followed Gillian could have told her that Gillian was making for a dilapidated apartment house—a house that Claridge had once entered. To the same place Strange had already been followed by what looked like a newspaper boy wheeling a motor-cycle.

For ten minutes Gillian and Strange were together, then they came out walking towards a very sporty looking sports-car with a stream-line that promised eighty with the wind. Strange was apparently trying to persuade her to do something—to go somewhere...

The newspaper boy was reading the address on his parcel and admiring the car's bonnet.

"If you don't come with me, it's the police," he heard Strange say finally, in a tone low enough, but so charged with anger that it carried like a shout. "Take your choice."

Evidently the girl found this difficult. Terror and hope seemed to be struggling inside her as she looked at the car—the man—the street. But she was shrinking away from the car—and the man—when a taxi buzzed round a corner. Yet another taxi appeared behind it, but to pass on—and stop out of sight around a bend. Mrs. de Souza leaned forward. She was in the first of the two.

"Miss Dundas!" she called, as though in great surprise. "How lucky to have run across you! I've heard of such a good post for you. Do come and lunch at Harrod's with me while I tell you all about it. You'll love it."

Gillian did not look as though she loved anything in the world as she moved away from the young man's car. Strange looked sullen. His lips were moving, urging the girl to jump in and let him show what his car could do. But Gillian turned to Mrs. de Souza, and now looked steadily into the other's plump, cheerful face.

"Yes, I'll come. Thank you very much." And with what looked like a sudden spurt of resolution, she opened the taxi door, jumped in, and slammed it shut on the two of them. Mrs. de Souza, still smiling, gave the order to the driver and they were off. The newsboy, too, had gone on, this time mounting his bicycle, and the taxi waiting round the corner moved off. Yet another taxi, the one that had followed Miss Dundas—made for Harrod's and arrived there at the same time as the one in which Gillian sat. The fare jumped out, said a word to an errand-boy peering in at the first big window, and then talked for a minute with the cab-driver who had followed Mrs. de Souza. He drove off.

Meanwhile Strange, muttering oaths in keeping with his name, had leapt into his car. For a short distance he was followed by the same boy who had shadowed him to the apartment house, then, when an empty furniture van pulled out from the curb and took the road alongside the sporting-car, the boy stopped and returned to the house where. Strange and Gillian had met, and where she had finally left him.

He was kept waiting a long time at the door, but finally it was opened by a slovenly-looking man with a puffy, lined face, the face of an habitual drinker.

"Mr. Strange? He's gone out." He put out his hand.

"When'll he be in?"

"Can't say." The man shook a tousled head. "Keeps any old hours."

"But he lives here, doesn't he?" The boy looked... startled.

The servant nodded. "if you can call it living. He comes in every now and then for letters and so on.

"When do you expect him back?"

"No saying. Never no saying. May be hours, may. be days, may be weeks, see?"

"Do you forward packages for him?"

Again a shake of the head.

"He calls for them. If there are any. Very few come for him here. Lives in the country, does Mr. Strange, and just drops in here every now and then for convenience."

"How about that lady I saw just now drive up, stoutish, middle-aged party? Doesn't she live here either? I don't like to leave me parcel just to no one."

"You mean his aunt? No, she doesn't live here. Comes to see him every now and then."

The detective decided that he could ask no more for the moment. His orders were to be exceedingly careful.

Pointer himself, meanwhile, had received word that Mrs. de Souza and her maid had both left the flat in Mount Street. This was the first time since he knew of the lady's existence that the rooms had been deserted. The maid, his watcher phoned him, had gone off in the opposite direction to her mistress. Pointer hurried to the building. It was a flat which had been taken furnished for six months, and as he had learned, there had been no workmen in it since she took it In other words, he did not think it likely that there was any secret biding-hole fitted in to wall or floor or ceiling. A question to the owners, put apparently by a dealer trying to please a collector, had negatived the idea that he possessed any article of furniture or old picture frame with a secret drawer or concealed space in it. All this might not have been true of the house in Palace Green, and Pointer determined to do his best to avoid having to search it too He had already sent a window-cleaner, and a gas-inspector to look over the flat, but each had found the maid beside them all the time of their round.

It was a stormy day threatening, to grow worse. As he pulled up, he saw lights in the flat above Mrs. de Souza's, belonging, as he knew, to a young actor-manager. Asking for him, he and his companion were allowed to pass up. A luncheon party, was on. Pointer decided he could chance it So he and Inspector Watts walked up the stairs and stopped at the floor below. A twist with his master key, and he stepped into the flat and shut the door behind them. He had a search warrant, but he did not want to use it. The two men worked swiftly and carefully. After an hour and a half they looked at one another. They had found nothing. It was possible that Mrs. de Souza, supposing her to be the supplier of the poison as Pointer did, might, have kept her stock in some other place, but he expected it to be within easy reach. The flat was not abandoned. Nor was it difficult to search. Something about the paucity of personal belongings suggested that mistress and maid were more or less prepared to leave quickly. He knew from the expert that the poison would probably be in powder form, putty-colored powder with a faint smell as of horse-radish. He did not waste time going over the furniture a second time. If he and Watts could not find it the first time they would not the hundredth. He stood, head bent, eyes on his shoes, deep in reverie, while Watts stood by the door listening for footsteps. Pointer was swiftly running over the objects in the rooms before his mind's eye again. Suddenly he took a step forward. He remembered a smart scarlet inkstand in the dining-room with penholders of jade and blue. The ink was red, so were the nibs. The sort of thing that is for decoration, not for use.

"Did you look in the ink-well?" he asked Watts.

"Yes. Full to the brim," was the, reply. Pointer went to it, inserted a pencil and felt the smooth glass sides and bottom. It was shallower than one would have expected.

He lifted it out. It too was of opaque scarlet glass, and fitted exactly into the silver holder. The bottom must be unusually thick. He poured the ink into a tumbler, and, as he inverted it, out fell a flat capsule about an inch thick, the exact size of the bottom of the well. Drying it carefully so as not to let a drop fall, he found the box had a. screw lid fastened with a narrow strip of surgical plaster, the latter of quite recent date. The inside of the glass was full of putty-colored powder with a faint horse-radish smell. Pointer emptied it into a glass box of his own, wiped it, and put back into it a powder similar in appearance and smell, but harmless as chalk, of which it was made. He had with him quite a little beauty parlor of complexion powders of shades which ranged from cream to nigger, and he was careful to mix what he wanted to the exact tint of that in the glass. Everything put back, the two men hurried out of the flat and sauntered down the stairs, looking at peace with all the world. The powder was carried at once to the expert analyst. It was the poison described by Dr. Angelli and found in Tait's dead body.

While waiting a few minutes for this, Pointer was told that Miss Dundas had left the house in Great Cumberland Place with Miss Henrietta Naylor. That seemed all right. The sharpest scrutiny that had been possible in the short time since Tait's death had failed to find any hidden acquaintanceship between any member of his household and the three around whom the Yard's suspicions gathered. As long, therefore, as Gillian was with any of the Naylors she should be safe, and Pointer wanted to save her, if that was possible. But he did not like the emptiness of Mrs. de Souza's flat. He could now ask for a warrant against her, and Lady Ida, and Strange, and he intended to do so at once. They would not wait long, he feared, that clever trio. Though another death would not do, coming directly after Tait's death by poison, he believed that, had that passed as heart failure as they had expected, Gillian Dundas would not be alive now. They held her silence, it was true, because of the threat of disclosing the fact that she had taken part in blackmail, but if, as Pointer felt sure, Mrs. de Souza was in that too, for Gillian Dundas was really too stupid to have found out by herself what men to blackmail, and how to set about doing it, even Gillian must know that they could not use that weapon without themselves being cut in using it. She had complicated matters, from their point of view, by going to the same house as their victim Tait. That was clever of her, so clever that it struck an odd note.

Every hour she was in Lady Tait's house must be an hour of terror for the three. But though he did not think she would be killed in the house itself, he was afraid that, by some means, she would be decoyed away, or kidnapped, in order to take her to some place where she would "disappear." He would have liked to arrest her, but he had nothing on which to get a warrant. He decided to try again for a talk with her. Though he could not promise her immunity from punishment for blackmail, the punishment she so richly deserved—for Pointer was certain in his own mind that because of her Lord Mills had shot himself—yet he could assure her that the police would do their best to see that the fact that she had helped them to bring the poisoners of John Tait to punishment, would be taken into account. There must be good in the girl. He would get the warrant, execute it as soon as Mrs. de Souza was within reach, and then try for a word with Gillian.

A message came for him on the telephone while he was at the Yard getting the warrant. It was of first-rate importance. Pointer had had errand boys questioned who were known.-to have delivered parcels in the street around the hour when Tait had collapsed. Working through their own clubs, and the shops, he had succeeded in rounding up quite a number, and two of these had undoubtedly seen Tait. One had noticed a big dark man, overtake him, stop, him and light his cigarette at Tait's cigarette. As the wind was strong, he had had to come quite close for this. The boy could not swear that he had touched him, but he thought he had put a hand on his arm. As to identifying the man, his back had been to the boy, who had also not noticed whether he wore gloves or whether there was a buttonhole in his coat. This might or might not be useful, but the time was just a few minutes before Tait collapsed, for the clock was striking three. There was more to come. Another boy had seen a gentleman whom he had identified from his pictures as Mr. Tait, standing still. It was just after the hour had struck, therefore just after the other boy had seen the man lighting his cigarette. Mr. Tait, this second boy saw, was fumbling in his pocket—he had no gloves on—and after a second, with a jerk as though something had hurt him, had flung an envelope into the gutter.

The boy had picked it up, and found inside a very pretty artificial sprig of lily-of-the-valley. It was slightly damaged. He had not touched it beyond drawing it out by its silver stalk, intending to wear it next Sunday. He let the Yard man have the whole for half-a-crown. So Pointer now had his proof that it was by means of one of the pretty little Ricci buttonholes that the poison had been given, for a careful test showed that the whole sprig had been thickly coated with it after it was made up.

On the back of the envelope was the printed address of the Ricci's shop. Now, when Pointer and his taxi-driver had bought theirs, neither had been furnished with an envelope. A man was sent down at once to buy some trifle, and, when paying, ask if it could be put in an envelope for him. This was done, but the envelope was not the same kind as that which Tait had been seen to fling away. The man, however, had obtained a similar one from a pigeon-hole filled with printed stationery on the top of the paying-in desk.

Pointer examined the envelope carefully. On the inside the analyst found some traces of the poison, but besides that invisible substance, there was a faint round red mark the size of a penny, and two tiny red smears rather like thick pencil strokes, without apparent meaning. The round red mark turned out to be rouge of a good French make, especially suitable for a blonde, and the two red dabs were lipstick, also of a kind used by fair women. Miss Dundas was blonde, with soft fair hair and a lovely fair skin.

Pointer put the precious envelope in another, and went off to Great Cumberland Place. His watcher told him what he knew already, that Miss Henrietta Naylor and Miss Dundas were not yet back, that Miss Scott, his woman detective, was "in attendance." Pointer went on into the house. He showed the envelope to Mrs. Burnham and Lady Tait, but to neither, to no one, did he mention what had been inside it, but he did say that Mr. Tait had been seen to throw it away as he walked from the house after lunch.

Mrs. Burnham caught it up at once at the words. "The last thing possibly that John touched. You'll let me have it back when it's all over?"

He promised that she should have it. Both she and Lady Tait said they had no recollection of ever having seen it before. Both, on reading the name of the shop on the flap, looked disturbed.

"Where is Miss Dundas? She may have seen it by chance." Pointer's tone suggested one who misses an unimportant member of the household for the first time.

"She's gone out with one of the Misses Naylor," Mrs. Burnham said, speaking a little awkwardly, and with her back to the chief inspector, "they said something about Selfridge's florist shop."

"In my opinion, Chief Inspector, Miss Dundas has run away," Lady Tait put in sharply, "because my niece, too, refuses to see the obvious—sorry, Puss—she's gone out with her, to be given the slip, of course, at the first opportunity, and left to come home alone. I saw them both go out, and I saw their faces. Two conspirators."

"How can you say such things!" Mrs. Burnham spoke with warmth.

"My dear," the elder woman replied firmly, "kindness to some people is weakness."

"But, Lady Tait," Mrs. Burnham protested, "this envelope—Miss Dundas doesn't—can't—know these Italians, and it is Mrs. Ricci, you know. We all know."

Lady Tait blanched as always at that name, however gently spoken. Naylor came in during the painful little silence that followed. He examined the envelope carefully, and said that he had never seen it before. "The Ricci's... perhaps what poisoned him was inside... you haven't told us yet what did poison him, something practically undetectable, according to the woman herself."

Pointer was wanted on the telephone. An urgent message from Miss Scott. Pointer listened to a very unusual report from her of failure, absolute and possibly irretrievable. He was now told that Mrs. de Souza's "shadow" had seen a man enter Harrod's who was very much wanted by the police, and who had for quite a long time been in hiding. He had asked Miss Scott if she could manage both women for a few minutes, just to give him time to telephone, after which he would pick up Mrs. de Souza again. Miss Scott had been quite sure she could manage—easily. She had been too sure, and she had lost both.

Pointer listened with his usual immobile face, but he was greatly disturbed.

"They changed the hats they were wearing for others," she said with bitterness, "must have done, or else took their hats and cloaks off, dropped them somewhere and went on as saleswomen—anyway, one moment I had them well in sight, Miss Dundas in her orange and black little hat and her coat with the ermine collar, and Mrs. de Souza in purple velvet hat and coat, and the next moment they were nowhere to be seen. There's a sale on, unfortunately, and the place was packed."

"I told you to be sure not to let Miss Dundas out of your sight," Pointer said with ominous calm. Then he hung up. The woman was a good detective, but this was a ghastly enough failure. His face was very grave as he hurried back to the house. The only hope was that the man following Strange would link up again with the two women, and Pointer rather expected Strange to join Mrs. de Souza ultimately, for he did not think the latter would herself actually murder Gillian Dundas. He read her as a woman who would shrink from physical violence, also Gillian was, or should be, the stronger of the two. But Strange... his rather terrible figure struck a sinister note...

Pointer returned to the room with a set face.

"I think you're right, Lady Tait, and that Miss Dundas has run away. She may have met some one and gone with them unwillingly, cowed, or she may think she's with a friend, and yet be in the hands of the murderer of Mr. Tait."

Mrs. Burnham gave a little cry. Even Lady Tait gave a gasp.

"Where would she be likely to go? To make for?" he asked the former. "Have you any idea, however faint or improbable?"

"She spoke of going to Brussels, she must have a passport, of course, and I have an idea her parents live near there. They are caretakers at a cottage in the Ardennes, I believe, or rather I fancy. I wish I knew the place; she didn't go into details... Oh, why is she so reserved? Why doesn't she confide in one of us here? We're all her friends. We all want to help her." Lucy Burnham actually wrung her pretty hands. "I'm beginning to I think that Gillian must be connected in some way with the murder of my John." She spoke slowly, almost fearfully. "But not in any guilty way. She knows something, and loyalty won't let her speak. That's possible, though even that seems a dreadful thought. For she came here—to me—as I thought, but now I think she came to try and warn John. To save him." Her voice broke. Lady Tait took her hand and held it close.

"Dearest Lucy," she began, then stopped as the door was flung open and Etta Naylor stood in the opening. "That girl has got away!" She spoke in a voice quite unlike the gentle tones Pointer had hitherto heard from her. "I wondered if she had crawled back here. No? Then I'm off to look for her in my car." There seemed strangely little of the compassionate friend who had begged Gillian to confide in her in the angry, handsome woman who faced them at that moment with flashing eye and bright carmine cheeks.

"Yes, yes!" Lucy urged. "Do try and catch up with her. She'll make for the boat train, of course, or else for wherever an Ostend boat starts from—she'll make for Brussels... she told us so."

"Did she tell you that too, Miss Naylor?" Pointer asked.

"She told me nothing," was the reply.

"But you were with me when she said she wanted to go to Brussels. Alone. She said it over and over!" Mrs. Burnham looked amazed. "We both said Brussels was out of the question and you said—"

"I didn't hear her say a word about Brussels," Etta repeated firmly. This time Mrs. Burnham's eyes widened in earnest. How could Etta pretend that she had not heard Gillian say she wanted to go to Brussels? Why did she now claim, before the detective officer, that she had no idea where the girl would go first?

"I believe that dreadful. Italian woman has got hold of her," Etta now went on, "or that Gillian went there because of something—some message, perhaps—anyway, I'm going to try in Soho first. I want you"—she turned to the two women—"to come along. If we're in force we may one or other of us stumble on something—you see"—it was Pointer now on whom her eyes rested—"I feel responsible for her in a way. I tried, to help her. I thought she needed to get away to some quiet place."

"You can hardly expect me to go to Soho," Lady Tait said crisply. But Mrs. Burnham threw herself into the project.

"I don't believe she's there. I know she's going to try and reach her parents in Belgium, but I'll come with you. There may be something we can find, out, and after all, she once turned to me, she may again." Mrs. Burnham hurried away to return almost immediately, she had not an ounce of vanity in her, and never wasted time on arrangements of hat or scarf. The two fairly ran out of the house into Etta's car outside. A much swifter, bigger car, as she noticed, than Mrs. Burnham had ever known her to drive before.

On the step Etta turned. "I'm going to the Ricci's first, then to her studio, and then the round of all the. shipping offices that have to do with Ostend or Calais," she told her brother, who had silently followed them out. Pointer saw them dash off, and saw a small delivery car with the name of a well-known brand of cigarettes on it just behind them. It was a ramshackle looking, concern but it could beat Miss Naylor's big hired car on three wheels.

Pointer had no intention of letting Mrs. Burnham run into danger, and though, so far, there seemed no danger from Etta Naylor, nor any reason why Mrs. Burnham should be in peril, from the first he had had her followed by a good man who, in case of necessity, would defend her...

Alysia came back just as her sister's car sped off. She found Lady Tait intensely indignant at the fact that one of her nieces should deliberately, and against her express desire, thrust herself forward as a friend of Gillian Dundas's.

"Even Lucy was coming round, slowly, of course, dear thing, to the sensible point of view," the elder woman began, and Alysia looked as though she quite agreed with her aunt as to Etta's uncalled-for interference in the dark mystery, surrounding Gillian, but Pointer was in a hurry.

"May I have a word with the servants?" he asked. "I want to show them this envelope, and see if by chance any of them ever saw it in Mr. Tait's possession. Have you yourself ever seen it, Miss Naylor?"

Alysia looked at it. She was told where, and when, it was picked up, and scrutinized it closely.

"Yes, I know it by those two dabs of red. You'll find a round smear of rouge inside from a pad. It's an envelope that Etta has had for weeks. I think she brought the receipt away in it last time she paid the Ricci's the quarterly present from John, anyway, she put a couple of lipsticks and a rouge pad in it and, kept them all in a tortoiseshell box on her dressing. table. She tried the lipsticks on it once while I was in the room."

Naylor, who was back in the room, listened attentively, and shot a keen glance at the tense figure beside them. Something about it struck him. The maid who looked after Etta was hastily summoned, Pointer seemed in a rare rush. She also recognized the envelope by its marks. She ran up and then hurried down to say that it was no longer in the box. She could not remember when she had it last. Certainly not for some days, but on the other hand, she did not think it as long ago as a week.

Pointer wheeled on Naylor. "I'm going to see if I can pick up Miss Dundas's traces, yet I must have a word with you. Please come with me and we can talk in the car."

For a second Naylor hung back. Then he followed the other in his rush to the pavement, where Pointer said a few sentences to his driver.

"You think she's in danger?" The words seemed to burst from Naylor without his willing them.

Pointer was in the car, and somehow Naylor found himself beside him, and being whirled off silently and swiftly.

"I think she's dead," Pointer replied in a low tense, voice. "I may be wrong. I shall act as though I expected to be. in time. And if there is a chance it will be largely because you tell me everything that passed between you and Mr. Tait yesterday morning."

CHAPTER THIRTEEN

NAYLOR looked as though he could not speak for a moment.

"Come, Mr. Naylor," Pointer went on, still in the same driving voice of concentrated power that seemed to lift the other man along with him, low though it was. "As I see it, there are two crimes here, though closely linked. Blackmail in which Miss Dundas was concerned along with others, and murder, in which she had no part, or, at most, the part of a catspaw. We believe that Lord Mills was being blackmailed, if not by her, then through her, and the same is true of Mr. Tait. I think Mr. Tait told you as much the day he died. The only question in his mind was, who was behind her. I think he meant to drag that name out and pillory it in order to save Brown, though it meant acknowledging that he himself had suffered in the same way. Am I right?" The question came like a whip lash.

Naylor did not speak. His lips set tight, he sat with his eyes staring straight ahead of him.

"I believe she has paid in full by now," Pointer went on very gravely, "but if she has a chance it may depend on whether I know everything you can tell me."

A look of positive agony crossed Naylor's face. Something like sweat stood out on his forehead.

"As far as we can, we shall not press the charge of blackmail," Pointer went on, realizing the dreadful dilemma of the other, his fear lest he should give information to the police that would send Gillian to prison. And, however much she deserved to go there, Naylor could not send her there; he was under her spell, though he refused to let it blind or even entirely bind him to her. His good sense, all that was sane in him, struggled against it, and by no means ineffectually.

"Why do you think she has paid in full—by now?" Naylor asked under his breath.

"Because, in my opinion, she's been kidnapped by very desperate people and, owing to the fact that she took part in blackmail, cannot turn for help to the only power that might save her, the power, of the law. My belief is that Mr. Tait was summoned by Lord Mills just before the latter shot himself. He was summoned by a telephone call and Mills himself let him in. I think he warned your cousin, against having anything to do with Miss Dundas or he would pay for it dearly. Mr. Tait had paid in the past on two occasions. I think Mr. Tait went away and found to his horror Miss Dundas installed in his aunt's house as Mrs. Burnham's protégée, and taxed her with the truth. Her replies did not satisfy him, or their talk was interrupted before he had finished."

Pointer felt Naylor start, but the barrister did not speak. "Anyway," Pointer went on, "he went to her studio next morning—must have"—Pointer was speaking slowly now, groping, half to himself—"and learned from her, or found for himself, something for knowing which, or for having which, he was poisoned. I think she told him she could not help herself. And he believed her. I think that was why he asked you if you believed in the devil... I take it Mr. Tait referred to the person behind the blackmailing of Lord Mills, and of himself, behind Miss Dundas. You see, Mr. Naylor, we know most of the facts, but among those we don't know may be something that will help— just now—in this moment of real emergency."

Naylor drew a deep breath.

"You're quite right," he said, speaking clearly and coldly, in his most impersonal tone. "As far as I can check it, all you've said is absolutely true. Mills sent my cousin a telephone message asking him to come and see him at once. He got it while at his own house, looking over it with my sisters and Lady Tait. He hurried to Mills' flat and found him alone. He told my cousin that he was being bled by blackmail on account of a visit to a gambling den with Miss Dundas. That he had just learned, by chance, that he, Tait, had been seen talking to her in a corner of the links at Vichy. He warned John to have nothing to do with her, and said that he himself had been bled so white that he had decided to cut it all and leave England. When he shot himself, not an hour later, John understood what he meant by 'leaving England.' Full of the tragic story and of alarm at his own position, John found, on his arrival at his aunt's house that night, that Miss Dundas was there. Ran into her in the dining-room and arranged for an interview when the house should be quiet at night. He taxed her with being the blackmailer of Mills and himself. I interrupted the talk. Next morning he went to her studio and had it out with her. She seemed beside herself with anxiety and horror over Mills' death and with something more, John thought it sheer terror. At any rate, she broke down after that, and confessed that she was a party to the blackmailing, but said she acted under compulsion. She drew a touching picture of herself as a slave with a father and mother who would be turned out if she disobeyed orders." Naylor's lip curled. "She refused to say where they lived, but my cousin was tremendously sorry for her. He was an awfully good chap... At lunch he spoke to me afterwards with a sort of fury of the man or people behind Miss Dundas. I've never seen him so wrought up. But he didn't go into details. It—it was a blow in a way. I stopped him later to ask for particulars when he was hurrying out. He told me that on his return he would want to consult me most urgently as to what steps to take about an action he wanted to bring. Those were his words. Some idea of preventing scandal spreading was in his mind evidently, but he rushed away, telling me he wouldn't be long—to wait for him... That was the last I saw of him."

There was a short silence.

"I was afraid that Miss Dundas would be suspected of having poisoned John. The motive might seem so obvious. To escape being found out." He went on heavily.

"You didn't think so yourself?"

"No. But then, I saw no terror. It was more than fear of punishment. It was"—his voice fell a note "fear of death.. Nothing less."

"You don't believe Signora Ricci murdered your cousin, do you?" Pointer asked.

"No. I do not. But I wanted time—and a chance for Miss Dundas to pull herself together. She knows the truth. She must. I hoped she would yet speak out to you."

After that, there was a long silence.

"About Mr. Tait and his friend Mr. Westmacott, can you give me any notion of why your cousin came. to take less interest in Lady Ida? It's not curiosity that prompts the question, needless to say."

Naylor replied flat he could give no explanation. "I suppose you know that Westmacott wanted to marry my sister Etta," he went on. "I've sometimes wondered if there lay the reason. Though exactly what it would be is beyond me. For it was Tait who strongly supported Westmacott in his sudden idea of leaving England and going first to Honduras, and then to China. That certainly ought to've made Lady Ida his for life!"

"Mr. Tait supported Mr. Westmacott?" Pointer repeated.

Naylor nodded. He was glad to deaden thought by chatter.

"Etta wouldn't look at him for a couple of mouths. But she got over her indignation, or seems to have. She grew to be quite fond of John lately."

Another silence fell. The car rushed on and on. The sky was black. They seemed to be in the heart of a storm.

Pointer was busy writing in his corner, filling a couple of pages with his neat, copperplate writing. Part of the time, he was making a carbon copy. Naylor automatically noticed. It could not be what he, Naylor, had just told him, for Pointer had known that already. The young barrister closed his eyes. Suddenly the chief inspector leaned forward and spoke in the other's ear. The wind was howling as in a gale at sea.

"Mr. Naylor, will you be kind enough to take this envelope"—he held out one—"and keep it very carefully. You see that it's addressed to the Yard. Should anything happen to me today, I want it posted."

Naylor nodded and slipped the envelope, addressed as Pointer had just said, into an inner pocket, which he buttoned shut. An extra strong burst of wind crashed a tree down behind them. It was a terrific storm which slowed down even the Bentley, and they seemed to be in the midst of it.

"Where are we?" he shouted to Pointer, finding that with all his might he could barely get the words across the few inches to the other.

"Not far from Tor Cottage."

"Tor Cottage! Why Tor Cottage!"

"Mr. Tait was having a hard tennis court made there," Pointer roared in reply. "I had a man posted down there as soon as I heard of it." He spoke as though hard tennis courts were outside the pale.

Naylor made some reply, or ejaculation, which was drowned in a yet more terrific crash. A tree was down in front of them. The ground quivered where it struck, and a cloud of earth rose from the ground to be whirled away by the howling wind. The rain lashed at the car, pounding on the roof and the glass as though it were hail. Something in the tumult, something in the noise around him, in what he had just heard, seemed to daze Naylor. His usually swift wits were numbed. That terrible reply about the hard tennis court was running in his brain. There was another road across the common on which they now were.

Pointer ran for it. Out of the storm a car roared forward along it. The chief inspector had a fog lamp in his hand and waved it. The car did not slacken; like an express train it kept to the center of the road, and Pointer had just time to leap aside as it rushed past him.

At the wheel sat a big shouldered man. It was Strange Just a glimpse of him, and the car was blotted out. To hear was impossible when standing in the open. Pointer ran back to the other two crouched in the shelter of the car. He seized Naylor's arm and drew, him close.

"We ought to strike a road in a few minutes that leads to Tor Cottage—to the right."

Naylor stumbled on blindly. He lost Pointer, he lost the road, and the common, but somehow he crashed into a wooden fence, knew that Tor Cottage had one just like it, and groped his way by it to a swing gate. A car stood beside it. It was the cottage. Bent double, he forced his way up the drive Another ear, Etta's car, stood in front of the door. Into the portico he stumbled, and rang. No one answered. He rang again. No reply. He broke the pane of the bow window beside him, and, opening it, jumped in. It was the drawing-room. Empty.

What followed was a nightmare. Amid the din of the storm he heard voices calling Etta's voice, Mrs. Burnham's, he could not tell which. The electric light was useless owing to a breakdown in the cable. He struck matches in vain, each time the wind blew them out. Then he was outside, calling Gillian Dundas's name as these other voices seemed to be calling it. The storm seemed to be abating its violence He could now see the rhododendrons, behind which the hard court was being made. That ghastly word of the chief inspector as to its being the reason for his having come to Tor Cottage... Naylor jumped a bed of flowers and ran. As he fairly flung himself around the end, he saw Mrs. Burnham and the chief inspector struggling together, to get something out of a large barrel filled with cement bags. Even as he reached them, they lifted something long—difficult to handle.

Another moment and Gillian Dundas's body was laid on the ground. There had been a tarpaulin over the barrel, and the cement was dry. It rose in the air, it fell in heaps at the feet of the men, it dropped from Gillian Dundas's white face and fan hair, and fell from her crumpled frock, except where it clung like a big bouquet of crimson flowers at her breast and her back. She had been shot through the heart from the back, the bullet they found afterwards had lodged in an arm which she must have had pressed against her heart, to still some transport of fear.

"Dead!" Naylor said hoarsely, his own face nearly as white as that at his feet. "But she's still warm. Still flexible. She's—"

Pointer had seized Mrs. Burnham. "Did you see any one? Any one? He must have gone round these buildings." She only shook her head. For the moment she was past speech, but she rushed with him in the direction of his finger. There was no one to be seen. The wind was falling. Behind the shelter of the pavilion he paused.

"Quick, Mrs. Burnham, think quick! Didn't you see any one? At any time in the garden?"

"I saw some one—I think a man—but it was only an outline—no face—"

Pointer put a hand swiftly into his pocket. He drew out a bulky envelope. His name was on it, in Miss Dundas's smart, small writing—or in his best imitation of her writing.

"Then I must open this. Evidently, from its thickness, it contains a full confession from Miss Dundas."

He ran a finger under the flap. She fumbled in her handbag.

Another moment and she was lifted off her feet, her two wrists caught together in Pointer's one hand. Something fell to the ground with a clatter of metal. This was what Naylor saw as he rushed to join in the hunt for the murderer of the girl now growing cold behind him. He was aware of a big-shouldered, tall young man plunging in the same direction. One of Pointer's men evidently. He had a revolver in his hand. As he flung himself round the

little garden shelter, Pointer fairly tossed Mrs. Burnham
to the barrister. "Hold her fast," he called. And Naylor
did. The chief inspector leapt past him at the newcomer,
the man with the revolver, the man of the studio, the
mouthing horror of Westmacott's house. Something
clicked. The two went down in a heap. A shot rang out,
but the man now, twisted and tore at bracelets of steel on
his wrists.

"You fool!" There was foam on his lips as he got to his
feet and advanced, manacled as he was. "Let me get at
her! At the devil who's done this." He was advancing at a
rush. Pointer flung him back. "Stand where you are!" he
thundered.

"I tried to get at a revolver to threaten him with. I
saw him coming. He was aiming straight at you," Mrs.
Burnham said. She was holding Naylor's protecting arm,
quite as much as he was holding her. "I brought it to give
Gillian—oh, poor, poor Gillian!"

"Why didn't you let me shoot her?" the man who had
shot and missed, thanks to Pointer, said savagely.

"Because there's evidently some mistake," Pointer
said to that. "Perhaps a mistake all round. This lady
befriended Miss Dundas."

"Befriended her! Good God!" The man gnashed his
teeth, a thing that Naylor had thought was only a figure
of speech. As for Mrs. Burnham, her usually gentle timid
eyes were alight, with indignation.

"Pray, who are you?" she asked, turning to Strange
and eyeing him from head to foot.

"One of your creatures"—the man took still another
step forward—"just as she was."

"He's mad," Mrs. Burnham said in a tone of pity. "He's
raving I never, saw him before Oh, yes, I have, though." A
look of recognition for the first time crossed her face
which was very pale, but otherwise looked untroubled. "I
know who he is. He's Mr. Jack Westmacott, Mr.
Westmacott's mad son who has intervals of sanity, and is
mad all the rest of the time. His keeper could identify

him. Lady Ida Westmacott can identify him. Miss Dundas pointed him out to me in the park one morning and said he was madly in love with her. Evidently he murdered her because she would have nothing to do with him."

"He certainly sounds mad," Pointer said shortly. "Come, sir, what have you to say against my arresting you on the spot for the murder of Miss Gillian Dundas?"

The man gave a laugh that certainly sounded the maddest thing that Naylor had ever heard.

"You think I murdered my Gilly! Gilly who never had a chance; who couldn't help herself once she got into her hands." He rocked a second on his feet.

"If you didn't murder her, can you give us information as to who did?" Pointer demanded. "Information, Mr. Strange, not rantings. Information that you can swear to, that can be proved?"

"I want to tell you now—everything—I don't want to be able to draw back," Strange said to that, his breath coming in gasps "I know what I'm saying and the consequences. I only make one bargain with you —get her! Don't let her slip through! They talk against hanging, it's too good for her. And what I say I can prove up to the hilt."

Pointer looked at him keenly. The man's eyes met his firmly. Yes, Strange would tell everything, though he was well aware that it meant penal servitude for himself possibly. Certain of that, Pointer turned to the women.

"Mrs. Burnham, I arrest you for the murder of John Tait by poison, and of Gillian Dundas by shooting." Followed the usual warning.

"Arrested on that creature's information?" Lucy Burnham asked scornfully. "He's mad. Look at his eyes. Certainly no sane person would believe such a statement."

Naylor felt as though the ground under him rocked. But he noticed that Etta, who seemed to have joined the group, stood behind Mrs. Burnham with a hand out ready to grasp her, if need be.

A man, draggled, and torn, and muddy, and bleeding from a cut on the head, now appeared; he looked at Pointer. It was the man told off to follow Mrs. Burnham. Only the storm which had overturned his car had kept him back. Pointer said a couple of words that conveyed nothing to the others. The detective turned to her civilly enough.

"Will you come with me, please? We can drive back in the car that is at the front door."

"You'll drive me to the commissioner's rooms at Scotland Yard," Mrs. Burnham said firmly. "This is an incredible outrage."

"Ah, here's Miss Scott," said the man beside her. "She did get through the hedge, then."

A tall, quietly-dressed woman, looking neat in spite of a torn cloak and muddy hat, was running towards them. Again Pointer said a word, and she too went up to Mrs. Burnham.

"Will you come with me into the house, please?" She and, the man on the other side each laid a hand on one of Mrs. Burnham's arms.

Mrs. Burnham looked first atone, then at the other, then at Pointer.

"I don't envy you your feelings, Chief Inspector, when I have had my talk with the commissioner," she said gently. "I don't think you'll be called by that title after today."

"As for you," she turned with something very sad in her voice and eye to Etta Naylor, "you disliked me from the first. But you might have stood by me in such a moment as this."

Etta Naylor had covered her face with her hands. Now she turned even her covered face away. Mrs. Burnham walked quietly to the house. There to be searched by the woman detective, and then, when they knew that she had no poison nor any weapon on herself, to be taken as she had requested to Scotland Yard, there to have an interview, with the assistant commissioner.

Pointer stepped over to where she had been standing. Into a rose-bush; all broken by the storm, he put. his hand and torch. Another minute and he lifted out a little roll of gray. It was a pair of rubber gloves tightly rolled together.

Etta went up to her brother.

"I thought it was she who poisoned John. I wanted to save Gillian Dundas. That's why I took her off with me. But Gillian wouldn't be saved."

Claud hardly heard her. But the man from whom Pointer was taking the handcuffs, only put on to prevent him from trying again to shoot Mrs. Burnham, heard her...

"No, she wouldn't be saved. She wouldn't come with me either. She thought my brain couldn't beat Mrs. Burnham's. I'd been drinking. She wouldn't come!" A sob choked him but he went on: "I'll tell you everything."

"Come into the house and I'll write it down and have you sign it," Pointer said to that. He wanted witnesses who were not of the police for such an important explanation as might be coming. "You understand, of course, that it will have to be used against you?"

Strange only nodded, with a look that said that he did not care what became of himself. Between the three men, Naylor white but silent, they carried Gillian Dundas's body into the nearest room and laid it on a blanket, covering it with another. And in the same room, Pointer, writing swiftly in his speedhand, Strange began.

"That woman you've got, and Mrs. de Souza, are sisters—and blackmailers. The one you've got is the elder. Mrs. Burnham married a solicitor who left Wales, came to town and did well. He was a family solicitor and had some smart people among his clients. When he died, she went through his deed-boxes, I was his head clerk, and what she learned she used. She used! I hadn't had time to straighten out a muddled, account"—his voice was muffled here "she chose to take it the wrong way— couldn't refund the money on the spot—she got me in her power, and promised not to prosecute if I obeyed orders. I had to write the blackmailing letters for her which she dictated from what she learned in her husband's papers. Her sister got on to the idea too, and met Gillian at her mother's studio. Gilly used to help with the china there. Mrs. de Souza soon found that maids bringing things to be repaired used to gossip to her. Then she took her traveling with her as a very useful companion. Meantime, I took to the films with what was paid me to write the letters and receive the payments. I might have done well, only drink got me, so I had nothing but writing to their victims to fall back on. Then one day Mrs. Burnham told me that her sister could offer me a very well paid, easy post. I was to go at once to Genoa to see her about it. Of course I had to go, and of course, I had to take what was offered me. I was deep in their clutches by that time. They had me on toast, and I had nothing to prove the truth about either of them. Mrs. de Souza told me that she had met a Lady Ida Westmacott, had made friends with her, and learned that she was terrified of her brother-in-law marrying again, in which case her own son, now considered as the heir presumptive, would have nothing and she would have nothing. As long as his idiot son lived, he wouldn't marry, now that he had found out that the son couldn't be cured. He had said so."

Etta Naylor gave a sort of strangled moan. Then she stood as before, rejecting the chair that Pointer had placed for her.

"This boy, or rather young man, was ill. She was afraid he might die at any time. Mrs. de Souza had passed this on to Mrs. Burnham, the cleverer devil of the two, and it was she who had suggested supplying a fake idiot should the son die. He did die while I was in Mrs. de Souza's villa by the sea. They kept the death dark, dropped the body into the water, and I was fetched at once. The terms offered me were fine. It wasn't an impersonation, really. But I could make up enough like him in coloring and general build, and if any one who knew the son should see me, I only had to keep on twisting my face into grimaces. Lady Ida had done most of the nursing herself. She really was devoted to her nephew, really loved him and was intensely sorry for him. The valet-nurse was easily persuaded—by Miss Dundas—to put in most of his time at the gaming-tables, and then was found out and dismissed. Another man was engaged in his place over whom Mrs. Burnham had a stranglehold.

"We came to town and the house was divided in half. Westmacott discharged the man we had, and left old Craven to take his place. I refused to be waited on. I refused to let him touch me, but otherwise I was quite tractable. The old chap soon found that the less he saw of me, the better I seemed to be, and, the more attention he gave me the more violent I grew. But he's as stupid as he's faithful. He hasn't the faintest suspicion. For one thing, I've kept on the old Jacky's little games and pretty ways, biting and clawing halls, and so on... Rooms were taken for me where I could go, except for the hour that Craven played with me or when the commissioners came or Mr. Tait would look in at me from the cage by the door, in response to a letter from Westmacott. By the way, that was a mistake, Lady Ida's letting me play with her fountain pen last time. I felt it incumbent on me to paw and bite it, and the result was Tait took the top away with him.

"By the way"—he looked around him with glassy eyes, he had been drinking recently, Pointer thought, and found it hard to concentrate on what he really wanted to say—"by the way—funny world, isn't it?—Tait was taken with Lady Ida, but I know why it came to nothing. Once, before Tait, she let out a bit at me when I was making rather more of a fool of myself than was necessary. I saw the startled look in his eyes. And as far as he was concerned her lack of sympathy with her poor half-witted nephew—that was me—tore it. Funny world! She loathed me because she had genuinely loved the real boy and hated having to palm me off as him. But about other things—I met Miss Dundas at Genoa.

"She was as much in their clutches as I was. I don't say she was an angel, but what could she do? She liked the easy life and the easy money. Then she thought she could get a bit more for herself than the ten per cent allowed her, and put the screw on to Lord Mills herself. I suppose you know all this? She overdid it. He shot himself. Gillian was in for the devil of a time with Mrs. Burnham and Mrs. dc Souza. She got rattled, and overlooked a paper in her studio. It was a note to me from Mrs. Burnham about two years old, on the back of which I had jotted down the directions for a face-pack actresses often use after a fatiguing night. She left it, my directions uppermost, on her table. Tait came to the studio the morning after Mills shot himself, brushed it off by accident, picked it up, recognized Mrs. Burnham's writing, and must have seen a word here and there. Anyway, he read it, standing before her and asked its meaning. Now, though guarded, it would have put any friend of Westmacott on to the right track—about me. Gillian said she had never seen it before. He didn't believe her and took it to show to Mrs. Burnham, who promptly said it was a forgery, you may be sure. I don't know how she explained that talk to you that Tait had with her, after lunch. It was about the note. When she said it was a forgery, he believed her, and went to fetch Miss Dundas to confront her, feeling sure that it was she who had forged Mrs. Burnham's writing. But Mrs. Burnham had seen to it somehow that though he was to leave the house all right, he would never return.

"It was Mrs. Burnham, of course, who ordered Gillian to come to her, so as to have her under her own eye and be able constantly to direct her. For Gilly lost her head. Completely. When Tait was poisoned she knew her turn would come next. She knew Mrs. Burnham would never forgive her for having left that piece of paper lying about which forced her to kill Taft, and with him do away with all her chances of a good marriage. That engagement had been a piece of most unexpected good luck for her. Mrs. Burnham told her that if she obeyed all orders she would overlook her carelessness. Much Gilly believed she would! But she had no other alternative than to obey. Mrs. Burnham had destroyed the paper, of course. Told Tait, you may be sure, to leave it with her while he went for Gilly. Oh, she was a clever devil, with the face of a dear little parson's wife. But there was one thing she didn't know. That I loved Gully. She told me, thinking I was completely under her thumb, that Gillian was a danger to all of us. That she must be silenced for all our sakes. Mrs. de Souza would bring her down to Tor Cottage, which was shut up for the week. Mrs. Burnham had a key to it and had a couple of extra keys made. I was to come down, shoot her, and shove her dead body into the cement!" His eyes were like a madman's.

"Knowing the danger to Gillian, I pretended to agree and then tried to get her to come with me. I'd have hidden her safely where even those two devils couldn't have got at her. But they got her first. They had frightened her of me. Telling her some damned lies. Mrs. de Souza took her down here, and then lit out, leaving her fastened up, I'll bet, for her sister to finish. I thought I could get here first. But that damned storm..." He broke down and sobbed wildly.

"And what about those lily-of-the-valley buttonholes you bought at the Ricci's shop?" Pointer broke in. "Who told you to buy them?"

Strange raised his despairing face as though to refuse to answer, such a trivial question.

"It's important," Pointer said quietly, and Strange looked at him more sharply.

"Is it? Do you know I fancied there was something about them... Mrs. de Souza made such a scene. when she found I had one in my own buttonhole—she saw me with it at my rooms. Mrs. de Souza had told me that I was to have my hair cut at the Ricci's shop in Soho and there buy a couple of artificial little lily-of-the-Valley buttonholes and leave, them done up in a box at the studio. I did it, bought a third one for myself, and that's all I know about them."

Pointer turned to. Miss Naylor, who was now sitting at the window, her back to the room. He had to touch her arm before she heard him. When she did it was she who spoke first, and as though continuing a talk.

"The boy died! And all the time we've been separated by a fraud!" Her eyes, too, were flame. "It broke our hearts nearly. But he wouldn't marry, as that horrible creature there says, while the boy lived. The taint was in his mother's blood. But he wouldn't chance having a son who would have to stand second to an idiot. And so he went off to Honduras and China and I—I tried to change into something worthy of a saint. I don't doubt I overdid it. There was such a lot to change that every one thought me a canting humbug. And all the time these devils"—she choked on the words.

"What about Mrs. Burnham down here?" Pointer urged. "She must have slipped away from you and shot the girl just now."

Etta dropped her personal feelings at once. Yes, knowing of some short cuts, she had come straight to the cottage and found it, apparently shut up. They had tried to find Gillian. Mrs. Burnham pretended to think she might be hiding in one of the rooms. In the storm and the darkness, Etta missed the widow. "How could she have done it so quickly?" she asked in hushed tones of the chief inspector.

"She evidently came prepared for any eventuality — though she expected to find Strange had relieved her of the necessity for doing it herself. But finding Miss Dundas alive, tied up somewhere and gagged, left so by Mrs. de Souza—the traces are still on her cheeks and wrists—I think Mrs. Burnham untied her and told her to hide in the barrel, that I was on her track. I think she may have shown her a revolver and seemed about to hand it to her, perhaps saying 'Take this, and get away while you can. He's after you!' Mrs. Burnham is no revolver artist to have shot her through her pocket, and I don't see how else she got that shot in without your hearing a cry. Her revolver would of course have a silencer on it. Then she covered her with bags of cement that were standing around. She was doing this when I got here, and I of course, turned it into trying to get the bags out of the barrel. She helped me to lift the body out—-still warm, but unfortunately dead."

"Have you got the revolver with which she did it?" Strange broke the silence of sheer horror that had followed on the chief inspector's words.

Pointer had. It had been dropped into the cement. It was of foreign make, and would, he fancied rightly— probably turn out to be Miss Dundas's own revolver, which Mrs. Burnham had hidden.

"But fingerprints?" Etta asked.

"There aren't any. She wore rubber, gloves." He looked at Naylor. "Just as she had them on when she tried to shoot me before I could read what I had told her. was Miss Dundas's confession just now. You see, I didn't know that Mr. Strange would appear at that moment, and I wanted to catch her in the act. But, of course, his evidence was what I needed most... I let her tell us that she had seen Strange and intended to threaten him with a revolver... it was the best lie she could tell... by the way." He turned to Etta. "Did Miss Dundas tell you she was going to Brussels? Of course, all that scene was 'arranged' by Mrs. Burnham beforehand."

"Just so." Etta agreed with him. "I was sure from Miss Dundas's manner, voice, look, that she was repeating what she had been told to say, and that was why I wouldn't let you know, that I had heard her speak of Brussels. I was afraid it might mislead you. Poor Gillian Dundas! Despicable enough she was, but I knew she was frightened of Mrs. Burnham. And that she hated her. You could feel both welling up in her every time Mrs.

Burnham came near her. And because of that, when John
was poisoned, I wondered—well, something of the truth.
But it seemed mad to suspect Mrs. Burnham. And she
seemed so sweet and good. She really was a solicitor's
daughter and widow... It all seemed so mad... my
suspicions, I mean...

"How did you come to go down here, to Tor Cottage?"

"I had missed my key three days ago. John gave us
each a key. The only three there were. Alysia's was in a
locked bag where she keeps keys. Mine were always kept
in a little tortoiseshell box of odds and ends on my
dressing-table."

"Did you miss anything else at the same time as the
key?"

"Yes, but nothing of any importance, only an envelope.
When Mrs. Burnham kept insisting that Gillian had gone
to Brussels, I thought of that key that some one had
taken. And I decided she was being kept down here till it
would be safe to get her out of the country. When I told
Mrs. Burnham where we were going, she looked odd."
Etta's lips tightened at the memory. "I think she was half
unwilling to come, and half fearfully excited to find out
and have it over and done with. I only know that though
she pretended to scoff at the idea, she took the wheel
from me part of the way and drove through the storm like
a woman possessed."

"As she was. By a devil," Pointer said gravely. The
idea of Lucy Burnham hurrying to the slaughter of
Gillian Dundas was a terrible one.

"Of course, she expected to find a corpse——" he went
on, "and trusted to your presence to give her an alibi.
But—well—there she slipped up. Ah, here comes the
police I had Smith telephone for."

Etta laid a hand on her brother's arm. "Shall we go
now?" she asked gently. "We're not needed any more."

He did not reply. Just for a second he strode to the
dead girl and looked down on her. Then, turning as a

blind man might have done, he made his way down the garden path.

Another woman might have tried a word of consolation, or at least some sentence such as that he had nothing to reproach himself with, that he was quite right that it wouldn't have done, but Etta said nothing. Claud was saying all this to himself, she knew, or would say it when time had worn off the first shock of what he had just seen. He. did not love Gillian, but that was only because he would not, because he refused to give way to the. strange attraction she had for him, an attraction which he believed was of the senses, but which had some strange, deeper root that he himself, never understood.

Only as they stopped at the house in Great Cumberland Place did Etta venture a word.

"You won't do anything foolish?" she whispered. He shook his head scornfully, and whether he did it or not depended on one's point of view. Within the year, he was engaged to a wealthy commonplace girl of unimpeachable family, married her at the same time that Etta married Westmacott, and within another year became a K.C., and was spoken of as a man who would go far, because he was all brain and no heart.

But he never would go near a hard court, and to the end of his life he grew white when he saw bags of cement standing on the ground.

Back at the Yard, the Assistant Commissioner was waiting for Pointer. Superintendent Dartmoor came in for a second too.

You're asking where the lady is?" Pelham saw the eyes of the chief inspector sweep the room. "Taken away, of course. You should have seen her gentle indignation, her pathetic efforts to understand what I meant by not believing her story. Though she wilted a bit when Dartmoor here brought in Mrs. de Souza."

"Good idea of yours, Pointer," the superintendent said, "to have had Mrs. de Souza's horn disarranged so that she tooted a peculiar note which we could tell our men to look out for. Seething a kid in its mother's milk to help hounds on to the right trail. Neat idea."

"As you found with Miss Dundas's hat, so both Mrs. de Souza and her sister wore ones that could be turned inside out to make apparently a different hat. Their cloaks too were reversible. Silk one side, different colored cloth the other. That was how the Dundas girl and Mrs. de Souza got away from your watcher at Harrod's of course. They were prepared for anything. I wonder why Gillian Dundas went along with the other?"

"She hadn't much choice," Pointer said thoughtfully. "and there was the possibility of it really being another post, a good one. The higher the place, the more useful she could be to them. Mrs. de Souza would have told her some well gilded tale, I fancy, when she drove her down to the cottage to call on the dear Dowager Duchess probably. What about the maid, she must have been in the blackmailing?"

"She's slipped through our fingers," Dartmoor said regretfully, "for the present."

"But her absence allowed the superintendent and me to put some very telling guesses into her mouth," Pelham added with a faint smile. "Egged on by what they thought she had revealed, the two women fairly turned and rent each other to shreds. It was rather unpleasant."

It had been a horrid scene.

"But I have had one treat," the assistant commissioner went on more cheerfully, "almost the happiest moment of my life, in some respects. When I had a word with Lady Ida... of course, she won't be prosecuted, Westmacott will see to that, but I talked as if penal servitude were a certainty. However, to come back to the case in hand, how did you come to telephone for a warrant to be made out in Mrs. Burnham's name? What put you on to her before you went down to Tor Cottage? I don't mind saying that I was sure at first that the superintendent couldn't have got the name right."

"I wondered myself!" Dartmoor said stolidly.

"I'd have come up and explained, of course, sir," Pointer hastened to say, "but, if I was right, no further time would be wasted. I always feared that the first chance they got to get Miss Dundas out of town and to themselves would be the end."

"Yes, but how did you come to pitch on that dear, pretty little woman who had lost a handsome husband and five thousand a year by Tait's death?" Pelham persisted. "When did you drop the notion that the motive for his murder was to hide the Lady Ida—Strange—Mrs. de Souza trickery?"

"The instant I learned that the envelope in which Tait was carrying the buttonhole had come from the house in Great Cumberland Place, sir. I confess, the solid, earth seemed to rock under me." Pointer's eyes were on his shoes, he was living again through that second of amazing revelation. "It wasn't a fresh envelope,. which he might have taken himself for another reason, or had in his pocket. It was one which had been..in Miss Etta's toilet box for weeks. That meant that all my theory of Lady Ida—Mrs. dc Souza—Strange trio was wrong None of them would have taken this particular envelope. It would have been simple to get a fresh one from the Ricci shop It pointed straight to some one in the Great Cumberland house itself, who wanted to keep to the Ricci trail, and who was pressed for time

"Yes, yes," Pelham put in "But why suspect Mrs. Burnham? Why not one of the Naylors? They benefited through Tait's death, or even, why not Lady Tait?"

"Ah, I had two clues, sir. The first, the bitten pen top had led me wrong, but there was still the second one—the clue of Gillian Dundas's terror. We all agreed that Miss Dundas was but the underling—the decoy, and that the blackmailing in which she had taken part went back at least a year—Lord Mill's first payment was about a year ago—well, as for the Naylors or Lady Tait, we couldn't trace any previous connection between them and Miss Dundas."

"But why wasn't Mrs. de Souza good enough for you as an explanation of the girl's terror?" Pelham insisted pushing a box of cigars across the table..

"She had been until that envelope told of some one else in the house who had been the actual poisoner of Tait, sir. Yet we knew that Mrs. de Souza was in the poisoning too. I thought Lady Ida was, but I *knew* Mrs. de Souza was. So I looked around—mentally—for some one linked with her as well as Gillian Dundas and actually at Great Cumberland house."

"You did some swift 'mental' looking," Dartmoor said with a faint smile.

"I had to!" Pointer said with an inward shiver. "Now Mrs. Burnham had gone openly, to Mrs. de Souza's flat—to ask about Miss Dundas's reference. No one but Mrs. Burnham wanted Gillian Dundas in the house. She did. She insisted on her being there—under her eye. She alone of those at the Great Cumberland house went to Miss Dundas's studio, where also Mrs. de Souza went. Her great idea seems to've always been, as far as possible, to do things openly. In short, sir, given that envelope everything pointed that her account of the last talk with Mr. Tait was false. She could easily have handed him envelope and poisoned twig then...

"She overreached herself when in stealing the key of the Tor Cottage she also took that envelope. She didn't realize that the hardest thing in the world is to lay a false trail. She wanted the Riccis' to be suspected from the first, which was why she told me of Tait's talk with her about threatening letters. She must have known about them, apart from what he told her. Before she blackmailed any one, we may be sure she made all her inquiries, and the detail of his half-brother's unwelcome marriage wouldn't have been missed."

"Clever of her to have blackmailed Tait again after the engagement was announced," Dartmoor said appreciatively.

"I suppose her idea in going to Vichy was to see Lady Tait for herself, so as to know the exact amount of money Tait would pay, if need be," Pelham thought. "She seems to've understood the rule that attention to detail marks the good business man or woman."

"Just so, sir, that's why she took two revolvers with her down to Tor Cottage. One of Miss Dundas's, we think, to be used on her, if need be, or on Strange. One to have with her when she left. She knew that Miss Naylor mistrusted her."

"And how do you think the buttonhole was actually given to Tait?" Pelham asked after a pause, in the tone of a man who knows the answer, and glancing with a ball smile at the superintendent behind Pointer.

"From the fact that she made so much to me of the threatening letters, I feel pretty sure that she played that card with Tait. I take it, she listened to his outpouring about Gillian Dundas and Lord Mills, took the paper with her writing on it from him—to keep till he should he back—and then insisted on his waiting a moment while she showed him a mysterious spray that she had just received, probably told him it had some word or other pinned to it, such as 'Revenge' or 'Beware.' It had come to her enclosed in another envelope which she would tell him, she had unfortunately tossed in the fire. The envelope in which the sprig was found, has a worried looking slit at the side. I feel sure that the leaf was pulled through this, so that Tait would be sure to find it a little difficult to get it out and have a look at it, sure to get splinters into his fingers while doing it. Of course, this is only guesswork, but—"

"It's absolutely borne out by what Mrs. de Souza shrieked at her sister just now." Pelham told him and the superintendent nodded.

"Well played, Pointer!" Dartmoor said warmly, "and then?"

"Apparently, Tait stuffed it into his pocket, felt there for a match when the man asked for a light, and tossed it away. In his opinion, the Ricci's threatening letters meant nothing He refused to take them seriously.-He was concerned with a much graver matter—Miss Dundas's backer in her blackmail, and at the moment the idea that Miss Dundas herself was actually forging Mrs. Burnham's handwriting for some black scheme of her own."

"You're probably right. Well, well!"

"To think the tremendous Westmacott motive wasn't the right one," Dartmoor said thoughtfully, getting up, preparatory to going back to other work. "That Mrs. Ricci was just trying to frighten her husband, as he thought, and that Tait's poisoner should have been his fiancée, the dear little woman who seemed to lose so much by his death."

"She lost a long sentence of penal servitude, by it, at any rate, sir ," Pointer reminded him. "Tait would have stuck at nothing to clear Brown, and to do that he would have had to put Gillian Dundas in the dock. He would have done it without hesitation. Once there, Gillian would have told, of course. And Mrs. Burnham couldn't have murdered Gillian after Tait had told her of the paper found in the studio without arousing even his suspicions. She couldn't run away, for she has laid by no large sum of money. These people never, do. She didn't need capital, her, income was quite a splendid one. A true blackmailer's income."

"And as to the paper which she claimed was forged," Dartmoor went on, "she would know that her denial of it wouldn't hold water for long, apart from the possibility of it leading to the detection of the fraud on Westmacott. She certainly was in a hole, and decided to cut her losses."

"Yes, it must have been a wrench to get rid of Tait after he had miraculously fallen in love with her," Pelham agreed dryly, "but, as you say, by far the lesser of two evils. But why did you take the trouble to post this nice long letter to us? It's just arrived."

Pointer looked a trifle awkward. Naylor had exceeded his instructions.

"I thought that she might have more of the poisoned buttonholes ready," he confessed. "Not knowing that Strange would come up to scratch just when he did, I had to have something on which to arrest her. I believed Miss Dundas would he dead, *spurlos versenckt*, and I had to have some proof. So I arranged a wad of accounts which I'd got ready to hand in, wrote my name, in something like her writing, on the envelope, and then showed it to Mrs. Burnham when we were nicely off by ourselves. She fished in her bag—for a revolver, as it proved. She had woolen driving gloves still on over her rubber gloves. I knew it would be for something effective to prevent my reading what she thought was inside. And as I wasn't sure in all that storm of my men being handy, I thought it better not to chance my pockets being picked, should she get me. But it was unnecessary trouble."

Six months later, the proprietor of the Hotel Imperial at Vichy faced an Arab in flowing robes and shook his head decidedly.

"Impossible! Impossible! The fee you ask is much too high. You do not earn it. That American lady whose fortune you told last time you were here wrote to tell us that it had not come true, and that she had been put to great expense getting a trousseau and new furniture."

The chief magician of Abd-el-Krim gazed haughtily out of sooty eyes.

"What has my gift to do with her expenses? Where is the letter I left with you at that same time? You know what happened to those English guests of yours. I heard the servants here talking of it only last night. They have read all about it in the papers. Open that letter, Monsieur, and see if Ibrahim does not read the future, and it is not cheap at double what he charges."

"Childish!" snorted the proprietor, but he fished in a cupboard and finally brought out an envelope with a huge seal on it. He opened it disdainfully and read:

"Of the English party whose fortunes I have just declined to read, this last day but one of April, three will die unnatural deaths. The man called Tait, the young woman who stood beside him, beautiful and treacherous, and the woman standing next to her. I looked no further. I stood in the presence of three about to die before three months are past, and such influences are unwholesome. Written and sealed for the proprietor of the Hotel Imperial, to be opened by him a year from this date, or when he hears bad news of this group."

The proprietor looked at him. "*Eh bien*, perhaps I will try you at the higher fee. But see to it that no one complains?" Alone, he read the letter again, then carefully dropped it on the fire, shrugged his shoulders, and turned back to his accounts.

THE END

Other Resurrected Press Books in *The Chief Inspector Pointer Mystery* Series

Murder at Bridge

When an afternoon bridge party attended by some of Hamilton's leading citizens ends with the hostess being murdered in her boudoir, Special Investigator Dundee of the District Attorney's office is called in. But one of the attendees is guilty? There are plenty of suspects: the victim's former lover, her current suitor, the retired judge who is being blackmailed, the victim's maid who had been horribly disfigured accidentally by the murdered woman, or any of the women who's husbands had flirted with the victim. Or was she murdered by an outsider whose motive had nothing to do with the town of Hamilton. Find the answer in... **Murder at Bridge**

One Drop of Blood

When Dr. Koenig, head of Mayfield Sanitarium is murdered, the District Attorney's Special Investigator, "Bonnie" Dundee must go undercover to find the killer. Were any of the inmates of the asylum insane enough to have committed the crime? Or, was it one of the staff, motivated by jealousy? And what was is the secret in the murdered man's past. Find the answer in... **One Drop of Blood**

AVAILABLE FROM RESURRECTED PRESS!

The Edwardian Detectives
Literary Sleuths of the Edwardian Era

The exploits of the great Victorian Detectives, Poe's C. Auguste Dupin, Gaboriau's Lecoq, and most famously, Arthur Conan Doyle's Sherlock Holmes, are well known. But what of those fictional detectives that came after, those of the Edwardian Age? The period between the death of Queen Victoria and the First World War had been called the Golden Age of the detective short story, but how familiar is the modern reader with the sleuths of this era? And such an extraordinary group they were, including in their numbers an unassuming English priest, a blind man, a master of disguises, a lecturer in medical jurisprudence, a noble woman working for Scotland Yard, and a savant so brilliant he was known as "The Thinking Machine."

To introduce readers to these detectives, Resurrected Press has assembled a collection of stories featuring these and other remarkable sleuths in The Edwardian Detectives.

- The Case of Laker, Absconded by Arthur Morrison
- The Fenchurch Street Mystery by Baroness Orczy
- The Crime of the French Café by Nick Carter
- The Man with Nailed Shoes by R Austin Freeman
- The Blue Cross by G. K. Chesterton
- The Case of the Pocket Diary Found in the Snow by Augusta Groner
- The Ninescore Mystery by Baroness Orczy
- The Riddle of the Ninth Finger by Thomas W. Hanshew
- The Knight's Cross Signal Problem by Ernest Bramah

- The Problem of Cell 13 by Jacques Futrelle
- The Conundrum of the Golf Links by Percy James Brebner
- The Silkworms of Florence by Clifford Ashdown
- The Gateway of the Monster by William Hope Hodgson
- The Affair at the Semiramis Hotel by A. E. W. Mason
- The Affair of the Avalanche Bicycle & Tyre Co., LTD by Arthur Morrison

RESURRECTED PRESS CLASSIC MYSTERY CATALOGUE

Journeys into Mystery
Travel and Mystery in a More Elegant Time

The Edwardian Detectives
Literary Sleuths of the Edwardian Era

Gems of Mystery
Lost Jewels from a More Elegant Age

E. C. Bentley
Trent's Last Case: The Woman in Black

Ernest Bramah
Max Carrados Resurrected:
The Detective Stories of Max Carrados

Agatha Christie
The Secret Adversary
The Mysterious Affair at Styles

Octavus Roy Cohen
Midnight

Freeman Wills Croft
The Ponson Case
The Pit Prop Syndicate

J. S. Fletcher
The Herapath Property
The Rayner-Slade Amalgamation
The Chestermarke Instinct
The Paradise Mystery
Dead Men's Money

The Middle of Things
Ravensdene Court
Scarhaven Keep
The Orange-Yellow Diamond
The Middle Temple Murder
The Tallyrand Maxim
The Borough Treasurer
In the Mayor's Parlour
The Saftey Pin

R. Austin Freeman
*The Mystery of 31 New Inn from the Dr. Thorndyke
Series*
*John Thorndyke's Cases from the Dr. Thorndyke
Series*
The Red Thumb Mark from The Dr. Thorndyke Series
The Eye of Osiris from The Dr. Thorndyke Series
A Silent Witness from the Dr. John Thorndyke Series
The Cat's Eye from the Dr. John Thorndyke Series
*Helen Vardon's Confession: A Dr. John Thorndyke
Story*
As a Thief in the Night: A Dr. John Thorndyke Story
*Mr. Pottermack's Oversight: A Dr. John Thorndyke
Story*
*Dr. Thorndyke Intervenes: A Dr. John Thorndyke
Story*
The Singing Bone: The Adventures of Dr. Thorndyke
The Stoneware Monkey: A Dr. John Thorndyke Story
*The Great Portrait Mystery, and Other Stories: A
Collection of Dr. John Thorndyke and Other Stories*
The Penrose Mystery: A Dr. John Thorndyke Story
The Uttermost Farthing: A Savant's Vendetta

Arthur Griffiths
The Passenger From Calais
The Rome Express

Fergus Hume
The Mystery of a Hansom Cab
The Green Mummy
The Silent House
The Secret Passage

Edgar Jepson
The Loudwater Mystery

A. E. W. Mason
At the Villa Rose

A. A. Milne
The Red House Mystery
Baroness Emma Orczy
The Old Man in the Corner

Edgar Allan Poe
The Detective Stories of Edgar Allan Poe

Arthur J. Rees
The Hampstead Mystery
The Shrieking Pit
The Hand In The Dark
The Moon Rock
The Mystery of the Downs

Mary Roberts Rinehart
Sight Unseen and The Confession

Dorothy L. Sayers
Whose Body?

Sir William Magnay
The Hunt Ball Mystery

Mabel and Paul Thorne
The Sheridan Road Mystery

Louis Tracy
The Strange Case of Mortimer Fenley
The Albert Gate Mystery
The Bartlett Mystery
The Postmaster's Daughter
The House of Peril
The Sandling Case: What Would You Have Done?
Charles Edmonds Walk
The Paternoster Ruby

John R. Watson
The Mystery of the Downs
The Hampstead Mystery

Edgar Wallace
The Daffodil Mystery
The Crimson Circle

Carolyn Wells
Vicky Van
The Man Who Fell Through the Earth
In the Onyx Lobby
Raspberry Jam
The Clue
The Room with the Tassels
The Vanishing of Betty Varian
The Mystery Girl
The White Alley
The Curved Blades
Anybody but Anne
The Bride of a Moment
Faulkner's Folly
The Diamond Pin
The Gold Bag
The Mystery of the Sycamore
The Come Backy

Raoul Whitfield
Death in a Bowl

And much more!
Visit ResurrectedPress.com
for our complete catalogue

About Resurrected Press

A division of Intrepid Ink, LLC, Resurrected Press is dedicated to bringing high quality, vintage books back into publication. See our entire catalogue and find out more at www.ResurrectedPress.com.

About Intrepid Ink, LLC

Intrepid Ink, LLC provides full publishing services to authors of fiction and non-fiction books, eBooks and websites. From editing to formatting, from publishing to marketing, Intrepid Ink gets your creative works into the hands of the people who want to read them. Find out more at www.IntrepidInk.com.